The Green Monster

A Johnny Denovo Mystery

By Andrew Kent

For SNA and EKA.

First published by Dog Ear Publishing
4010 W. 86th Street, Ste H
Indianapolis, IN 46268
www.dogearpublishing.net

ISBN: 978-160844-115-0

Printed in the United States of America

The Green Monster

A Johnny Denovo Mystery

By Andrew Kent

To Lisa —
Your friends should
be green with envy!

—akent

Chapter 1
First Pitch

In the shade of a massive green stanchion, surrounded by thousands of strangers, he felt alone at last. Safe.

With his baseball cap pulled down over his trademark shock of black hair, his gray eyes skulking in the brim's shadow, Johnny Denovo was placid, his pulse rate low.

He was happy to be blending in with the crowd.

The ironic haven was exactly what he needed after the past few weeks – a case had just closed, and he'd had his fill of the stabbing flashbulbs, beckoning voices, and glaring television lights that inevitably followed. The media circus felt like an ordeal every time his fame reignited, an exhausting and lonely crucible of forced smiles and fleeting connections.

Playing to the press was a necessary evil. He attended to it professionally, knowing his media image had to be nurtured and preserved. But after nearly two weeks of interviews, paparazzi, and reporters, this day came as a welcome relief, with its simple pleasures and blessed obscurity.

He needed to hide out and recharge.

Hiding came second-nature to him by now. Over the past few years, it had become a way of life. He'd once been an academic neuroscientist. Now, he was well-practiced at concealing his education and abilities under the guise of a superficial, world-famous detective.

The fact that the noise and the glare of his accidental fame helped obscure the truth added a satisfying dash of the perverse.

The emerald field below was ablaze in the afternoon sun. Green light slanted into his pale eyes, low and faintly pulsing. He had only his hat's brim to shield him from the blinding rays. He'd worn it partly for the game, partly to conceal his trademark tide of black hair. But in his haste to get to the game, he'd forgotten his sunglasses back at his condo. They would have added to his disguise, allowing him to relax even more.

He'd felt slightly exposed at first, but after an uneventful hour, his anxiety had evaporated.

He just wanted one full day of obscurity, blissful obscurity. Soon enough, his craving for endorphins and excitement would reignite. He would yearn for a case, fret and pace in agitation and boredom, hanker for a hit of adrenaline.

Today was an interlude, one that he knew wouldn't last.

For the past half-hour, the heat from the sun, the field, and the enthusiastic crowd had been vulcanizing him. Lazy breezes couldn't shift the air blanketing the seats. Yet even in the sluggish heat, he remained amazed by the verdant splendor around him.

Where he'd grown up, with his given name of John Novarro, a glorious jewel of a park like this wouldn't have endured. Sagebrush and scrub would have quickly overrun it in the dry, high-altitude air, the inevitable desiccation to be mourned only by lonely grasshoppers performing a mindless dirge, dry and rattling.

He'd sat spellbound for two hours now, fascinated and entertained by the game, its inspiring feats of athleticism, and the colorful and sometimes unruly crowd. When at last the light and heat of summer moved behind the stanchion's wedge of shade, he realized how uncomfortable he'd been. A few beers had done little to fend off the effects of this late-August furnace.

Suddenly, there was a loud retort, and the crowd gasped in surprise and anticipation, craning forward as one to see the effects from the violent interaction. Heads turned skyward and cheers began to percolate as thousands of hopeful brains rapidly and instinctively calculated distances and trajectories. Neuronal networks millions of years old pursued their natural ends – stereo vision resolving misaligned information, neurotransmitters bridging connections, and a common realization slowly emerging in the mix of consciousness and instinct each fan possessed. They stood higher as one, hands tensed in anticipation as the ball knifed into the crowd down the right field line with a dramatic arc. A foment of noise shook the sky, shoved upward by arms raised in joy.

Johnny shouted at the top of his lungs along with the rest of the sell-out crowd. This was a big game, and the contest was now into the late innings. A home run with men on was precisely what his beloved Red Sox needed to overcome a middle-innings struggle by their bullpen. Now the offense was roaring back, and with their closing pitcher warming in the bullpen, the Sox seemed poised to clinch the game.

Next to him, Tucker Thiesen's loud bellow of encouragement was partially muffled by a mouthful of nachos. His scorebook had dropped to the ground as he'd stood in unity with the cheering throng. Sloppily dressed and intensely watching the game, Tucker looked nothing like the renowned technologist and intelligence expert he was. His hands remained at waist level, trapped into holding the chip tray and large soda that inevitably accompanied him at games. But his joy at the developments on the field was unbounded. If Johnny was a Red Sox fan, Tucker was a fanatic. He'd named a dog Yaz once in honor of Carl Yastrzemski, the great Red Sox left-fielder and clutch hitter. When the Curse of the Bambino had finally been broken, Tucker had celebrated sporadically for months.

As a neuroscientist, Johnny had briefly studied curses and how they affected the brain and consequently the body. He'd focused on curses and superstitions in sports, where the tie of mind and body was the strongest. The neuroscience literature held a good amount on the topic, even if the references were somewhat oblique.

When he'd moved to Boston during his first case and just before a typo and some powerful friends changed his identity, the Sox had been about to break a curse, renewing his interest in the topic. He remembered digging into the research again, wanting to read it in light of the team's apparent ability to overcome a strong biological predisposition.

The biology behind curses probed the more primitive instincts humans carry in their three-layered brains, Johnny recalled. Curses worked because they exploited the middle of the three brains humans possessed, the limbic brain, the true home of emotional synthesis and action-oriented thinking. The logical cerebrum and the truly primitive reptilian brain functioned in their own ways, but when people were thinking on their feet, their limbic system ran the show. Belief in a baseball curse could poison a limbic brain and hence the mind-body connection, leading to insecurity, botched plays, and late-season collapses.

In a team situation, doubt could become contagious.

But at this particular moment, such theories were a fleeting thought, an unseen flash of neurotransmitters in the unlit recesses of his mind. There was a game to enjoy, and the Sox were winning once more.

From his vantage point, Johnny had a clear view of the scoreboard in left field, a venerable manual affair operated by people peeking through holes and inserting painted panels for runs and lighting bulbs for outs. The scoreboard enhanced the ambience of the timeless scene, reconciling old with new, exhibiting a reverence for tradition.

And it was huge, consuming most of the lower portion of the park's famous left-field wall, the Green Monster.

In recent years, the Green Monster had been refurbished so that fans could sit atop it in coveted seats complete with tables and counters, a new perch from which to see and be seen.

Despite the modernization and added capacity, the park had lost none of its charm.

The Red Sox kept the scorekeepers busy for the home half of the final innings while their relief pitchers drilled strikes and forced ground-outs. The game ended after the top of the ninth, the Red Sox ahead by six runs. It had turned into a rout.

"What a great game!" Tucker shouted to Johnny as they stood after the last out, nearly deafening him while all around other fans smiled and exchanged high-fives and fistbumps. Tucker closed the cover on his battered and stained scorekeeper's book, and slipped his mechanical pencil into its spiral binding. "Thanks for bringing me along again, Johnny. I love this team!"

A voice piped up behind them.

"Johnny? Johnny Denovo?"

Johnny cringed involuntarily. His cover had been blown in that instant. He was paying the price for forgetting his sunglasses. Today's respite was over.

He turned his head and saw a tall man peering over the crowd filing out, striving to make eye contact.

Johnny raised his eyebrows in acknowledgement and sidled onto the side of the stairs, letting the crowd pass. Many of them now gave him apprising looks, recognizing him but remaining respectful. Out of his peripheral vision, he could see some camera-phones raised and pointed in his direction.

"Why're you stopping?" Tucker asked, nearly running Johnny over, the brim of his hat striking Johnny in the neck. Tucker was about the same height as Johnny, but was now a step lower in the aisle. Johnny indicated with a twitch of his head the man coming toward them.

"Hi, Johnny," the man said, extending a hand from on high, reaching over a child ducking through the crowd. "I'm Tom McNaught. I was going to call you Monday, so I hope you don't mind me taking this opportunity."

"Not a problem," Johnny squinted, responding with a faint smile. "Mr. McNaught, this is my friend Tucker. He's a Red Sox fanatic I pack along for trivia and noise."

Tucker laughed as he and McNaught shook hands. Tucker nearly spilled his drink juggling it into his nacho tray, his score book tipping precariously under his arm.

"Good to meet you," McNaught said. "I'm fanatical about the Sox, too. Have been all my life."

Tucker just smiled in response.

"So," Johnny began, the crowd rapidly thinning around them. "Why were you planning on calling me? And I assume this is something we can discuss here?" He often had to remind clients that the walls had ears, eyes, and even brains. Just being seen talking with Johnny had caused some people problems in the past, and camera-phones had found him already today.

McNaught looked about furtively, almost reflexively. He was spooked, that was clear. "To some extent, certainly," he muttered, lowering his voice. His warm and gregarious approach had closed down noticeably. "I'm being blackmailed, and it's very messy. I need help."

Johnny had been turning the man's surname over in his mind and suddenly realized who he was speaking with. "Are you Thomas McNaught, the biotech mogul?" he asked.

"One and the same," McNaught replied. "I don't know if I'd say I was a mogul, though. Just a scientist who had an early hot streak at the research bench, and then a lot of good help making it all into a company. But you're right, I'm that guy."

By now they were standing in very thinly populated stands, most of the fans having either departed or gravitated down to be near the field. The cleaning crews were beginning to make their way through the seats, television crews were clustered around the few players who'd come out for appearances, and the grounds crew was laying out their rakes and lifting the bases out of their sockets.

"Well, as you probably know, McNaught," Johnny said in a professional tone, "I mostly deal with high-profile, twisted cases involving rich people. You sound like you might qualify for two out of three here. Care to tell me if this is twisted, if you're batting a thousand?"

McNaught laughed. "Oh, I'm batting a thousand, all right," he responded, but the levity drained away almost immediately. "I'm definitely batting a thousand if you throw 'twisted' into the equation."

Tucker looked from McNaught to Johnny and back again. "I think I'm going to head home, Johnny, and let you two discuss this. Nice meeting you, Mr. McNaught."

"Nice meeting you, too," McNaught replied. "I didn't mean to scare you off."

Tucker laughed his big laugh. "No worries," he said, turning to head up the stairs. "Johnny, thanks again. Great game!" And he let out one more victory whoop as he trudged away.

Johnny and McNaught turned to face each other again. McNaught had a cheerful face and sandy hair peeking out from under a battered baseball cap. He was lanky. He might be a bit clumsy, Johnny thought. Long nerves in the arms and legs often meant coordination problems.

"Impress me," Johnny challenged, his eyes taking on an aggressive aspect, his more compact build flexing a bit as he tried to convey a sense of gravity behind his statement.

McNaught cleared his throat. "I'd better be brief," he managed, his voice slightly tense. "I need to get home, and you're right, this isn't the place for a full conversation. Even being seen talking with you is probably a bit risky, but I couldn't resist myself when I caught sight of you. Essentially, I'm having an affair, someone found out, and they're blackmailing me. Worse still, there's a very awkward complication, and the blackmailer knows about it."

Johnny continued to peer up at McNaught, squinting in the bright afternoon sun. Like a lot of sheltered academics and scientists, McNaught was a little slow on his feet, a little too trusting. Someone wiser to the ways of the world would have known to wait to talk with him privately, realizing the risks of a public encounter from the start.

Johnny sympathized. He'd been a scientist once, albeit one specializing in applied research. He'd never lost his common sense, never accrued that distracted and insulated habit of the mind plaguing so many pure thinkers, but he knew the type well. This guy would need some hand-holding.

McNaught adjusted his baseball cap and shifted his feet uncomfortably, then slowly regained some resolve in his demeanor.

"I'm sorry, I can't tell you here," McNaught said definitively, his eyes meeting Johnny's. "Monday. May I come by Monday? I mean, tomorrow. I'm losing track of the days."

Johnny scowled and pondered. A part of him didn't want another case right now, so soon after one just wrapped up. He was a little spent from the rounds of interviews he'd just finished – the airplanes and lonely nights in strange hotel rooms had worn him down. Yet, here was another case, standing right before him, imploring him for help. Even if the timing was bad, he felt like he needed to hear more. His personal creed was at stake. He'd studied neuroscience to help people and had pledged to do the same as a detective.

Besides, the familiar tingle of endorphins – the human opiate – had surged again as McNaught outlined his problem and hinted at something more intriguing. The infusion felt good. He knew he couldn't resist it.

Feigning reluctance, Johnny reached into his wallet for a business card. McNaught would need his address.

"Sure," he said, handing the card to McNaught. "Tomorrow, Monday. But don't be early. Be late. I sleep in."

Chapter 2
Line Up

Leaving Fenway, Johnny hoofed it home, aware that he was a little behind schedule. He'd arranged for an early Sunday dinner with his agent and current girlfriend, Mona Landau, and he didn't want to be late. He wanted to recapture the feeling of privacy and intimacy his recent media tour had shattered.

He'd envisioned dinner with Mona as a perfect extension of a fine summer day – first, male bonding and baseball, then time with a favorite female. Now, it would mean even more, helping to restore his lost sense of hiatus. She would take his mind off his fatigue and McNaught's interruption.

He quickly stopped by his condo to clean up, change into something other than a sweaty t-shirt and ratty shorts, and get his sunglasses. He needed to be at least bistro-ready. He had a reputation to preserve at Maurice's, their favorite dinner spot. He had an image to uphold.

Mona had been Johnny's agent for months, but was now much more. Since their relationship had blossomed in France, during what Johnny chose to call the Case of Spam and Eggs, he and Mona had tried to keep things to a low boil, limiting their dating to weekends and, even then, mostly to Saturday nights.

Tonight was the rare double-header, a Sunday follow-up. Last night had been a simple dinner and a movie, culminating in a nice brunch at a downtown eatery.

They were both left wanting more. It was part of the fun of limiting their interactions.

Johnny knew it would be an early evening in any event. Mona ran a busy agency managing local superstar clients, and she'd been feeling pressure from some of them. And now Johnny had McNaught coming over in the morning. He knew he'd be distracted. The potential case meant detective work was back on the agenda.

Even though a case had just closed, knowing another might be brewing had quickly changed his attitude. Walking to meet Mona, he unexpectedly felt ready for another case, his brain fighting back inertia. Mindless interviews and media events hadn't kept him from getting bored. A new case would reestablish his focus and distance him from the media circus. His brain had spent a couple of weeks roasting in the relentless media oven, after all. It was time to get back into the game.

He felt energized as he walked into Maurice's cool, air conditioned lobby.

He removed his sunglasses and glanced instinctively over at their usual table. Mona had already arrived. She looked lovely, her auburn hair tumbling over her soft taupe shoulders, her dark eyes resplendent with the bright light glinting in at end of day. It was the tail end of summer, and she'd browned nicely. She wore a soft yellow shift, tasteful, stylish, and sexy. He never tired of looking at her. She greeted him with a dazzling smile, and he stooped over for a soft kiss. He scratched his head as he sat down, tousling his hair into a new style of mess.

"Did they win?" Mona asked.

"Did they win?!" Johnny mocked. "You mean you weren't glued to the television, pitch by pitch?"

Mona laughed. "Maybe someday you'll take me to a game, but I expect that will be a cold day in hell," she taunted.

Just a couple of months ago, Johnny had been of the opinion that Mona might have once worked as purgatory's meteorologist, rising through the ranks to the exalted title of she-devil. To him, Mona had been a cold, calculating agent who cared little for him beyond the percentage they shared. Now he knew better. That had merely been her professional façade, something she invoked at will. Beneath it resided an interesting and beautiful woman.

"I owe Tucker a lot for everything he's done lately, and he's a huge fan," Johnny pointed out. "He comes first, sorry. Where's Ivan?" he asked, looking for his favorite bartender and waiter.

"He'll be back," Mona answered. "I think he had to go take a delivery."

Just then, Ivan emerged from the kitchen, recognized Johnny, and smiled in his direction.

"The usual, Mr. Denovo?" he asked in a light Russian accent, wiping his hands on his apron.

"Please, Ivan," Johnny replied. "You make the best ones."

Ivan smiled at the compliment and went behind the bar to fix Johnny's drink, a gin and tonic with lemon. Mona was already sipping from a glass of red wine.

"The money from the last case keeps coming in," Mona noted. "Since we agreed not to talk business on date nights, I didn't tell you last night. I just got confirmation Friday that the French insurers are sending you something sized in the low six figures, so it's on my mind," Mona related.

"Fine, fine," Johnny said. "Most of it to the foundation, please, and some to me for cash on hand. You keep your share. I think I'll have another case tomorrow."

Mona took another sip of her wine as Ivan set Johnny's drink in front of the detective.

"Another case already?" she asked, lowering her wine glass. "That's quick."

"Somebody at the game stopped me," Johnny said after tasting his own drink. "A guy named Tom McNaught. He's a biotech hotshot."

Mona arched her eyebrows at him over her wine. "And a very handsome one at that," she said suggestively.

"You think so?" Johnny responded. "He's tall and lanky. I guess you could call him handsome. I didn't take him for your type. Kind of scrawny."

Mona smiled an inscrutable smile. "Like I keep telling you, you have a lot to learn, Mr. Denovo," she said in a voice shading to the sultry. "What's his issue?"

Johnny sipped again from his gin. "Extra-marital affair," he mumbled, chewing on a piece of ice. "Someone's blackmailing him. That's all pretty boring. But he said there's a twist, something he wouldn't divulge it in public."

"I'm surprised he told you that much," Mona noted.

"He's been sheltered. I don't think he realized the stakes. But it was pretty safe," Johnny assured her. "He seemed a little desperate for help, and definitely jumpy. But I'm hoping for a real bombshell tomorrow when we meet. I don't do petty adultery."

Johnny was sound asleep when his phone rang the next morning. He slapped at it blearily. After a brief struggle, he managed to grasp it clumsily, fighting to recognize the device so that he put the right end to his ear. Satisfied after another moment of fumbling, he pressed a button and cleared his throat.

"Denovo," he croaked.

"Johnny, it's Tom McNaught," said the voice on the other end. "I hope I didn't wake you."

Johnny rubbed his eyes with his thumb and forefinger. "What time is it?"

"Six in the morning," McNaught said. "Sorry, I'm an early riser. Could I stop by to continue our conversation?"

Johnny stifled a yawn. "How long will it take you to get here?" he asked.

"I'm right outside your building," McNaught said. "I can be up in five minutes."

Johnny groaned. Damn type-A personalities, they were adrenaline junkies. If their blood pressure wasn't pushed to the max, they'd find a way to elevate it.

"Give me ten," Johnny responded and hung up. He'd have to wake up fast. Fortunately, he'd been able to afford a system that controlled window shades and lighting. He reached for the remote he kept near his bed, fumbled with a few buttons, and accelerated his morning program. The blinds opened with a hum, sunlight pouring in. He heard his coffee maker click on and his computer boot. He flopped back down on his pillow and shut his eyes tight, stretching his legs and back to help himself wake up. After taking a deep breath, he flung his legs over the side of the bed. He scratched his scalp, then stretched his arms overhead, fingers intertwined. Dropping them back to his sides, he was officially awake.

Picking the phone up off the bed where he'd tossed it, Johnny called Wei Chou. Wei lived in and owned the restaurant on the main level of the building. In addition to being a great cook, Wei kept an eye out for problems.

The phone was answered on the second ring. Wei was already at work, something that subliminally annoyed and impressed Johnny as he glanced at his clock.

"Wei, it's Johnny."

"Oh, you sound bad, Denovo," Wei joked. "Too early for you?"

"Yes, far too early," Johnny admitted in a fading voice. "Wei, a man is coming up to see me. Let him through, and forget you saw him."

"OK, Johnny, no problem," Wei confirmed. "You want something to eat? I could fix something, I guess."

"Maybe later, thanks. Start thinking about what you'd recommend," Johnny replied with a short laugh. Wei always intuited Johnny's meals for him.

Nine minutes later, Johnny ushered McNaught into his condominium, sunlight now filling the windows that just minutes earlier had been sealed against the day. The smell of coffee dominated the foyer.

McNaught was dressed in a sharp dark suit but no tie, looking every bit the CEO, his lankiness modified by his attire into an air of fitness and approachable authority.

"You should know," Johnny said grimly as he stepped aside to let his potential client enter, "you are not conforming to Denovo hours, McNaught. In the future, if I take your case, I would kindly ask you to not call on me until after 10 a.m., unless it's literally a matter of life or death."

McNaught looked sincerely abashed at Johnny's upbraiding. "I'm very sorry, Johnny. I just have to consult with you at an hour that isn't likely to raise suspicions with anyone – my wife, my company, anyone."

"I'll let it go this time," Johnny replied brusquely, pouring himself a cup of coffee. "Would you like some?" he offered in a friendlier tone.

"No, thanks," McNaught said, waving his hand. "Already on high-octane."

"OK," Johnny said, the coffee searing his throat and tingling his nerves. "Now, tell me why you're batting a thousand on the bizarre front."

McNaught again grew uncomfortable and began to exhibit every sign of circumnavigating the story rather than plunging right into it. Perhaps it was the early hour or the fact that he'd been awakened so harshly, but Johnny was having none of it.

"Listen, McNaught, you woke me from my coffin," Johnny snarled. "Either tell me now what's going on or hit the road. Neither of us has time for a slow dance."

McNaught seemed to galvanize with the reproach, his eyes taking on an adamantine quality.

"You're right. Let's cut to the chase," he replied. "So, I'm having an affair. You know that. I'm being blackmailed over it. You know that as well. Now, here are some things you don't know yet."

Seating himself in an armchair, McNaught paused, gathering his thoughts into an efficient sentence or two. Johnny sat opposite him.

"The first bit of news is that I've learned that my mistress is my wife's long-lost little sister. The second bit of news is that I think the blackmailer is also engaging in eco-terrorism of some kind, attacking my firm with one hand while he extorts money from me with the other."

Johnny smiled, swallowing a large gulp of coffee. "You are batting a thousand, McNaught. I'm sorry if I ever doubted you."

McNaught stood suddenly, towering over Johnny. "Now it's my turn," he said in a powerful, authoritative voice. "I've told you my story, and shown contrition for my early intrusion into your indulgent lifestyle. What I need from you is for you to take this matter seriously, and to drop the insouciant tone. Can we agree on that?"

Johnny had remained smiling at McNaught during the outburst, and sat in silence for a moment after McNaught finished, sipping from his coffee thoughtfully.

"Let's be clear, McNaught," Johnny finally replied in a dead-level voice, staring hard into McNaught's eyes. "You need me. You don't boss me around. I bat a thousand, too, on my terms. If you don't like how I work, you can go to Dipshit Detective Agency and get Flunky Flatfoot to take your money and botch your case. Or you can engage me, on my terms. Are we clear? My terms, or no terms."

McNaught had lowered himself into the chair once more during Johnny's lecture. He looked contrite again, like a sullen teen, hunched in the armchair across from Johnny, his suit bunched up around his thin shoulders.

"I'm sorry," he said quietly. "You're absolutely right. I just haven't stated my problem to anyone in such certain terms. I think hearing it echo back to me got under my skin. Apologies."

"Apology accepted," Johnny replied. "Now, I need to ask some questions. Just the standard fare. OK?"

"Right," McNaught said, sinking back into the cushions, his long frame like a rolled carpet flopped over the chair.

Johnny started with the most obvious question. "Do you know who the blackmailer is?"

"No idea," McNaught answered. "Absolutely no idea."

"But you know it's a man," Johnny asked.

"The one time I heard a voice, it was male," McNaught acknowledged.

"How does he communicate with you?" Johnny asked.

McNaught glanced downward. "Through a social networking site, a fan site," he said with some level of embarrassment.

Johnny perked up. "What do you mean?" he inquired.

"Well," McNaught explained, "there's a page he's set up at one of the larger social networking providers. I have to check it daily. If he wants money, he'll post a photo of a sunset and a number, like 50. If this were the example, I'd have 24 hours to get $50,000 into his account, or he'd go public. If I pay, the page reverts to being an innocent little social networking page devoted to a kids' cartoon character. I've never dared see what would happen if I failed to pay. I have too much to lose."

Johnny whistled. "Brazen," he stated. "When and how did he first contact you?"

"That first phone call, no caller ID," McNaught replied. "He gave me the web site address and some bank information, then told me his plan. It's been going on for about three months now."

"You have bank information?" Johnny asked.

"It's a dead-end," McNaught replied. "I asked our accounts payable to check it out under another pretense. They said it's an offshore shell account of some kind, and they couldn't get any further."

"Interesting. And why do you think he has the goods on you?" Johnny asked.

McNaught gave a bitter laugh. "Oh, I've seen what he has. He posts pictures on the site as proof, but only briefly and in an obscure area. They're incriminating. He's also posted other evidence that only I would be able to appreciate. I'll get to that in a minute."

"Do you have the URL?" Johnny asked.

"Oh, I'll never forget it," McNaught sighed. "I travel a lot, and I don't want to bookmark it, so I've memorized it. I use Internet cafés or hotel business centers to check it. I don't want it on any computer I'm associated with."

"Very wise," Johnny said approvingly. "There's a pen on the table. Can you jot the URL on that notepad there next to you?" he asked, motioning to the end table nearest McNaught.

McNaught picked up the pen and scribbled for a moment, then handed the paper to Johnny.

"Does the owner have a profile or email address?" Johnny asked, glancing at the URL. It was innocuous.

"Nothing real that I could find," McNaught answered. "I've checked around the site, and there's nothing that seemed to tie back to anyone in the real world."

"And the pictures," Johnny continued. "Where has he taken your picture with your mistress?"

McNaught shifted his weight. "Lots of places, which is what's so puzzling," McNaught elaborated. "Some very compromising, intimate moments, some public moments, many different places. She travels for her organization occasionally, so we sometimes rendezvous on my business trips. But I haven't seen any signs of anyone following me."

"And he knows your mistress and your wife are sisters?"

McNaught scratched his throat nervously. "Yes, he does. A picture he posted recently showed them both together, a digital cut-and-paste job. They've never met as far I know, but yes, he knows. And he started to up the ante after that, doubling the requested money."

"Does your wife know?" Johnny asked.

"I don't think so," McNaught said, scowling. "She and I began to grow apart a few years ago. She wasn't the same person I fell in love with. Something bitter and angry started to work on her, and it turned me off. I guess I found someone who reminded me of her, but without the growing hostility. I ended up a little too close to home, though."

Johnny shifted the subject slightly. "What are their names?"

"Who?" McNaught puzzled.

"Your wife. Your mistress."

McNaught squirmed perceptibly. "I suppose you need to know that. Absolutely right. Well, my wife's name is Heather, Heather McNaught. My mistress' name is Ivy, last name Thomson. Thomson is the name of the family that adopted her as an infant. The house where she grew up with them was covered in ivy. She was told that's how she got her name."

"And Ivy is your wife's long-lost sister?" Johnny asked.

McNaught laughed loudly and awkwardly. "Crazy, isn't it? I mean, talk about lightning striking twice. Ivy has short, cropped hair, but there's definitely a resemblance. I thought that was all there was to it. Then, I learned of the link after my wife had some genetic screening done, purely informative for breast cancer genes, back about six months ago. Because of my line of work, I had a friend who used to be our company physician administer and manage the testing. He spends most of his time running a small genetics company on the side. Unbeknownst to me, my mistress had a genetics test done that went through this guy's private company as part of a health screening, too. A quality control procedure picked up what it thought was an error, but it was really the familial relationship. Our physician confirmed it, kept it under wraps, and told me about it. He was the only one in a position to know, really."

"And this physician is not your blackmailer?" Johnny asked, testing the obvious.

McNaught laughed again, his body relaxing for the first time since he'd arrived. "No, no, most definitely not," he insisted. "Jim's not capable. He's one of the most honest people I've ever met. Besides, he's independently wealthy himself. Owns his own genetics company, Schwartz Genetics. He doesn't need my money."

Johnny wondered at this answer. Independent businessmen had a knack for keeping up appearances of prosperity even while burying themselves in financial troubles. When things got desperate, they could go to great lengths attempting to save themselves, their egos, and their reputations. He'd seen it many times over the years.

"So his name's Jim?" Johnny asked.

"Yes, Jim Schwartz," McNaught answered. "You can investigate him if you want to, but you'll be wasting your time."

Johnny nodded, jotting the name on the same piece of paper carrying the URL.

"Who else should I know about?" Johnny asked. "Your wife came from a family that gave up a daughter for adoption? Why didn't they keep their second daughter?"

McNaught was clearly not enjoying being grilled. "You ask a lot of questions, but I guess that's your job," he said as preamble to his response. "My wife grew up in New Hampshire on a farm. I don't think she even knows she has a long-lost sister. I'm certainly not going to ask her, and she's never brought it up. But through birth records I was able to confirm that her mother did have another female baby, and the age checks out, so I feel like that confirms the genetic testing. All I can guess, knowing her family and their history, is that the farm went through a tough few years when my wife was a toddler and her sister was born. I think her mother gave up the baby because she couldn't afford to keep her," McNaught speculated. "I've never even met her mother. She stays holed up in New Hampshire. They're not a close family."

Johnny nodded, thinking about what a terrible choice giving up a child must have been. Family woes were nothing new to him, and he knew how they sat in your mind like a hot cinder in the carpet, threatening to burst into flame at any moment.

"Are your wife's parents still alive?" Johnny asked.

"Her mother is," McNaught answered. "Her father died many years ago, when Heather was a toddler and just before her sister would have been born. Drowned on a boating trip with friends. That probably contributed to the decision to put Ivy up for adoption."

"Probably so," Johnny nodded. "Does your mistress have any siblings via her adoptive parents?"

"No siblings," McNaught answered. "She was the Thomson's only child. Her adoptive parents were older, and both died a couple of years ago, her father first, her mother soon after. They were never in great health, but they raised a great daughter. She's never even tried to find out who her birth parents were. She's very well-adjusted."

"OK," Johnny uttered distractedly. "If I were to ask you again point-blank who is blackmailing you, who would you accuse?"

McNaught looked startled. "You asked that before, but saying all this makes me rethink the answer," he replied, looking thoughtful. "Off the top of my head, I'd say I think it's some functionary at either my company or Jim's, someone who got hold of the information, doesn't have a lot of money or scruples, and saw this as a way to make a fast buck."

Johnny thought about this. It was a pretty safe answer, and not unreasonable. It seemed McNaught was truly stymied. He doubted his client would be a source of leads around this key question.

"Now, tell me about the attacks on your company. Why do you think it's eco-terrorism?" Johnny said to McNaught.

"Ah yes, that," McNaught responded. "I didn't know if you'd remember."

Johnny remained silent.

"Well, about the same time as the blackmail started," McNaught said, "we started to see a concerted set of attacks on our manufacturing facilities, shipping routes, and labs. Nothing major, but persistent and focused. Everything was aimed at the side of the business that has to do with agriculture, like genetically modified seeds and disease-resistant crops. There haven't been any attacks on any other part of the business, so our security people are operating under the assumption that these are eco-terrorists. At every attack site, there has been a green flag stuck in the ground, one of those landscaping flags on a thin wire. But nobody's stepped forward to brag about it yet."

"So," Johnny said conclusively, "you've been trying to handle it privately so that you don't scare off investors. The police have no idea."

"Right," McNaught confirmed. "The damage in each case has been in the hundreds or thousands of dollars, nobody's been hurt, and we've been able to sweep it under the rug. But they've been getting more daring recently."

"And you think these things are linked?"

"Someone's trying to hurt me," McNaught replied, an edge to his voice. "I think they're attacking on two fronts. They started at about the same time. Call me paranoid, but it felt like a two-pronged attack when it started, so that's what I think it is."

Johnny paused in his interrogation, letting the facts sink in. Things were happening simultaneously – the blackmail, the vandalism. It was tempting to link them together but he needed to know more first.

"OK," Johnny finally offered. "I think I need to talk with some people. This is a good start. You probably need to get back to your daily routine. How urgent is this?"

McNaught thought for a moment himself. "Given the fact that the blackmailer is becoming more demanding, the sabotage is costing my company thousands each week, and I see no end in sight otherwise, I'll tell you what, Denovo – you solve this while keeping my name out of the media, and I'll sign off on whatever dollar amount it takes."

Johnny wasn't impressed by the open coffers, and it showed, perhaps to McNaught's dismay.

"All right, that's fine," Johnny said. "The sooner the better is what I get from that. This is growing in severity, not getting any better. I'll work fast."

Chapter 3
Clean Up

After McNaught left, Johnny closed the heavy door to his condo with a gentle push and leaned against the doorframe, lost in thought. This was an interesting situation. McNaught seemed to be telling him everything he knew. There were no evasive metaphors, only statements – no fanciful language, no comparisons, nothing theoretical. Fanciful descriptions weren't always a sign of insincerity or disingenuous behavior, but with body language and other signals, they raised warnings that someone might be lying or knew more than they were telling. Johnny had been on his guard, knowing McNaught was capable of cheating on his wife.

It was worrisome.

After a few pensive moments, Johnny walked over to his computer and typed in the URL McNaught had given him. The site that appeared was innocuous, an infantile tribute site to a popular children's cartoon character.

Johnny began to probe. The source code of the site wasn't helpful, most of it concealed in templates driven by the social networking tool, too opaque to reveal any hand at work.

The layout was another template, barely customized and revealing nothing of particular interest. The wording on the site was standard. Judging from the comments users had left, the site's fan base ranged from children to potheads.

Sometimes, the two were difficult to distinguish.

Checking for related domains and sites linking to it yielded nothing helpful. The usual logins he used to probe access only delivered error messages.

He considered setting Tucker loose on it, but he didn't know enough yet to believe it would be worthwhile. Better to keep the big guns for when you need them, he thought. Besides, Tucker had just finished saving his hide on the Fabergé eggs case. He didn't want to go to the well too often.

After a shower and shave, Johnny pondered his next step – approaching the genetics company owned by Dr. James Schwartz.

As McNaught's company physician, friend, and confidant, Schwartz was in a pivotal position. His technical knowledge of genetics might shed some light, and Johnny needed to assess for himself how trustworthy and affluent Schwartz really was.

Friends were easy to fool.

It would also be nice to spend some time with a fellow scientist, Johnny thought, even if he wouldn't be representing himself as a member of that global fraternity.

He deliberated about how to approach Schwartz, deciding the best course was the direct approach. He wanted to see his offices and the man in a natural state – what the moat around the place was like, how the guards inside the walls behaved. If it was a tense, high-security environment, the paranoia itself would tell him something. Announcing his arrival would skew the facts, allow them to adjust, perhaps concealing factors and behaviors he'd want to see firsthand.

Johnny found Schwartz Genetics' address online and entered it into his phone for reference. He left his condo, climbed into his car, put the top down, and drove west out of the city, Boston's sloping and extended skyline receding in his rearview mirror.

The sun gleamed overhead. The day was warm, almost mild, not hot enough to smell pavement but warm enough to feel heat off it.

Schwartz's small company was tucked into the woods along the inner beltway northwest of the city. This was Boston's business corridor, where companies large and small headquartered, their logos peering over the treetops, gazing down haughtily on the passing traffic.

Because Schwartz's company wasn't a multinational goliath, his offices were relatively modest and nondescript given the neighborhood. Hidden away, the secluded building might have housed anything – a shipping company, a cosmetics warehouse, a skating rink. Only when Johnny was almost on top of the place did the words "Schwartz Genetics" become clear, etched on a small sign near the front door, a red dot in an embossed chromosome serving as its logo.

Johnny pulled into the narrow, shaded drive and parked his car in one of the dozen or so spaces designated for visitors, noting how quiet the woods became once his engine's noise died away. Birds and the soft rush from the distant freeway were the only sounds that lingered.

It was a peaceful scene.

The immediate area sported a minimum number of surveillance cameras, a good sign. The place wasn't bristling with electronic surveillance at least. There had been no security gate. The loading docks were behind the back, down a narrow access drive. The small underground garage tucked beneath the building had simple passkey gates.

Johnny walked slowly up the sidewalk and strode through the front doors, headed for the reception desk. The lone observable security guard, a man probably in his 70s, looked up with watery eyes as Johnny approached. The guard looked more like a tattered sock puppet than a robust defense against intrusion.

"Good morning," the guard beamed, apparently happy to see anyone at all. "Welcome to Schwartz Genetics. May I help you?"

"Good morning," Johnny echoed. "I'd like to see Dr. Jim Schwartz. My name's Johnny Denovo."

The security guard's eyebrows arched involuntarily. "Indeed you are! I should have recognized you. I guess my eyesight isn't what it used to be, but now that you're closer, I can see it plain as day. My, are we in any trouble?"

Johnny smiled. "No, no trouble. Just working on a case involving genetics, and Dr. Schwartz's name came up. You can tell him Tom McNaught suggested I see him. It's a private matter."

"Tom McNaught," the guard confirmed as he reached for the phone. He punched a few digits and waited, the receiver resting lightly against his ear, as if it were uncomfortably warm and might burn him if he let it get too close. There was a pause, then the guard perked up and said, "Robert, I have someone here to see Dr. Schwartz. He said it's a private matter. Sure, I'll hold."

The guard gave Johnny a pained, apologetic shrug, and they waited. A moment later, the guard said, "Dr. Schwartz, Johnny Denovo is here to see you. A Tom McNaught suggested he speak with you. Yes sir. I'll ask him to wait a moment."

The guard lowered the phone back into its cradle gingerly. "Well, you must have the magic key," the guard said, bemused and smiling. "Nobody just drops by on Dr. Schwartz, but he said he'll be right up. You can have a seat over there." The guard motioned vaguely with one hand.

Johnny went over to a chair in the modern lobby and sat down, contemplating the dense foliage around him, amazed once again at how green and lush New England was compared to where he had grown up. He'd been in Boston for many years now, but a recent news story from back home and the memories it triggered had made him aware of both his past and present. Juxtaposing the two – verdant forest-covered hills and barren wind-blown desert fringe – had been jarring, sensitizing him to appreciate the dense forests and green lawns of Boston.

Before Johnny could probe the memories deeply, his reverie was broken when a door flew open down a hallway behind the security desk, the rush of air almost palpable the force was so great. A short, muscular man emerged, glasses somewhat askew and a white lab coat gusting behind him. His sandy, thinning hair floated in the breeze created by his brisk, energetic steps. Before he even reached the periphery of the lobby, he shouted a greeting in Johnny's direction and doffed his eyeglasses, jamming them in his shirt's breast pocket.

"Mr. Denovo? Jim Schwartz, my pleasure to make your acquaintance, and please call me Jim," the man said, reaching Johnny as his words raced ahead of him, the volume decreasing as the distance closed. Now that Schwartz was standing with Johnny, his voice had acquired a warm and intimate tone, softening as if they shared a secret.

"Jim, please call me Johnny. It's a pleasure to meet you. Tom McNaught suggested I stop by to speak with you."

"Say no more, say no more," Schwartz said cheerfully but pointedly. "Let's go to my private office and discuss what's on your mind."

"Lead the way," Johnny replied with a wave of his hand, and the two strode silently down the hall, Schwartz shedding his lab coat as they walked, revealing a taut weightlifter's physique under the researcher's cloak.

Schwartz reached a reception desk staffed by a pale, thin man with black hair, slicked back and shiny. He looked sallow and undernourished, almost ghoulish in his matching black wardrobe. Johnny could easily imagine him in a spotlight, reciting self-possessed poems on free evenings at some basement dive in Kendall Square.

"Robert, not a word to anyone about who I'm meeting with," Schwartz snapped as he and Johnny passed the desk. Robert gave Johnny an appraising look but otherwise behaved as instructed, giving off a slightly snippish air.

Schwartz strode through a sleek maple door, held it open to allow Johnny to pass through, and then closed it tightly behind them.

The office was large but not ostentatious, lined with books and what appeared to be souvenirs from years of travel, artifacts from many cultures and regions mixed haphazardly around the room.

"You've been a lot of places," Johnny remarked, gazing admiringly at the objects adorning the bookcases.

"Yes, a benefit of years of field research," Schwartz responded. "Each one has a project associated with it. If the project went well, I can appreciate the beauty of the object. If the project went badly, I keep the object to remind myself to do better next time. It's a mixed bag, but more winners than losers. Can I get you something? A coffee? Water? It's too early for much else."

"No thanks," Johnny demurred. "I'm all set. I'm on a tight schedule today, so if it's all right with you, I'd like to dive right in to why Tom McNaught sent me your way. It's about the affair and the blackmailing."

Schwartz smiled. "I like that, no nonsense. Yes, let's get right to it. No need for small talk. He mentioned he might be looking for some help with this delicate matter. Blackmail is nothing to take lightly. You should know that I know the whole story. Who would have suspected that such a genetic surprise lurked in his mistress' DNA?"

Johnny smiled in return, enjoying the energy Schwartz exhibited. Everything was fired off rapidly and with sharp aim. This was a man not intimidated by ideas or the world at large.

"Exactly. How confident are you in the results?" Johnny asked.

"Oh, 100%. There's no doubt. It's not a case of chimerism – you know, when a twin absorbed by a surviving embryo might confound a simple genetic test. It's not a case of laboratory or human error. No, the test is solid, the results true. Plus," Schwartz continued, "there's plenty of anecdotal evidence about the family to confirm it all. I'm sure he told you about it, right? Not only that, but there's a clear family resemblance. They are sisters, phenotypically as well as genotypically."

Johnny nodded. It seemed like a solid conclusion, and Schwartz obviously knew his stuff.

"All right," Johnny responded. "So, let's agree that the testing is accurate and there's a familial connection. Then the question centers on who got the information and is using it to blackmail McNaught."

Schwartz's countenance clouded. "You know, that's been bothering me, and for the life of me I can't figure it out. Tom and I have been very careful with the information. We met in a public place to discuss it, and then only spoke in the quietest of tones. Nobody could have heard us. I did the testing myself, and once the findings were clear and I'd gone over them with Tom, I destroyed the report. Burned it after shredding it. And it wasn't in any machine here during that time, so nobody could have accessed it. The testing device isn't linked to the network. It prints reports, but then you have to physically move data via a thumb drive to the network if you want to keep it. I could recreate the test any time. I didn't destroy the evidence, just the report of the evidence, if you follow me. So, I don't know how anybody found out about the existence of the link."

Johnny thought about what Schwartz had just said, especially the fact that they had discussed the issues in public. "Where did you meet to discuss the results?" he asked.

"A very busy place – Grand Central station. You can't get much more public than that. It just happened that we were both in New York City that day and decided to catch lunch at one of the posh new restaurants in the revamped station. It's a real jewel now, you know. I'd just finished the testing the night before. We went downstairs and talked it over while we waited for a table. We were in the heart of the public area and must have looked like two businessmen talking about the news of the day. There was nobody nearby, nobody in earshot."

Johnny smiled. The word "earshot" set flares alight in his mind. It was a carefully chosen word with a precise meaning. It was a range metaphor. It connoted an opponent, adversary, or accomplice. At the very least, it suggested a target. Schwartz had set it apart grammatically through emphasis and parallelism. These unconscious cues made the term stand out to Johnny. His limbic brain was shining a spotlight on it. It meant something. It wasn't just a gaffe, an elaboration, or a meaningless linguistic flourish. Language revealed thought and betrayed knowledge. The brain sought to express itself. This was a peek inside.

Schwartz was reassuring him that because nobody was in their immediate proximity, they couldn't have been overheard. But Johnny knew there were other ways to acquire a voice signal, techniques that made range meaningless.

This was especially true in Grand Central station. He'd been in the location Schwartz had described. He knew what was possible, and he was betting Schwartz did as well.

In a flash, Johnny harbored deep suspicions that Schwartz was playing another role in the blackmail scheme, exploiting his friendship with McNaught in a manner Johnny couldn't yet fully see.

Johnny looked at Schwartz from behind his smile. Could Schwartz be a two-faced confidant? Did he set up a circumstance for someone else to benefit from the information?

In an instant, Johnny's brain initiated a new pathway, one that began to evaluate Schwartz and his abilities to deceive.

But he let none of this show in his expression or voice.

"Yes, I see," Johnny intoned seriously. "Very puzzling."

"And," Schwartz continued, "there's still the eco-terrorism angle. Tom told you about that, I'm sure."

"Yes, he did," Johnny answered, viewing Schwartz differently now in his mind's eye.

Schwartz strode behind his desk, tall windows overlooking the forest behind him, his silhouette wrapped in light, casting a long shadow into the room.

"Now, I haven't told Tom this, but I know other companies that are suffering from the same types of vandalism and eco-terrorism he's seeing," Schwartz said gravely. "I have investors, friends, board members. Because I'm a physician, they feel they can confide in me. I know they aren't talking about this to each other, that's clear. And they swear me to secrecy, so I keep my mouth shut. But they are all having issues with low-level and sometimes larger rounds of vandalism, theft, and espionage. It's actually fairly wide-ranging. And in each case, the targets are agribusiness lines, petroleum-based products, and energy facilities. The same green flags are stuck in the ground after each incident. To each CEO, it looks like they're on the bad side of an eco-terror group. They are all putting the facts together in the same manner, but keeping it from the public eye, so nobody's been able to really tie it all together."

Johnny watched Schwartz without responding.

"Did you hear me?" Schwartz asked finally.

"Yes, yes," Johnny answered. "Widespread espionage at many corporations. Looks like eco-terrorism. All hush-hush. You're sworn to secrecy. That's all very interesting."

"Precisely," Schwartz continued. "These people, whoever's doing this, know how to annoy without raising allergic titers, if you follow. No cops, just a lot of pissed off executives who begin to flinch at their own shadows. Very effective."

"Very effective," Johnny echoed rhetorically.

"So," Schwartz asked. "What's your plan?"

Johnny let the question hang in the air for a minute before responding. He wanted to convey the sense that he was considering many options simultaneously when in fact he already knew the course of action before him.

"I'm a bit stymied," Johnny finally responded in measured tones. "This is all very confusing. I have a few directions I could go at once, and I need to ask other people some questions before deciding how to proceed. But I won't take any more of your time, Jim. You've been very helpful."

"Very well, then," Schwartz said, coming around the desk to shake Johnny's hand. "Feel free to call me if you need anything, or stop by any time. Here's my card," he finished, handing Johnny a sleek plasticized business card with beveled corners. A stylized double-helix with one bright codon highlighted in red decorated the front. "Robert will show you out."

"Great, and thanks again for seeing me with no notice," Johnny said, turning. His hand struck a heavy wooden collectible as he turned, sending it to the floor with a reverberating clatter.

"Damn!" he said, reaching desperately for the falling statuette. He hastened to retrieve it. "I'm very sorry. If it's damaged, I'll gladly pay to replace it."

Schwartz was next to Johnny by this time and helped him lift the item, ultimately taking it from Johnny's hands. He examined it a moment, then smiled.

"No need. This one has no real value, either material or sentimental. Besides," he finished, "I think this one could survive a nuclear blast. It's made out of an Asian wood that's as hard as steel."

"Glad to hear it," Johnny intoned. "That's a relief. Again, thanks for your time." As he opened the door, Robert rose from his chair nearby, giving Johnny a wan smile.

The door to Schwartz's office closed behind Johnny with a click. Robert strode forward. "May I show you out?" he inquired politely.

Johnny smiled. "Sure," he responded, looking down the hall and out the windows. "Nice day. You going to be able to get outside?"

"Probably. Today's schedule is pretty tame," Robert answered, his voice monotone.

"Have you worked here long?" Johnny continued in a conversational tone.

"Too long," Robert said in a weary manner. "I've been here since I interned in college. I'm 28 now, so that's about eight years. The benefits are good, and Dr. Schwartz is easy to work for. He's gone a lot, and all I have to do is manage a little bit of office work. I have short days mostly."

"It sounds like a good gig," Johnny agreed. "Say, maybe you can help me. Do you happen to know where Dr. Schwartz goes to relax?"

Robert stopped at the mouth of the hallway, the security desk directly in front of them, the guard scrupulously minding his own business. He thought for a moment. "Well, there are three things he does for relaxation. First is work. He really likes to work. Second is weight-lifting. And third is drinking. He works here, lifts weights at the sports club around the corner, and drinks at the Top of the Hub. He likes the views, he says."

"Really? That's an odd choice of bars, but I guess if I could afford it, I'd do it, too," Johnny admitted, thinking that views from the city's highest point would be even more spectacular after a few adult beverages. "Well, thanks for leading me out."

Robert gave his closed mouth smile again. It was even less convincing than before.

"Certainly," he said. "Good luck with whatever you're working on, Mr. Denovo."

Johnny squeezed around the security desk and smiled in farewell to the guard.

Climbing into his convertible, he gunned it down the short hill leading from the nondescript genetics headquarters. The day had heated up, and so had this case. His head was pulsing with thoughts and scenarios. This was always how he felt when his theories exposed a brilliant, two-faced liar.

Chapter 4
Insurance Run

Johnny drove away from Schwartz Genetics in a relatively agitated state, the wind angrily strafing over the windshield as he pushed his car up to speed. Two observations connected to convince him that Schwartz was more involved in this than McNaught would probably ever be able to bring himself to believe.

"Earshot." There was the use of the word "earshot." It was an unusually precise word to use, and the way he'd introduced it suggested that latent brain activity lay behind it, as if it were a proxy for a secret success, a brag he couldn't reveal but that still leaked through. It suggested calculation, disassociation from events, planning, taking aim.

It was a plotter's word.

The second observation was that when Johnny purposely swept the wooden souvenir off Schwartz's bookcase, the loud clatter hadn't brought Robert in, and he hadn't inquired about the noise as they had walked out together. It was one of the oldest tricks in the book, but Johnny had wanted to make sure that Schwartz's assistant wasn't able to listen in. Sound-proofing an office to that degree wasn't something done lightly. It showed intent, planning.

So, Schwartz didn't have an eavesdropper, and he really was hush-hush, someone who was sensitized to how sounds and voices carried. It had shown in his choice of words and in how his office was soundproofed.

Schwartz had secrets.

Now the question was whether he kept them.

It was going to be a busy day, Johnny thought, shifting his mind into a more action-oriented mode as his sped down the freeway, the traffic thin as summer snoozed to its conclusion. It was time to consult with his old friend in the insurance industry, Daniel Mayfair. This case involved property crimes sneaking under the radar of the police. The insurers might have picked up a scent, and Daniel could help him find it.

Daniel Mayfair, a towering, robust older man with red hair and a jowly face, was jovial, avuncular, and always available, but Johnny liked to give him fair warning. Daniel loved helping Johnny, but he was a busy man, a respected member of his trade, and he deserved the courtesy. Just dropping by was not appropriate and carried no benefit. Besides, Johnny knew how formal and old-fashioned Daniel could be. He required a little special handling.

Johnny opened his cell phone and speed-dialed the number, one hand gripping the steering wheel as he flew down the wide open outer lane.

The phone was answered by Daniel's assistant, Diane, a brusque older woman who, beneath her stately outer shell, had a wicked sense of humor. When Johnny needed to secure her cooperation, a dirty joke or ribald comment was often enough. Over the years, the two had developed a sort of patter, like a comedy duo. Diane had been on vacation most of the month of August, so Johnny was expecting her to be in top form today.

"Daniel Mayfair's office," Diane intoned.

"Hi, hot stuff," Johnny said casually. "The tower of power around?"

"Is that you, Pedro, you hot stud?"

"Yes, it is I," Johnny replied, adopting a poor Spanish accent. "Have you yearned for me, my little jalapeno?"

"Oh Pedro," Diane exhaled in a quiet whisper. "You are my love burrito."

Johnny burst out laughing, knowing he had lost this competition.

"Pedro?" Johnny asked, still laughing. "Who the hell is Pedro?"

"My imaginary Latin lover," Diane whispered back. "But I guess it's just you, Johnny. Too bad."

"Did you miss me on vacation?" Johnny asked.

"Nope. I didn't miss any of this. Cabo was great. I could have stayed there forever. But no Pedro. Just my mother and kids. Being divorced sucks, you know?"

"I can only sympathize. Glad you had fun. We missed you."

"Aw, you're so nice when you want something, Denovo," Diane prodded. "And I guess you want some time with my boss?"

"Does he have about 15 minutes for me today?"

"Can you be here in about an hour?" she asked. "He has a break for about 30 minutes then."

"I'll see you then. Can I bring you anything?"

"Just bring me a Pedro, about six feet tall, thin, and 23. That would do."

"You're a dirty bird, Diane," Johnny laughed. "See you soon."

"Bye," she said. Johnny clicked his phone shut and tossed it on the passenger seat.

He could make the timing work, Johnny thought. It gave him at least half an hour to eat, something he hadn't done today unless coffee counted as food.

He crossed three lanes of traffic at high speed and headed back into downtown Boston for a quick lunch at a favorite seafood establishment.

After a bucket of steamers and a few shrimp, he was feeling much better.

As he prepared to leave for the drive out to Daniel's offices, he put the top up on his car to deflect the growing heat of the day. Air conditioning was in order. Daniel worked inland, away from the cooling breezes of the harbor that made Boston so pleasant.

When Johnny arrived, Diane was away from her desk. The young brunette who had filled in for her on vacation was in her place. She smiled at Johnny as he arrived.

"Hi Wendy," Johnny said as he entered. "Is Daniel expecting me?"

The girl glanced down at a sheet of paper. "Sure is, Johnny," she said. "Diane went out for a smoke and a stroll. You didn't see her coming in, did you?"

"Nope. She must have gone around the block," Johnny answered.

"Must have," Wendy muttered. "Vacations are tough on her, you know. Her Mom is hard to deal with, and add in both kids and the pressure to entertain, and it's not much of a vacation for her."

"That's too bad. Her husband was a bum, and it's not fair to her that she has to carry the whole load now."

"You said it," Wendy agreed wholeheartedly, her pretty smile widening. She glanced back through the glass at Daniel, who was just hanging up the phone. "I think he's ready for you now," she said, standing to open the door for him.

As Johnny was ushered into the glass-walled office, Daniel was just putting away a file. He still kept paper files, insisting they were faster for him than computerized systems. Johnny knew Diane scanned everything into her computer as a fail-safe, carrying her boss secretly into the digital age, no argument allowed.

"Johnny, my boy," Daniel effused in a loud tenor. "How is the great detective? Those eggs from a few weeks ago are still the talk of the industry, I can tell you that. If you ever need a job as an insurance investigator, you're set for life."

"Thanks, Daniel," Johnny smiled. "You were invaluable in cracking that case. I hope you know I couldn't have done it without you."

"Oh, posh," Daniel snorted. "I didn't do anything any old insurance man couldn't have done. It was my pleasure. And those Swiss chocolates you sent over as a token of appreciation went down very well with the missus, you know. She's very glad I know you."

"I'm happy you both enjoyed them," Johnny replied.

"Yes, very much," Daniel said in his low rumble of a voice. "If I don't miss my guess, this is another case crossing my threshold. Am I right?"

"You surmise correctly, my insightful friend," Johnny said, his own vocabulary taking on a more formal aspect in Daniel's presence. "This may be a quick interview, though, because if I'm mistaken, I'll be speeding off to look elsewhere. I'm on a tight deadline with a high-profile client. So, if we can keep this between us, I'd be very grateful."

"Of course," Daniel rumbled. "I won't tell a soul. Now, what do you need to know?"

Johnny paused significantly. "Tell me, does everything claimed in insurance require a police report be filed?"

Daniel laughed. "Johnny, you know the answer to that. Of course not. A photo of the damage and a large policy is usually enough. Is this individual insurance or corporate?"

"Corporate, not individual," Johnny answered. "There seems to be a string of vandalism occurring at various corporations around the country, but at a low level, so police don't get involved. And each company wants to keep it quiet. I was thinking I could verify the trend using an insurance database. You see why I asked the question."

"Of course," Daniel said, donning a pair of reading glasses and turning to his computer. "It would have been a wild goose chase if the answer had been different, and nobody has time for one of those. Now, let me run a query and see what there is to see. I haven't heard of any unusual trends, but if it's something like what you're describing, the trend may have been missed. Run of the mill claims tend to be treated as such. They're nothing sensational. And as you know, we insurance people respond to sensationalism just like everybody else!"

Daniel's eyes twinkled in his ruddy face. He typed commands into his computer with the same distinctive two-fingered style he always used, peering up at the monitor to verify his entries and hitting the Enter key with a definite passion.

"Hmmm, interesting," he growled, looking at the screen. "You might be on to something, Johnny."

"What do you mean?"

"Well, I can only access a small slice of the insurance market right now, but it's there. Petty claims, but a lot of them, all starting back in May, maybe April," Daniel said ponderously, absorbed in the data he was interpreting. "Nobody would think twice about any of these. Sliced tires, cut fences, small fires, claims on damaged lab equipment, damaged electrical conduit, no pattern I can see. All corporate, but all types of corporations. Seems random, but in aggregate the level of activity is much higher than normal. With more time, I could access many more databases. Now," Daniel said, turning from his computer and peering hard at Johnny over the glasses perched at the end of his nose, "tell me what's going on."

Johnny smiled. "You know I can't do that," he said to his friend. "I need to know what you know, and you get to learn all the facts later. That's how this detective game works."

Daniel smiled good-naturedly. "Yes, yes, I had to give it a try, though, attempt to get something out of the great detective. Almost caught you off-guard, didn't I?"

Johnny laughed with a bravado that matched his friend's. He'd learned long ago that Daniel responded best to a refined, gentlemanly approach. "Actually, yes, you almost did, I must confess. But only almost."

Daniel was laughing, as well. "Oh, I do enjoy your visits. Great, interesting questions. I usually end up looking into things for days afterwards. Well, I suppose you'll be wanting some data now, is that right?"

"That's right," Johnny confirmed.

Daniel tapped at the keyboard a little more. "I can't reveal too much. Even though I'm predisposed to help you, limits exist. Let me see here," he said, typing more, then hitting Enter very firmly. "Give me about an hour. I'll email you a flat file of all the data I can get my hands on – but only the addresses, dates, times, photos of the damages, and amounts claimed, all jumbled so you can't tell which is which. That should keep us in daylight."

Johnny smiled at his old friend as he turned to leave. "Thanks, Daniel. Once again, you're a peerless resource."

Daniel beamed back and waved as Johnny left, his phone ringing once more as Diane, who had returned from her walk, began to let calls through again.

Chapter 5
Curveball

After a few minutes of playful banter with Diane, Johnny returned to his car. Pulling out of Daniel's offices, he realized that by boomeranging from the outskirts back downtown and again to the suburbs again, he was just a few miles from Schwartz Genetics if he used the back roads up through Waltham.

He had scolded himself earlier over lunch – he'd taken such a direct approach to interviewing Schwartz that he hadn't done any reconnaissance. He'd seen enough to know that security was fairly lax, and he'd met Robert and the security guard, as well as Schwartz himself, but he knew little else about Schwartz or the property.

He decided to take a detour back to the non-descript office building tucked away in the woods and do some real detective work. He'd at least drive through the parking lot, he told himself. If Schwartz were up to no good, knowing what he drove and a few other details might help at some point.

It was mid-afternoon by the time he arrived at Schwartz Genetics. Some employees were already leaving, probably to deal with child-care issues, Johnny thought. He'd left the workforce just as childcare was becoming an issue for a small subset of his peers, and having them leave early from the lab had held few consequences. Researchers controlled their own schedules for the most part. Here in private enterprise, Johnny noticed that people seemed to have more flexible schedules thanks to communication technologies. The people leaving each held a cell phone to their ear or in their hand as they drove, and he was sure they'd all be on email when they got home. People had learned to slice time wafer-thin.

Driving swiftly through the back of the parking lot, he whipped his little convertible around and slotted into a space at the far end of a parking row. The lot around him was about half full and very quiet. He glanced over at the underground garage tucked beneath the offices.

Getting out of his car, he walked downhill, away from the building's main entrance He snaked around the lowered barrier arm and into the small underground garage, its cool air almost dank in the residue of summer's humidity.

The lighting was dim. Coming in from dappled sunlight, his vision took a moment to adjust. Casting his eyes about, he saw that the interior had been recently refinished and repainted, the parking stripes and walls bright and new. The company was apparently doing well enough to attend to routine maintenance, something that usually slipped if hard times struck.

Walking toward a set of numbered spaces, he found one labeled "President."

Schwartz's car was a large American sports sedan, maroon, with aggressive angles that evoked a sense of tasteful power. It was a status car, a choice Johnny could appreciate. Image mattered. There were stickers in the rear window, a harbor permit and a parking permit for a Back Bay neighborhood. The interior was clean, nothing on the seats, nothing in the cupholders.

Johnny turned to walk out the opposite side of the garage. Pivoting to the right, he was surprised to see Robert moving quickly out of a basement exit and running lithely to a car parked across the lot from Johnny.

It was strange to see the man move this way, Johnny felt, a sense of unease filling him. He couldn't reconcile what he was seeing with how he'd pigeonholed Robert, who had seemed reptilian, with his sallow face, slicked back black hair, and effete mannerisms. The way he moved looked alien and unnatural. He was sprinting fitly and aggressively to his small foreign car, not a slither to be found, his head up and eyes extremely focused.

Johnny ducked down between two cars and watched. Robert seemed to be nervous, especially when compared to the smooth, almost phlegmatic disposition he'd exhibited earlier in the day.

As his car started, loud music pounded and Johnny could see him toweling his head, apparently removing the gel that had kept his hair shellacked to his head like a swim cap. The car peeled out loudly in the garage, the music's volume increasing as the vehicle approached Johnny's hiding place. As the car tore by, tires squealing on the painted floor, Johnny only caught the slightest glimpse of Robert's silhouette, the poor lighting and car's speed making any more observations impossible. Robert was a shadowy blur.

Standing up, Johnny smiled inwardly and sympathized. He could remember his early jobs. Apparently, Robert put on airs at work but was a bit of a wild man outside the office.

Johnny shrugged involuntarily in response to his thoughts, then turned and continued walking through the parking garage, checking for other details and avoiding the security cameras, an easy task as they lazily traced badly timed arcs. There was nothing more to see. Documenting Schwartz's car choice had been the main point of the return visit, and now he'd know the car if he ever saw it – whether he was following it or was being followed.

Leaving the garage and climbing back into his car, Johnny looked around quickly to be sure nobody had spotted him returning. He was glad he had put the roof up on the convertible, obscuring him inside and making it harder to identify the car as the same one that had visited earlier in the day. Fame cut both ways. He enjoyed slipping through undetected.

The afternoon had worn on a bit, and he still had tasks ahead of him if he was going to close McNaught's case quickly. He'd promised he would, and he wanted to return to his interrupted summer break as soon as possible. Already the case had become significantly more complicated.

It wasn't just an adulterer being blackmailed anymore. There was much more at work here. The high level of coordinated damages suggested a network, a plan, something far beyond McNaught's parochial interests.

It was time to bring in the big guns.

Tucker Thiesen – also known as Tucker the Titan, Tucker the Triumphant, Tucker the Tumultuous – was one of the biggest guns Johnny could call on. Since childhood, Tucker had attracted nicknames, mostly alliterative. The fact that he'd developed into one of the nation's top computer intelligence officers did nothing to change how Johnny thought about him – a portly adolescent, the brilliant, witty, and fun-loving kid he'd grown up with. Tucker had incredible security clearances now. He worked freelance with officials at the highest levels.

Johnny didn't have to call ahead to visit Tucker. He had the same probability of getting time with him whether he called or not, so didn't bother with the extra effort.

Besides, catching Tucker unawares had always been a bit of sport.

Tucker lived near the harbor, along one of the larger piers in Boston. It was an enviable location, cooled in the summers and warmed in the winters by the moderating waters. With improvements to Boston's bayfront, the location had only become more desirable.

Once Johnny parked, he put the roof of his convertible down again, the breezes from the bay washing the heat from the day around him. He quickly donned his baseball cap, hoping to avoid being recognized even in the few steps it would take to get inside Tucker's building.

Tucker rented an entire floor, an unparalleled situation for residents in this expensive area of high-end properties. Most condos were more like apartments, a few rooms with neighbors, making Tucker's apartment an estate by comparison.

Over the years in Boston, Johnny had learned that Tucker's apartment also had secret capabilities. It was armored, soundproofed, and protected by an elaborate yet unobtrusive security system.

Riding the elevator up, Johnny snorted slightly. If Tucker's superiors knew what a muttonhead his friend had been as a kid, they wouldn't let him near an ice cube tray, much less some of the most sophisticated technology and information in the world.

The elevator reached Tucker's floor, the doors opening mechanically. The hallway was eerily silent. Usually, loud music, either of Tucker's making or from his sound system, reverberated through his insulated space. Tucker was as much an intuitive thinker as an analyst, and music helped inspire his muses, he claimed.

Instead, only a mortuary's hush greeted Johnny.

It was so quiet that Johnny dared not speak, his body reacting with a surge of primal anxiety. Cautiously, he strode forward, feet lightly rolling on the dense carpeting, reverent of the silence, as if some holy rites were being performed and he, a philistine, were striving to pass through unmolested.

Suddenly, there was a loud groan, a thunderous bang that shook the floor, and a scream of triumph.

"Hot damn," Tucker yelled at the top of his lungs. "Yes! Yes!"

Moving quickly now, Johnny followed the sound down the hall and peered into the only open door on the floor. As he approached the door, his mind raced with the possibilities this situation portended. What kind of compromising position might he find his friend in this time?

As Johnny arrived at the open door, Tucker was still carrying on vocally.

"Ooh, who's the man? Who's the man?" he was chanting.

Catching sight of his friend, Johnny nearly burst out laughing, but caught himself, instead relishing the moment and hoping to exploit it to grand effect.

Tucker was dressed in a ragged t-shirt and Scottish highland gear, including a kilt. He was dancing around a large steel ball in sheer delight, flexing angrily in its direction occasionally.

"Well, Mr. Mac-Thiesen, you certainly seem overjoyed at your manly feat," Johnny interjected when the time was right.

Tucker nearly leaped out his kilt in surprise.

"How long have you been watching me?" Tucker demanded as he spun about, his eyes wild under a sweaty brow.

"Long enough to know that you're no Scotsman," Johnny laughed, leaning against the door frame.

"About that, you may be wrong," Tucker replied. "I have become the Scot incarnate! This may be my claim to fame. World's strongest man. You watch. I'm in training."

Johnny nearly rolled his eyes, but had seen this often enough that he took it in stride. Tucker's brilliance was partially fed by his frequent fascinations and obsessions. Last month, it had been fitness and health, and before that topiary and yoga. These things came and went, but they kept Tucker sharp and alive. He had a diverse knowledge of obscure topics. He was a deep well of arcane knowledge. It often came in handy.

"Where'd you get the kilt?" Johnny asked practically, his eyes on the tartan wrap his friend sported.

"Online," Tucker answered. "And, no, I'm not wearing underwear, so you can cram that question back into your brain." Tucker's voice took on a more whimsical tone. "It's breezy. You'd like it."

Johnny laughed again. "Maybe another day. Today, I have questions."

Tucker heaved a great sigh and wiped the sweat from his brow and face with a large white towel that had been lying on a stool nearby.

"Looks like my strongman training has to stop for a bit," Tucker muttered, his voice partially muffled by the towel as he wiped rivulets of sweat from his face and chin.

"Just for a little bit," Johnny reassured him. "Think of it as recovery."

"Need a snack," Tucker said distractedly, and disappeared through an interior door. "Come on in, Denovo. You can leave that door open. You've been reintegrated, as you'll recall."

Tucker's formidable security systems had factored into Johnny's last case. A systems breach had forced Tucker to recreate his whitelist of allowed persons. Not being on the list could be painful, Johnny had witnessed, and he knew he never wanted to learn firsthand what could happen. He'd also learned that leaving one door open was somehow integral to the security system.

Johnny followed Tucker and found himself in his friend's spacious kitchen. It was surprisingly and sparklingly clean. Tucker was pulling a package of cheese out of the refrigerator.

"Needs some protein, I do," he stated, pulling some slices free, his voice taking on a faint brogue. "Want some?"

"Not now, I just ate," Johnny answered, raising a hand in refusal. "Can I grab an email on your computer? It has some files attached that I want you to look at."

Tucker, his mouth full, motioned Johnny toward another door across the kitchen. Passing through it, Johnny found himself in the familiar living space and computer room Tucker seemed to frequent the most.

Johnny's gaze immediately went to his left. He gave the eye-catching artwork on the wall a baleful glance. It was a large grid of eight patterned squares with a blank square in the center. Each occupied square was filled with uniform diagonal shapes, a bit jagged, like small bolts of lightning.

Johnny knew this artwork actually served as a monitor of Tucker's apartment and security grid. He shuddered at what these electrical patterns might portend for intruders.

He looked back to his right at Tucker's computer stations, a moshpit of desks and monitors and cables. Tucker's sleek silver laptop was poised in the center, waiting with an almost palpable power.

Johnny went over, opened up a browser, and logged into his email. He found the message from Daniel and saved the attached files to Tucker's desktop. The file with photos of the damages was gigantic.

Just then, Tucker emerged from the other side of the room, this time wearing shorts and a clean t-shirt. He still had the towel over one shoulder and dabbed his face now and again.

"OK, Denovo," he growled. "Let's see why you've disturbed my training."

Johnny moved aside as Tucker swung into the computer bay like a fighter pilot swinging into a cockpit.

"Don't you want the backstory first?" Johnny asked.

"I figured you'd tell me while I fiddled," Tucker responded, his hands flying over the keyboard with great dexterity.

"I put some files on your desktop. The first is a file listing acts of corporate vandalism that have occurred over the last few months, just the insurance claims," Johnny explained. "All the dollar amounts are small, and from what I've learned, the police aren't involved yet. Each company is sweeping them under the rug. They don't want word leaking out that eco-terrorists are targeting them. Might hurt their equity positions. The second file is pictures of the damages."

"Why do you think it's eco-terrorism?" Tucker asked, clicking his computer's controls rapidly.

"My client said that everything targeted has been at the agricultural side of his biotech firm," Johnny commented. "Another source confirmed that the companies are having their agribusinesses, petroleum-based lines, and energy facilities targeted. At every scene, the vandals plant a small green flag. For each company, it would look like looming eco-terrorism, but each one is trying to keep it quiet. So there's no real terror yet, and nobody's claiming responsibility."

"These are the files?" he asked Johnny, pointing at his desktop.

"Those are the files," Johnny confirmed.

"All right, let's see what these little babies hold for us," Tucker mused, opening the spreadsheet. He looked disappointed. "Johnny, this is dead boring. It's a list of addresses, dollar amounts, dates, and times. Where's the encryption, the secret code, the hackery, the jiggery-pokery? I'm a professional, you know. I have my standards."

Johnny smiled. "I know, it's underwhelming. But from simple stone, grand cathedrals are built."

"Grand cathedrals, huh?" Tucker scoffed with a huff. "A child could analyze this."

Johnny paused and began to think out loud. "Well, maybe and maybe not. I think there's bound to be a pattern somewhere. But you're right, these data are too scant to hold the pattern themselves. So, I think we're looking for something that shares some pattern with this set, a complementary system. And you know more potentially complementary systems than any man alive."

Tucker let this sink in for a moment. "Gotcha. This is a footprint, and you want the foot."

"Couldn't have said it better myself," Johnny noted. He was always impressed to see high intelligence boiled down to such a practical level.

"OK, if we're going to do this, let's do it right," Tucker said enthusiastically. "Stand back!"

Johnny did as instructed and retreated to the other side of the computer tables, leaning against an armchair. There was a manic procession of keystrokes and mouse clicks. All the while Tucker presided over the scene like a grand marshal, his eyes watchful and intense. At last, still working, he glanced up at Johnny.

"Well, nothing with the dollar figures. Totally random, other than everything being under $5,000, if that helps. Probably some materiality issue with insurance. Yes, I see this file came from Daniel, so I know its source. I look at everything in a file, you know that. His computer needs an upgrade, you can tell him that from me. Old file format here. Can't blame him. Insurance business is pretty stodgy. OK, what else? I don't have company names, but from the addresses and cross-matching, I can infer them. It's a representative list of companies with multistate operations, some multinationals, nothing unusual, no clear industry skew. As time passes, it's moving west, like it's emanating from a single source along the Atlantic seaboard. Don't know if that helps." Tucker looked up for an indication of approval or comprehension. Johnny nodded.

"Yes, this all helps," Johnny confirmed. "What else do you have?"

"What else do you have?" Tucker mocked. "Always wanting more, eh, Donovo? Fine. I shall provide. Now, as for the dates and times, there are some patterns. The set starts in April. Fridays are the days of lowest activity. Also, most of the reports were filed early in the morning, which suggests the vandalism happened over night. Not surprising, since nighttime's a good time in general to vandalize things. But that means if Friday is the day of lowest activity in the file, then actually Thurday is the day of least vandalism, if you follow. N minus one for this data set. There is afternoon activity occasionally during the week, but that's almost always on the weekends. Now, what would explain that?"

Johnny stared at his friend blankly for a moment, then repeated the findings back. "Starts in April, mostly late night vandalism, nothing much emanating from Thursdays, some day activity, mostly on the weekends."

Tucker snapped his fingers. "Baseball."

Johnny blinked at the apparent nonsequitur. "What did you say?"

Tucker looked a little abashed now. "I said 'baseball.'"

Johnny remained silent, not wanting to chase a timorous inspiration away. He knew to trust instinct, and his limbic brain was firing again, giving him the same rush of confidence it had provided when he had flashed on Schwartz's use of the word "earshot." He had trained his brain to register these impulses, and he obeyed them.

"Why baseball?" he asked encouragingly.

"Well," Tucker replied more confidently, "what you just said sounds like a baseball schedule to me. Starts in late spring. Not much on Thursdays, day games on the weekends, an occasional day game on weekdays but it's rare. Maybe because we just went to a game I have it on my mind. Maybe this is an availability error, right, where you think data fits a model that you're familiar with? But if the shoe fits, you know? This might explain the footprint."

Johnny could see the sense of Tucker's inspired outburst. "Well, no harm running with it. Can you put the dates and times here against this year's baseball schedules?"

"Easily done. I keep a baseball database, you won't be surprised to learn," Tucker said, punching away at his keyboard. Shortly, he sighed, "Not a good enough match. Too many holes, but some intriguing linkages. What if it's not a team, but something related to a team?"

"A particular player? Maybe someone was traded?" Johnny speculated.

"Weird, but, OK, I can try that." Tucker punched more keys. "Nothing on that. These things continued after the trade deadline, with nothing changing in the pattern."

"An umpire?" Johnny suggested.

Tucker leaned back and sighed. "An umpire?" he said with disdain. Then, after staring off into space a moment, Tucker changed his tune. "It must be a boring job. Why not? Maybe we have a disgruntled umpire." More keystrokes, and then a verbal report. "Negative on that one, boss."

Both men sat in silence for a few ticks of the clock. Tucker was the first to tender a new suggestion.

"What if it's a place?"

"You mean a particular ballpark?" Johnny asked.

"On it!" Tucker bellowed. There was more clicking and tapping. "Well, if we're not the lucky ones. Home games only now, that's what I'm searching. Guess which park's schedule matches the times and dates on Daniel's report to a tee, if you assume the morning claim filings correlate to a game the night before?"

"Don't tell me," Johnny groaned, dreading the answer. It hurt him to think that something he loved might be entangled in this sordid affair. "Fenway."

"You called it," Tucker beamed. "None other. Our venerable and blessed old Fenway. Somehow, it's at the center of whatever you're investigating. It's like a beacon."

Chapter 6
Third Base

Johnny strode back over to the armchair and perched on its arm, reflecting for a moment on what Tucker had just deduced from Daniel's data set. How could it be that Fenway Park was somehow mixed up in a large network of eco-terrorism activities? How could the schedule of his beloved Red Sox be perverted into a source of nefarious commands issued to a large eco-terror network that so far had gone undetected? It seemed far-fetched and offensive, but Johnny knew how the motivation to conceal often created strange and bull-headed schemes. Plus, it was where the data had led them.

"You're sure about this?" Johnny said, almost to himself.

"Very confident," Tucker confirmed, glancing at a monitor. "Ninety-nine point five percent or better, if you must know."

Johnny sighed deeply. Fenway. His world of internecine schemes and terrifying plots had now struck at his favorite oasis, his sanctuary.

Was there was no place to hide from the creeps?

He felt a deep weight grow in his chest.

"Want to look at the pictures now?" Tucker asked, oblivious to Johnny's inner angst.

"Sure," Johnny said, forcing his emotions away and striding over to the computer monitor again. Tucker had opened the photos in a slideshow application, the kind that streamed them seamlessly from side to side. In a long sequence, there was photo after photo of burned vans, broken windows, smashed transformers, and sliced fences. In about half of the photos, a green landscaping flag could be seen planted in the grass nearby.

"They confirm what we've been told," Johnny shrugged, going back over to lean on the armchair. "The damages have been pretty minor, focused on transport and energy, quick in-and-out affairs."

"Well, I'll hold onto these," Tucker said. "Never know when you'll need a good vandalism photo for your holiday cards."

Johnny wanted more facts, new facts. The pictures only confirmed what he'd been told.

His best bet at this point was to keep stoking Tucker with information. Once Tucker was alight with excitement, it was best to not let the fire die out.

"Tucker," Johnny said. "Type in this URL." He struggled for an instant to remember the web address McNaught had given to him earlier in the day, but was able to reconstruct it after a moment. Tucker typed it in as he spoke.

"OK, a tribute page on a social networking site, honoring a favorite cartoon character of rugrats and stoners everywhere," Tucker confirmed. "So, what's that have to do with anything?"

"Tucker, remember the guy who flagged me down at the end of the game yesterday?" Johnny asked.

"Um, yeah, I guess I do," Tucker replied.

"Tom McNaught, the biotech mogul, remember? He's being blackmailed for something. The blackmailer sends McNaught to this URL to signal when he wants some hush money. McNaught's also had instances of eco-terrorism at his company. I was looking into the blackmail part when one of his contacts told me that the vandalism is much more widespread than most people know."

"I see," Tucker murmured, leaning back in his chair with a creak. "And you'd like me to break in and poke around?"

"If you so choose," Johnny offered.

"Oh, I so choose," Tucker replied, flipping forward in his chair. "You know I hate people who use computers for nefarious purposes. And I love breaking down amateurs. It's quite enjoyable. Must keep the pecking order straight in the realm of the spooks and technologists. Give me a moment."

There was another burst of keyboard activity from behind Tucker's terminals, a few curse words, and finally a huff of resignation.

"Well, these may be amateurs, but if they are, they're good," Tucker revealed. "They've hit upon something I can't solve with what I know now. Because they're using a public platform, it's architected all wrong for my techniques. It's in the cloud, hard to find. I need more information."

"We both do," Johnny enunciated softly, his voice nearly a whisper. "Here's what we have, as far as I can tell. Baseball, web site, blackmailer, and eco-terrorism network. We can buy our way into only one, and there's a game tonight. I'll grab a couple of tickets from a scalper and we'll go. Can you slap a tracer on this site so we can audit it later?"

"They won't feel a thing," Tucker assured him. "You want me to keep this quiet for now, I assume?"

"Right," Johnny confirmed. "We'll alert the proper authorities in due time. Like you said, we need more information."

Tucker chortled. "And I get a free baseball game in the bargain!"

"You'll pay for your own nachos, though," Johnny established. "Meet me at Fenway at 7 p.m. sharp, at the south end of Yawkey Way. See what you can do in the meantime."

"Sure thing," Tucker confirmed. "You can always use a free Red Sox game to bribe me. See you tonight."

Johnny turned to leave, with Tucker banging away at his computer, still trying to crack the site McNaught's blackmailer was using.

As he exited, he glanced once more at the strange artwork on his wall, its display a reminder of the morbid force humming within Tucker's odd habitation.

The afternoon was edging toward evening as Johnny returned to his car, shadows from the city stretching out, cool canyons mixed with harbor breezes generating that unique Boston feel he loved. The interplay of sea air and city bustle was energizing.

Yet, in the midst of this idyllic setting, a plot was growing, little weeds in the cracks all around them, small acts of vandalism across the country, each easily eradicated on its own. But the roots weren't being eliminated, and the weeds were spreading.

Tonight, he wanted to get into the root system.

He arrived back at his condo to find a voice message from Mona waiting.

"Hi Johnny," Mona's voice began. "I lucked into two tickets to see that comedian you were telling me about the other day. He's in town for one show only, at the Wilbur. It's tonight. Call me if you can make it. I got these for you, so I sure hope so, but I know you have a case, too. Anyhow, give me a call when you get this message, Mr. Detective."

Dialing her number, Johnny felt a small twinge of guilt. He had to refuse the offer. The case took precedence. Besides, he didn't want to act like an eager puppy, bounding to her in thoughtless joy every time she beckoned. Mona Landau was a complicated woman, and they had a complicated relationship. They had to work to retain its essential tension.

On the second ring, Mona picked up the phone with her usual business-like tone.

"Mr. Denovo, did you get my message?" she asked.

"Yes, I did," Johnny replied. "Listen Mona, I'd like to go with you tonight, but I've already made plans to go to the Sox game with Tucker."

"Really?" Mona said a little icily. "You'd take Tucker over me?"

Johnny felt his stomach knot. "That's not the point. This case has exploded. He and I need to go to the game. It's too much to explain right now, but it has to do with the case, and I promised McNaught I'd work on a tight timeline."

"OK," Mona said, her voice suddenly and inexplicably light-hearted. "I was just teasing you anyhow. It was a longshot. I made a backup plan just in case, so no big deal. You'll have to tell me about it some other time. Where are your seats?"

Johnny's stomach knotted again. He glanced at the digital clock on his stove. "No tickets yet. I'm going to get some from a scalper right now."

Mona was silent. "No tickets, and throwing me over for a case. OK, Denovo, I guess you're taking this 'cool it' mentality all the way."

"Mona, that's not it," Johnny said, sounding a little defensive. "It's just not the right night. We're still on for this weekend, right?"

"I suppose so," Mona replied. "Unless something comes up. Right now, I need to call my backup plan to make sure we're still on. Talk with you tomorrow."

Ending the call, Johnny felt in the back of his throat the bitter bile of a potential relationship problem. His only worry was that when relationships degraded, they could get ugly, and Mona and he still had a professional alliance to maintain. Having a relationship to worry over while on a case was the last thing he needed.

But he didn't have time to indulge these thoughts. He had tickets to get. He had to move now if he wanted some that provided a good view of the field.

Mona would wait.

Still, he felt his jaw clench as he departed for Fenway. Who was this "alternative" she mentioned? They'd set no prohibition on seeing other people. Johnny hadn't had any time or interest in diversifying, but Mona's life and attitudes might be different. They weren't spending much time together. Something might have changed. He knew she was able to master her feelings, marshaling and compartmentalizing them with alacrity. Perhaps she was moving on to a different compartment tonight, an awkward train metaphor springing to mind.

Johnny shook his head in an effort to force out the stray and jealous thoughts.

Whatever the situation, he hoped a romantic train wreck wasn't going to complicate matters further. He didn't need a burning and twisted pile-up of romance competing for his attention during a complicated case.

It was about two hours before game time once Johnny made it to Fenway Park. He prowled Yawkey Way, the bustling and jovial pregame crowd erasing the tension he'd been feeling ever since leaving Schwartz's office. Red Sox fans created a spectator event in and of themselves, with their boisterous voices and fan gear, an amalgam of ages, races, and attitudes. Charged up by a few beers and some junk food, they became a vibrant mosaic of fandom at its finest.

Johnny started looking for a scalper, a sole person in the crowd craning his head for eye contact. In fairly short order, he lucked out, finding a hefty man seeking to sell two field level tickets on the first base side. Johnny paid full asking price, not wanting to linger and have his identity revealed. The man didn't recognize him. Johnny had worn his baseball cap, some non-prescription eyeglasses, and a tattered Red Sox shirt drained of color by its many washings. Also, the shadows pouring into Yawkey Way helped obscure him in the late day's trailing light.

The tickets cost him a pretty penny. The seller almost laughed with glee at the lack of dickering and the price paid, but Johnny figured he'd put them on McNaught's expenses later. There was no time for a drawn out negotiation. Tonight, he needed to be inside Fenway.

During the day, Johnny's logical cerebrum had been hard at work, rationalizing and trying to bring order to his thinking. The ideas emanating from this section of his brain had cooled his notion that Schwartz was a knowing participant. The mental pathways inherent to his cerebrum wanted him to believe that Schwartz was innocent.

Yet, his limbic brain was impatient and unsatisfied with this tepid, logical trail-breaking. Its general disrespect for cerebral thinking made Johnny feel toward these rational thoughts as an exasperated judge would feel listening to a felon's daft alibi.

His limbic brain did not suffer fools gladly.

His gut feeling centered on what a logical thinker would dismiss as flimsy evidence, the single careful use of the word "earshot," a metaphor for sound that connoted calculation, like a gunnery sergeant's aim. As soon as Schwartz used that word, Johnny sensed accomplices, plausible deniability, and deceit.

His limbic brain kept fanning the suspicions around the word. It was a hot spot. He had to pay attention to it.

Slipping the scalped tickets into his hip pocket, Johnny checked the clock on his cell phone. He had time to kill before meeting Tucker. Glancing up, he saw the distinctive tower of the Prudential Center peeking through the low rooftops around Fenway, its massive spike of an antenna inoculating the sky, its top floors alight.

That was a spot he needed to visit.

Walking quickly from the circus environment of Yawkey Way, he hailed a passing taxi.

The ride over to visit the Top of the Hub took only minutes, the Jamaican cabbie jetting down the straight streets of Back Bay, hitting most of the lights and barely flinching as he brushed back some of the more adventurous pedestrians.

Alighting at the foot of the Prudential Center, Boston's tallest skyscraper, Johnny paid the fare and strolled into the magnificent lobby with its fountains and sparkling décor. The Prudential's tony tenants paid a premium to boast an address at the Pru.

The elevators up to the Top of the Hub were in a separate lobby tucked away behind a set of walls. It was an exclusive route to the bar, restaurant, and tourist trap with 360-degree panoramic views of Boston. As he rounded the corner to the elevator banks, an elevator opened, the white chevron pointing up, the sleek brass interior clean and sophisticated. The ride up was smooth and swift.

When he arrived, the top floor was quiet, almost deserted. Prior to a Red Sox game at season's peak and with school back in session, tourists and business people had other early agendas. A lone bartender busied himself behind the parabolic bar, restocking the liquor in anticipation of a busy night.

"Evening," Johnny said in greeting.

The bartender, his shaggy black hair flying up like an explosion as he lifted his head, shot him a sidelong glare, his countenance sallow and menacing. "Barely. You're starting early."

Johnny was taken aback. Hostility emanated from across the long, sweeping counter, a palpable misanthropic energy pulsing the air. This was the most antagonistic bartender he'd ever met.

"Well, it's time for a drink somewhere," Johnny joked, noting the tension privately but projecting a calm exterior. The bartender's attitude was meaningless, the threat empty.

"Oh Jesus, not that old cliché," the bartender snarled with an acid tongue, turning his back on Johnny and spitting in a sink at his waist. "Can't you think of anything new?"

Johnny was puzzled. This person was beyond antagonistic. The stoop of his shoulders, the way he ejected his words as if they were distasteful seeds – every nerve seemed to gap with negative energy. Yet this person worked in the hospitality industry. How could this be?

"Well, how about this for new?" Johnny responded, his voice hard as a hammer. "Pull your head out of your ass and get me a drink, you prick."

The bartender stood up straight and looked Johnny in the eye for the first time, his sunken cheeks, flaring nostrils, and glowering brow transmitting bitterness. He turned his head and spat in the sink to his right. There was a seething resentment about his entire aspect, as if he despised not only Johnny, his job, and himself, but Boston and even the world on which he found himself living.

"That's better," he finally managed, but the feeling of free-floating hatred didn't diminish. In fact, Johnny could see the bartender looking out the tall windows at Boston with an icy menace. "What do you want?"

"All right, let's cut this off right now," Johnny said coolly. "I get it. You hate the world. You have an attitude. That's great. How long do you think you're going to last in this job acting like this?"

"Long enough," the bartender rumbled flatly. "I've worked here three years already. Does that surprise you?"

"And you've acted like a dirtbag the entire time?" Johnny asked.

The bartender smiled, revealing teeth that looked very white and precise. It was not a pleasant smile. "Except for the interview," he answered, his voice low and suddenly silken.

Johnny smiled back. "OK, great, that's longer than I'd have expected. Now get me a gin and tonic with lemon."

The bartender sighed, spat again into the wash basin, and went a few steps down the bar to mix the drink, Johnny carefully watching the entire time where he spat. When he came back, Johnny reengaged him after taking a sip. It was a damn good drink, he had to admit. Along with an attitude that could actually provoke drinking in the clientele, his mixology skills might explain why there was some job security here for even this throwback.

"What's your name?" Johnny asked.

"Well, you're Johnny Denovo," the bartender said, his voice curdling the words. "That's all I need to know."

"I asked you for your name," Johnny pressed, staring unflinchingly at the man's skeletal countenance.

"Oh, you just assumed I'd know your name, is that why you didn't introduce yourself?" the bartender retorted with sarcasm.

"Pretty much," Johnny answered wearily. "Can you just answer the damn question."

"Paul," the bartender answered. "Call me Paul."

"OK, Paul," Johnny sighed. "Nice to meet you."

Paul didn't answer.

Johnny took a sip of his drink and continued. "Do you know a Dr. James Schwartz."

"Can't say that I do," Paul answered.

"Short man, sandy hair, lifts weights, would be a regular here," Johnny continued.

Paul looked up. "Yeah, him I know. I call him Jim. He still calls me Paul. It works out."

This guy is unbelievable, Johnny thought, taking another sip.

"Ever talk with him?" Johnny asked.

"Why? Will you be jealous if the answer's yes?" Paul mocked, spitting again.

"I'll take that as a yes," Johnny replied emotionlessly. He had to draw this out, and the best way to do that was to appear nonplussed by the jibes.

"Yes, he likes to talk," Paul stated. "He's traveled a lot, knows a lot of people, brings in friends and associates once in a while. Is that what you wanted to know?"

"That's good enough," Johnny said, putting a bill on the counter and taking one last sip of his drink. He'd barely touched it, but he'd had enough. "It's been awful talking with you."

"The feeling's mutual," Paul chided as Johnny left.

Chapter 7

Top Spin

Johnny was doubly irritated leaving the Top of the Hub. Not only had the encounter with the bartender been unpleasant and unproductive, but he hadn't been able to drink enough to blunt the stabs of anger and animosity he felt.

He needed to calm down.

Once he was seated in a cab headed back to Fenway, he concentrated on a tai-chi routine, knowing that remembering an activity, or even watching an activity, would cause his neurons to respond as if it were actually happening. In a few moments, the tai-chi worked its magic and he was feeling balanced again.

The streets had gotten busier as the cab wended a path back toward Yawkey Way. This driver had no choice but to weave slowly street to street.

The cab left Johnny just short of Fenway Park, the traffic growing too dense for the car to make any useful forward progress. Johnny walked briskly through the energized crowd, searching for Tucker.

His friend appeared out of the throng in full Red Sox regalia – ballplayer jersey, cap, and a glove for catching foul balls. He'd also brought along his official scorer's book, a practice he'd sustained since childhood. Even when all he could do was watch baseball on television, he kept his own version of the scoring. As a kid, the books had piled up in a corner of his bedroom, each one a season of memories distilled in pencil marks and eraser shavings.

Tucker could be meticulous about data, and he liked the cryptic, slightly arcane rituals of scorekeeping. After the game, with the book cast open and a beer at his elbow, he'd regale Johnny with the play-by-play, reconstructing it with astonishing accuracy using just the hash marks and numbers recorded in the journal.

Data was what Tucker specialized in – decoding information, making sense of the obscure. Baseball scorekeeping was a simplified version of his avocation. Over the years, he'd accumulated a vast database of play-by-play game scoring.

"Johnny, I have something for you," Tucker said, greeting his friend slightly breathlessly. "I did a little more digging. I found some new trends."

"Nice to see you, too, pal," Johnny replied, slapping Tucker on the shoulder. "Come on, let's get inside and find our seats. Then we can catch up."

Johnny reached into his pocket and handed Tucker his ticket. They passed through the turnstiles and headed up the concourse.

After grabbing a beer and hot dog and Tucker adding his nachos, they made their way through the capacity crowd to their seats – field-level, along the first base side. It was a glorious late summer evening, a zephyr breeze from the west threatening to deaden home runs, a purpling sky brushed apart by feathered clouds. Overall, it was flawless.

The lights in Fenway were already up. The crowd was crackling with excitement. The Red Sox were once again on the threshold of a strong playoff run, and the loyal, lifelong fans were edgy for another celebration.

Glancing about the brightly lit environs, Johnny breathed in Fenway – the old and new, the recent additions and changes blending in well and updating the park while preserving its essential character.

Johnny had always felt a special appreciation for the timeless aspect of Fenway. Even when he'd lived across the country and Boston had been a remote, unknown city, watching a game against the backdrop of Fenway elicited the romance of the sport like no other park. The fans, dappled behind the players and bundled against the fall breezes and chilly temperatures, complemented the gruff and gritty team. There was a connection between spectators and players at Fenway that sparked across any distance. Even watching on television in a dim basement hundreds of miles away, you could feel it.

As they seated themselves, Johnny gave Tucker time to arrange his extra food burden before inquiring further. He watched families settle in, young couples converse awkwardly getting to know each other, and die-hard fans sit stoically waiting for the familiar to-and-fro of action to begin. Finally, Tucker stopped arranging his food and scorekeeping materials. He glanced at Johnny with a sigh, worn out at the effort it had taken to nest.

"OK, Tuck," Johnny started. "What's the latest?"

"Well, I could say I'm a genius, but that's not news," Tucker began. "And I'm about to become the world's strongest man."

"All undoubtedly true," Johnny stated, giving his friend time to catch his breath.

"So," Tucker continued, taking his first bite of hot dog, the nachos balanced precariously on his opposite knee, "I looked at the data a little more. There are other trends. First, there have been three double-headers here at Fenway this season because of weather. Remember that $5,000 limit we found in the damages? Well, on the days of double-headers, not only did the attacks come significantly closer to that limit, but there were more of them. So there's a dose-response relationship, if you will. More proof that our theory holds. And if I trend the damages since the beginning, the damages are increasing over time, slowly but surely, and there are more attacks, like a net being cast or a ripple expanding across a pond. In fact, when I put it on a map," Tucker said portentously, "it's almost as if it has radiated from Boston outward."

"Genius," Johnny confirmed, absorbing the new information.

The fact that this was escalating and spreading made tonight even more important in his mind. Upward trends predictably reached some sort of peak or inflection point, a saturation, a crisis. The increasing frequency and intensity, as well as the broadening network, meant mobilization for some goal. This would create an emotional pressure in the participants that could only be relieved by catharsis, a release. There was an approaching crescendo. How it would come together, and when and how it might peak, he didn't know yet, but in his imagination he could feel the weight of the network growing, their efforts pointed toward some singular event.

"Don't 'genius' me yet. Here's the really weird part," Tucker said after quaffing some beer to wash down another bite of hot dog. "Just for kicks, I decided to look not only at each game, but within each game. I keep very detailed records of each Red Sox game, as you know," he noted, patting his scorekeeping book. "OK, now this is a bit of a reach, but there was one outlier to all of this from a Red Sox perspective. And, you know that outliers can be the exceptions that prove the rule, right?"

"Go on," Johnny urged.

Tucker smiled. "All right, I have your full attention. Sometimes it's hard to tell. You have denial issues."

"Do we need the psychoanalysis?" Johnny asked.

"Probably, but there's no time" Tucker commented. "Anyhow, here's the exception: After one game, there were no attacks. There was no vandalism reported, at least according to Daniel's database. That doesn't mean some didn't go undetected, but we only have the data we have."

"I'm with you, my man," Johnny encouraged. Tucker was getting a little worked up, and Johnny knew he was about to reveal his magician's feat, his disappearing lady.

"Great," Tucker continued, breathing slowly. "That one game had a single distinctive feature. It was the only game in which the third baseman – from either team – didn't make or assist in a defensive out." Tucker stopped to let the significance of his statement sink in.

Johnny looked at Tucker for a moment, staring hard. That was it? That was the great insight? One data point about third basemen? Johnny looked askance at his friend, his skepticism showing.

"OK, OK, and there's more," Tucker said, scrambling to regain the dramatic momentum he'd established. "Also, the more plays the third baseman made – again, from either team – the more attacks there were. It's something you'd only detect using a regression analysis tuned to see it, but it's real, and it's there. The third baseman has something to do with this. Not the person, but the position, and what he does during a game. And that's where I ran out of gas," Tucker finished with an anticlimactic flourish, sagging back into his seat and tossing back the remaining stub of his hot dog.

"Uh huh." It was all Johnny could muster. It was a strange insight, but Johnny trusted Tucker's analytical skills. Because it relied on data, he had to push his limbic brain to test the air, check for leaks or cracks. His limbic brain was a little slower to render judgments about these types of things. Language was a natural for it, but numbers and data were a bit alien. His limbic brain had to ruminate.

The two sat in silence for a moment, the ballpark filling around them, announcements buffeting the soft air. A moment later, they found themselves reflexively standing for the national anthem, the opening strains causing them to jump to their feet. Tucker nearly spilled his nachos in the process.

As the final notes faded away and Tucker replaced his baseball cap and balanced his nachos on his knee again, Johnny turned to his friend, speaking in a modulated tone so that his voice didn't carry.

"All right, T-man, I need to say this back to you," Johnny said thoughtfully. "Just to make sure I understand what you're saying, and to put it in my own words."

"Go for it," Tucker replied, munching a nacho and eyeing the cup of beer at his feet. It hadn't been kicked over during the national anthem, a small miracle.

"So, the story we're getting is that a nationwide network of corporate eco-terrorism is somehow taking its cues from Red Sox games held here at Fenway Park," Johnny stated quietly, his voice woven with threads of skepticism. "Not only that, but they are somehow using defensive plays at third base as a precise cue for action."

"That's what I said, albeit much more eloquently," Tucker chided. "You make it sound so sane, but I have to tell you man, discovering it was making me crazy with insights. I loved it!"

Johnny laughed at his friend's enthusiasm. He'd always treasured Tucker's open nature and plainspoken manner. But hearing the theory again, in his own words, had given his limbic brain more to work with.

It purred happily, satisfied with the direction they were headed.

"Well, my friend, we know what our job is tonight," Johnny stated calmly. "Wait for a play by the third baseman, then watch for something to happen."

Chapter 8
Hot Corner

Neither Johnny nor Tucker could enjoy the game. Each play seemed destined to result in a ball struck to third. With every batted ball or situation where third base was drawn into the action, they scanned the stands. They missed a number of spectacular plays during the tense game. But Tucker's theory was their focus.

Something was triggering a network of people attuned to plays at third. They needed to know what it was.

In the bottom of the fourth inning, a right-handed hitter for the Red Sox struck a ball sharply to third, where it was cleanly caught by a well-positioned third baseman. An unassisted put out.

Both Johnny and Tucker searched the stands for anything unusual after the play, but everyone they could see seemed more interested in the Red Sox's lost offensive opportunity. There wasn't a flinch anywhere to be seen, just fans reacting with disappointment, a unified groan rising from the stands.

"OK, one play to third so far, and nothing," Johnny noted.

"Five unassisted," Tucker muttered. "Unassisted. I didn't control for that. Maybe it has to include an assist?"

"Maybe. Or maybe we've missed something," Johnny pondered. Fenway was a large ballpark, and they couldn't see it all from their vantage point.

Besides, Johnny thought, the radio, television, and online coverage of the game offered different versions of the events. The live game might be the wrong one to watch. Or the conspirators might not even have to watch the game. Considering how much he'd paid for the tickets, he hoped not.

As the game progressed, he became increasingly concerned about Tucker's line of reasoning. It was beginning to look like a dead end. Statistics could deceive – the numbers could be right but the interpretation wrong.

It seemed to be a good night for right-handed hitters. Both starting pitchers were righties, so the hitters held a slight advantage. In the top of the sixth, there was another play on the third-base side. This time an opposing batter grounded to third, the third baseman arcing a long and deceptively lazy throw to first for the out.

Again, Johnny and Tucker looked around for unusual responses, but the fans seemed to be doing what fans do, cheering, waving signs, and whistling as their team displayed its defensive prowess.

As the cheers faded, Johnny caught out of the corner of his eye a sign across the field that stayed up a little longer than others. It was only a glimpse, momentary and fleeting, but it struck him as unusual enough to note. He trusted his instincts. Something out of the ordinary had flickered in the corner of his eye.

"Tucker, if there's another play involving the third baseman, look across to the top of the Green Monster," Johnny said. "I think I saw a sign there, something that stayed up a little too long, but I can't be sure."

"Definitely," Tucker replied. "Otherwise, I'm not seeing anything strange, other than a raggedy curveball from their rookie pitcher. That thing has no bite!"

In the late innings, the game began to drag as both starting pitchers tired and relief pitchers took over. The visiting team was struggling the most. In the bottom of the seventh, there was another play to the third-base side. The shift was on, so the third baseman was shading over toward second. The Red Sox batter hit a grounder to the third baseman, resulting in a double play.

"I see it!" Tucker said excitedly, elbowing Johnny. "Look, on top of the Green Monster."

There it was, a sign that looked like any other baseball fan's sign. Yet, in an odd way, it was almost too innocuous. It was a simple green sign, no lettering on it they could see, just a bright green piece of cardboard. If this had been a Celtics game, green would have made sense, but this was a Red Sox game. Green didn't fit the Red Sox. And the sign was held very high and a little longer than necessary. Everything about it seemed slightly exaggerated.

Johnny had been to a few games this season but had never noticed the sign before. If their theory was right, it would have been there all season. But the blankness of it rendered it almost beneath notice.

Thinking quickly, Johnny turned to the people behind them.

"Excuse me, are you season ticket holders?" he asked the man directly behind Tucker.

The guy emanated Weston wealth like a cologne. He acted a bit perturbed at being interrupted.

"Yes, we are."

"See that green sign on top of the Green Monster?" Johnny asked.

The man squinted across the diamond. The sign was still held aloft, even though the Red Sox had suffered the double play.

"Yes, now that you mention it, I've seen it a lot this season. It's become part of the surroundings," the man reflected.

"So it's here most games?" Johnny asked.

"Every game, I think," the man answered, now interested in Johnny's questions. "I've never given it much thought, though. I always figured it was somebody who printed lightly and I just couldn't read the letters. It never struck me as that odd, just another fan."

"Great, thanks," Johnny responded with a smile. "It looked a little out of place to me, that's all. Sorry for the interruption."

Johnny turned back to Tucker, who'd heard the entire exchange.

"That seals it," Johnny muttered, a strong hunch consuming him. "That's what we came to see."

"OK. I guess I agree. But what do we do about it?" Tucker answered. "Do we go over there and punch out the person with the sign, end the madness based on our theories and my brilliant analysis? Get a nice stint in the clink for assault and disorderly conduct, bringing shame and ridicule to our good names?"

Johnny sat back and brooded. He had a powerful suspicion that one of the perpetrators was about 500 feet from them.

There was plenty of game left.

"Tucker, let's go visit," Johnny said. "Let's see who is holding up that sign."

"Great, because I have to pee," Tucker said with evident relief. "That last beer went right through me."

After a pit stop, Johnny and Tucker worked their way upstairs toward the Green Monster seats. The long concourses of Fenway echoed with a mixture of voices inside and crowd noise outside, the air redolent with the smells of fried food and spilled beer.

As they approached the end of the concourse, a security guard confronted them, asking for their tickets.

"Sorry," Johnny lied. "I left them with my wife."

"What seat's she in?" the guard persisted, arching an eyebrow and not giving an inch.

"I forget the number," Johnny replied, feeling the moment slipping away. "Can you just let us through?"

"Sorry, pal," the guard said. "Call your wife and ask her to meet you out here. I need a ticket stub, or I don't let you through."

"Fine," Johnny replied, pulling out his phone as if to use it. "I'll be back." He turned on his heel and stalked away, putting the phone up to his ear. Tucker gave the guard a friendly, mystified shrug and followed.

"Now what?"

"We go back downstairs," Johnny said, pocketing his phone.

Descending a level, they gravitated toward the fabled wall but made no attempt to move to the seats. Angling for the best possible view, they located a spot where they could see the top of the Green Monster.

There, they stood and scanned.

"The sign came up toward the far right end," Johnny noted, nodding his head in that general direction.

"Agreed," Tucker said. "Who do we have there? Top row is a family. I doubt that's our ticket. Row below is a bunch of college hooligans with a wild-haired girl in tow. Bottom row is a nice set of retirees, out for a game and some reminiscing, I'd say."

Johnny thought for a moment. "Watch the field, Tucker," he said. "I'll watch the girl. She's the only piece that doesn't fit. And our job is to explain things that don't fit."

"Yes, I know," Tucker sighed, staring vacantly at the field below. "The Denovo quote machine is revving again. Save it for the media tour, man. Can I get Quote 74 with marinara sauce? It's delicious served warm with a little cheese."

"Hey, don't doubt the power," Johnny retorted. "It's served me well to this point. I don't see you quoted that often."

"True enough," Tucker grudgingly agreed. "I'm too shy, anyhow. But next time, I get to watch the girl."

At that moment, there was a surge of excitement from the crowd as a ball was put in play. Johnny watched the girl intently. She looked young and pretty, in a plain manner, her wild black hair detracting a little and obscuring her face as the breezes blew over the wall and through the park. He doubted she was there for the drunken company of the boys around her. She seemed oblivious to them, and they took no notice of her. She definitely didn't fit.

Johnny watched as the play started. As the crowd tensed, he saw her reach down reflexively under her seat. Then, as the play resolved, judging by the noise of the crowd, he saw her relax and bring both hands back up to the counter she was seated behind.

"Tucker, let me guess. Ground ball, but not to third."

"Correct," Tucker replied, turning to face Johnny again, the play over with. "High hopper, gobbled up by the shortstop. Throw out at first. Bang-bang play."

"All right, she's the one," Johnny stated with certainty. "She reached for something when the play started and let it go when it became clear it wasn't the right kind of play."

Suddenly, Johnny had an idea.

"Tucker, you record the games at home, don't you?" Johnny asked.

"Well, if I'd known I'd be here, I wouldn't have recorded this one, but this was so last-minute I didn't cancel it," Tucker said.

"I'll take that as a yes," Johnny finished, looking distractedly over Tucker's head, bobbing and weaving to catch sight of a certain type of person. Down the concourse, he zeroed in on his target. "I'll be right back."

Johnny loped over to a television cameraman wandering the concourse, looking for spontaneous fan shots, pictures that were part and parcel of the local television coverage, used to provide a backdrop for fascinating announcer insights or commercial transitions.

Reaching into his pocket for the few bills he had left after paying the scalper, Johnny approached the cameraman.

"Excuse me, can you do me a favor?" he said to the side of the man's head.

"I'm kind of busy now, pal," the man replied.

"I know, but I only have a minute, and I think you dropped this fifty," Johnny stated, bringing up a $50 bill in his hand.

"Hey, you're right," the cameraman said dryly, reaching out his hand to accept the bribe from Johnny. "I wondered where that went. Thanks, buddy. OK, now you've got my attention," the cameraman said, turning and taking a hard look at Johnny for the first time. "Hey, you're Johnny Denovo! Don't that beat all. You on a case?"

Johnny snorted. "You could say that," he replied.

The cameraman smiled. "Whatever it is, I'm happy to help. Wait until I tell my wife. She'll freak. She thinks you're wicked cool. But time's a-wastin'. What do you need?"

"A shot," Johnny replied with a grin, pleased to hear that his fan base was still solid. "See that girl in the middle row of the Green Monster seats, the wild-haired brunette in the midst of all the drunken frat boys on the right side?"

The cameraman hoisted his camera up and adjusted the focal range. "Got her," he confirmed.

"Are they flipping to you at commercial?" Johnny asked hopefully.

"At the end of the inning," the cameraman replied, lowering his camera from his shoulder again.

"Great," Johnny said. "Make your shot of her, and you'll have earned that $50. If you get grief, tell them you were infatuated for a moment. Young girls, you know. They're the bane of every man's existence."

"Oh, I know the story to tell," the cameraman laughed. "If she's an unfaithful wife, I don't want to know nothing about it, though. I just take the pictures."

Johnny snorted. "Nothing that dull, I assure you. And please, only tell your wife we met."

"Mum's the word," the cameraman replied conspiratorially. "Thanks for returning my money."

Johnny returned to where he had left Tucker just as the third out of the inning was recorded. "OK, when you get home, check to see if our ladyfriend up there is captured in the shots around this commercial break," Johnny said. "Can you port the image out?"

"Can a bird fly?" Tucker snorted. "Easy as pie."

"Great. Send me the footage when you get it."

"Why would I do that?" Tucker challenged. "You think you can ID her? Give me a break. Let me run the footage through some forensic software I have. I'll bet I can tell you who she is by the time you wake up tomorrow."

"Care to put real money on that?" Johnny proffered.

"A hundred bucks enough for you?" Tucker inquired.

"Deal. I just had a fifty fall out of my pocket, so I could used some cash," Johnny said, shaking Tucker's hand to seal the bet. "And with that, my friend, I think our work here is done."

"Good!" Tucker exclaimed. "Can we go back to our seats and watch the end of the game now?"

"Sure, my boy," Johnny mocked, turning and beginning the walk back to their seats. "Just do me a favor, Tucker," Johnny said seriously, turning to his friend. "Mark down any time you see the 'green' sign go up. We'll want to analyze the scorekeeping, too."

"Way ahead of you, my brother," Tucker said. "I'll analyze tonight's game and cross-reference it against other games. I won't have the sign to go by, but if we're right about the assists from third base, it should hold up."

"Tucker, I feel like I have a lot of facts but no story," Johnny groaned. "How does all this make sense?"

"Johnny, that's not my problem," Tucker laughed. "My job is to give you more facts and win a hundred dollars from you. Your job is to tell me what it all means and pay promptly."

Chapter 9
Bases Loaded

Back in their seats, Johnny knew Tucker was right. He had to find a way to make sense of what was happening. It didn't add up yet. The main problem was a lack of a theme, some unifying meaning.

Questions plagued him throughout the remaining innings. What did corporate eco-terrorism have to do with a sign held up atop the Green Monster? And what did any of this have to do with the blackmailing of a biotech executive for cheating on his wife with her long-lost and unknown sister? And was Schwartz innocent or a scheming evil genius?

He groaned as he stood, the game over. His head hurt. The Red Sox had won in a fairly dominating fashion, with an outburst of scoring in the eighth and strong closing pitching. But questions crowded out any high spirits.

Tucker slapped Johnny on the back after the victory, then headed off to a local watering hole to meet up with some friends of theirs. Johnny demurred, the case weighing on his mind.

He needed to be alone.

A stillness settled on the city once the game ended, a vestige of the fading summer. He walked home through the unusually quiet streets of Boston, the whispers of his thoughts disrupted occasionally by a booming car revving past. There were a few boisterous pubs going late into the night, the smells of liquor and hot food distracting him as he passed. Brushing the diversions aside, his thoughts returned to the maze he was attempting to navigate.

One aspect alarmed him – whatever plan had been put into motion, it was nearing its apogee. Plays at third base were the trigger. Plays at first would have meant something else, but third base was penultimate.

The plan was nearing its conclusion.

In addition, the data Tucker had gathered and analyzed independently indicated that the frequency and intensity of activity were both increasing, the range extending across the land from Boston. The network was growing. The plotters were working a progression, just like the bases in baseball.

If the plan was almost complete, having conceptually reached third base, the group responsible for it was poised the proverbial 90 feet away.

As he walked, Johnny also pondered how this case had started. Two women, one man. From McNaught's perspective, the case was all about adultery and the blackmail it had visited upon him. The eco-terrorism was an unrelated sidenote. But Johnny wasn't focused on blackmail or adultery at this juncture. Something much larger and potentially more sinister was in play.

Working fast made even more sense than it had at the beginning.

As his footfalls echoed in the nighttime streets, they seemed like time ticking away. Johnny felt an impatience well up inside him. Days weren't sufficient, hours were borderline.

He needed more, and in minutes.

Anxiety about falling behind the perpetrators was blossoming. They already had a sizeable head-start. He had to raise his metabolism for this case. He needed to speed things up.

Without realizing it, he had picked up his pace, his steps pounding the sleepy sidewalks with an urgent authority. He felt his pulse quicken, a glisten of sweat form on his brow.

He needed to work, needed an hour or two of uninterrupted focus.

Bursting into his condo, he flipped on the lights and glanced at his phone. The message light was flashing. He checked the display. It was from Mona.

His pent-up energy dissipated and was gone.

He'd forgotten about Mona. The events at Fenway had required his full attention. Yet a pall had hung over him all evening, he now realized, a sense that he'd made the wrong choice by putting a case over his new romance.

And she'd gone out with a friend, a fall-back position.

He knew what a strong personality she had, and how she could lapse into a cold-blooded, rational approach if provoked.

He felt his stomach knot. His eyes felt bloodless and dry.

It wasn't normal for him to have anxiety about a case and a woman at the same time. Women especially were rarely a source of worry.

He was supposed to be above romantic insecurity.

Maybe he had taken a new case too soon.

Reluctantly, he punched in the code to hear the message. There was no use beating around the bush.

"Johnny, it's Mona. I wanted to call to apologize about how I behaved earlier. I hope the game went well. My friend Izzy agreed to go with me to the comedy show, and then we went to the Top of the Hub for a drink. I'm home now. Call me tomorrow. Again, sorry."

Who was Izzy? Ending an evening at the Top of the Hub sounded very date-like to Johnny's ears. So, while it was an apology, it also seemed like a way of rubbing his nose in the fact that she was out with another man.

He felt senselessly irritated by this. The message seemed passive-aggressive.

He had to admit it – he was jealous.

He heaved his baseball cap hard into the back of the couch.

With his mind roiled by problems with the case and woman problems, he was not ready for sleep.

Going over to his fridge, he took out a beer and cracked it open. Taking a swig, he pushed thoughts of Mona from his mind. Thinking about her wasn't helping. It made him feel helpless and stupid. He didn't like it one bit.

Strolling over to his desk, he turned on his computer and seated himself in his stylish and expensive ergonomic chair. It greeted him with a brief sigh of hydraulics. He felt his pulse resume its normal pace, his adrenaline diluting, his corpuscles relaxing again.

Daniel's database was on his mind. Tucker had looked at the information but Johnny hadn't turned his own pattern-recognition skills loose on it yet.

Sometimes, he could surprise himself.

Gazing at the spreadsheet, Johnny focused on the structure of the document. He didn't look at the details, but let his mind take it all in, probing for softness, gray areas. He let his eyes lose focus, seeking shapes, contours, densities. It was a tried and true technique, a first-pass visual scenting of the terrain.

Suddenly, a hole appeared in his hazed vision, something described not by its presence but by its absence, a gap in the data that jumped out in contrast, yawning out before him.

What was missing was an update. He needed to keep adding to it. The data ended, yet the sign was still being held aloft, the signals were still being transmitted to the network.

He needed to keep gathering information. The static data set he possessed was only the beginning.

Quickly, he dashed off an email message to Daniel asking to know whether any damages occurred overnight. The vandals were probably at it even now, and he wanted early word once the reports started coming in.

Clearing his vision, he felt somewhat better having set another wheel in motion.

He turned away from his computer and began to contemplate another path in the maze – the possibility that Jim Schwartz might be double-dealing on his best friend.

Earshot was the clue. It was not only the metaphors it elicited, but the spot Schwartz had described when he and McNaught had spoken.

If Johnny recollected Grand Central station correctly, Schwartz had steered McNaught to the precise location where sound is subject to an acoustic sweet spot called a whisper gallery, an architectural rarity where sound – even the quietest whisper – is transmitted, even amplified, and projected intact to a spot far away, out of the proverbial "earshot" that Schwartz had so suggestively inserted into his speech. In whisper galleries, people near the speaker might not hear the words, but across an elliptical room someone in the sweet spot would hear them with absolute fidelity.

If Schwartz knew of this acoustic sweet spot, all he had to do was have a conversation with McNaught there and an accomplice could hear the whole thing, safely hidden across the large foyer in Grand Central station. By arranging it in this manner, Schwartz would be beyond reproach, his accomplice could carry out the blackmail without any suspicion falling on Schwartz, and both would benefit while McNaught remained in the dark.

Johnny weighed the alternatives as he stared out his dark windows, the lack of light matching his pensive isolation.

It seemed implausible that McNaught and Schwartz were secretly followed, that they stood accidentally and innocently in the precise location of an acoustic sweet spot while their pursuer stood opposite them across the wide foyer and eavesdropped, unobserved and unknown to either man.

It didn't ring true.

It didn't explain the betraying metaphor – the use of the word "earshot" and the pride with which it had been highlighted and uttered.

While some might dismiss these as subtleties, Johnny dealt in subtleties.

The brain leaked information. It worked to reveal itself.

Most significantly, Johnny's limbic brain rebelled at the notion that Schwartz was innocent. It required too many coincidences. It didn't square with how the world worked. It didn't explain things well enough. It didn't match the hunch.

Johnny finished his beer with one last hard swig, the warm dregs burning the back of his throat. His thoughts were beginning to ramble. It was past midnight, and the alcohol was going straight into his bloodstream.

Holding the empty brown beer bottle up, examining the glass and running his thumb over the raised patterns along the bottom, he thought of Mona going to the Top of the Hub with some guy named Izzy. What kind of name was Izzy? Rock stars were named Izzy or Ozzy or Iggy, not normal guys. Izzy. What a stupid name, he thought. He'd take some pleasure in socking Izzy squarely in his Izzyhole someday.

Had Izzy met Paul tonight? The malicious bartender at the Top of the Hub behaved as if he knew Schwartz in an intimate way, something more than the norm, something possibly lurid. But what was their relationship exactly? Paul seemed cruel and sociopathic enough to blackmail somebody, yet he possessed an anger that suggested he'd find the slow torture of blackmail unsatisfying and draining.

Paul would prefer a bite and slash attack to attrition and shame. He was full of poison, but would prefer darts to a slow drip.

Finally, there was the girl in the stands atop the Green Monster. Who was she? And what was her role in all this?

The beer bottle had lost its fascination. Answers were not forthcoming. Yet the time spent contemplating them and the beer had done the trick. He had put the day behind him.

It was time for sleep.

Alone, frustrated, and jealous, Johnny Denovo slunk off to bed for a fitful night of dreams and realizations.

Chapter 10
Signals Crossed

Johnny awoke later than usual, head aswim in a new metaphor. Green. It was all green. Green sign. Green Monster. The green-eyed monster of jealousy. Even third base fell into the category through a meandering set of connections – the progression as growth, the hot corner in baseball, global warming, the green movement, eco-terrorism. Green.

He wished he'd realized it last night, but limbic connections occurred on an unpredictable schedule. Agonizing over clues and evidence usually just frustrated him. He should have known better. He could have gotten to bed much earlier.

Over the years, he'd learned to accept insights as they came. Forcing them often generated mistakes, led him to jump to conclusions, made him shut out possibilities.

The rate at which the prior day had proceeded and the number of facts he'd absorbed had overpowered his limbic processing centers. They worked slowly. During sleep, these centers of synthesis had kept working at their processional pace, finally presenting a vital set of connections to him with the morning's light.

Suddenly, there was a faint metaphorical infrastructure emerging within these investigations.

Yet one thing didn't fit – the blackmail. Black as in nefarious, darkness, concealment, opaque, death. It was the antithesis of green.

It didn't fit for a reason, Johnny thought. It was off-theme. It was a distraction from the root cause.

He felt a surge of confidence. The blackmail was somehow different.

That felt right, felt like progress. He put it in the bank and focused on more pedestrian matters – it was time for breakfast.

Having consumed only one hot dog and a few beers the night before, he was starving. Propping himself on his elbow, he punched his control pad to change his condo to daytime mode, then picked up his phone and called downstairs to Wei Chou for a quick late breakfast.

"Wei Chou's, where the chow is way good," Wei answered. "Johnny, is that you?"

"Hi Wei," Johnny said. "I'm either very late for breakfast or very early for lunch."

"Well, we don't serve breakfast, so let's call it early for lunch," Wei suggested. "Let's see, I think you need some pot stickers and Happy Family. How does that sound?"

"Like a ticket to paradise, my friend," Johnny responded. Wei always intuited the most satisfying meal combination. It was a gift he seemed to hone as the years passed.

"OK, give me half an hour," Wei promised. "I'm still doing prep or it would be faster."

"No worries. I can await gustatory salvation," Johnny replied, and the call ended.

As he pressed the off button, the phone rang again, startling Johnny. He recoiled from answering it. He preferred to wake up slowly and was still partially in dreamland, processing the metaphors.

The phone chirped again. He wanted to set it aside. He averted his eyes from the caller ID.

His arm began the motion to put the phone down in its cradle when he remembered his pledge from the prior evening. Things were reaching a peak. He needed to pick up the pace.

Today was not the day for indulgences.

He gripped the phone tighter as it rang a third time. He answered.

"Denovo," he barked.

"Down boy!" Tucker yelped. "Up on the wrong side of the bed this morning, sunshine?"

Johnny laughed. "Barely up at all. Late night. Couldn't sleep. Too much on my mind."

"I know the feeling, man, but being in training has its virtues," Tucker enthused. "I was up at seven for oatmeal and lifting. I wish I had room in here to toss logs. I guess I'll have to go to the Common for that."

"In your kilt?" Johnny asked.

"Maybe," Tucker offered. "Anyhow, that's not why I called. It's about the lady on the Green Monster."

"Right," Johnny remembered. "Did the TV guy get a good shot of her?"

"He did his part," Tucker responded, sounding mournful. "But I couldn't do mine. I owe you a hundred clams."

"What do you mean?"

"Well," Tucker said uneasily. "Facial forensics demand that you get a good, clear picture of someone, with continuous tone and unbroken features so that the computer can extrapolate, compare, and so forth. We didn't get that."

"Why not? Wasn't the picture clear?"

"Oh, the picture was clear," Tucker corrected. "It was her hair. It was all over the place, and there wasn't any 2-3 second video grab I could get that gave me a clear shot of her face. I couldn't even splice one together. That wild mane of hair shattered her image like cracks shatter a window."

"So I win a hundred dollars because of wild hair, huh?" Johnny mused.

"Yes, you do. Just don't rub my nose in it. The wind on the top of the Green Monster really whips things around," Tucker noted. "It hardly ever dies down up there, with the updrafts and downdrafts colliding in left field. Last night, the west wind just kept pushing her hair over her face."

"Like a disguise," Johnny blurted out.

"You know, I'm glad you said that," Tucker responded. "Watching the footage, I had that same feeling. It could have been you under that wig, and I wouldn't really have been able to tell. It's a pretty effective bit of cover."

"Well, get back to your training, my friend," Johnny yawned. "If you find anything else, give a shout. I'll collect the winnings from you after you nab the Scottish Highland's Best Kilt award. I've pledged to redouble my efforts on this case, get it closed down fast. I think whoever's behind this is sprinting, too. It's just a feeling I have."

"That, and they're using third base," Tucker mentioned. "Don't think the significance of that was lost on me, Johnny. I've worked with you long enough. I know you're thinking about it. And I think you're right. Plus, the season is winding down. You have to take that into account, as well."

"That's right," Johnny agreed. "Hey, are you going to analyze the other baseball stats you mentioned last night?"

Tucker swore. "You don't forget anything, do you, Denovo? And you need them now, I suppose?"

"You suppose right," Johnny confirmed.

"I did some work on them last night. Let me double-check the results, and I'll call you back."

Hanging up the phone, Johnny glanced at the clock. Breakfast was still twenty minutes away.

He was making progress on the case, but it was time to address the other green in his life, the green-eyed monster on Mona's leash. He wanted to nip it in the bud. No playing patty-cake. Jealousy was insidious and predatory. It needed to be speared and gutted, its carcass left to rot.

Sitting up in bed now, he dialed Mona's cell phone.

She answered quickly.

"Good morning, Johnny," Mona said brightly. "Did you get my message last night?"

"All of them," Johnny replied.

"I only left the one," Mona said. "What do you mean?"

"You know what I mean," Johnny retorted. "You wanted me to know you were out on a date with some guy named Izzy while I was at the game. So, yes, one message to send a few messages. I got them all."

"Damn, you're grumpy this morning," Mona observed. "And you're wrong. I went to the show with my friend Izzy, the one from New Hampshire. Izzy is Isabel. She came into town over the weekend but was busy with family until last night. She'd never been to the Top of the Hub, so we went there after the show. It was a lot of fun, but no date. Believe me, with the bartender they have there these days, I'd never take a date there knowingly."

Johnny felt his insides untwist. "You must mean Paul," he observed.

"You know him?" Mona asked, surprised.

"We crossed paths yesterday afternoon," Johnny answered. "One of McNaught's friends apparently frequents the place too. He was obnoxious and angry when I met him, but he mixed a good drink."

"Well, a redeeming trait, I suppose," Mona said breezily. "He spits like a ballplayer. I think he's a jerk."

"No argument here," Johnny said. "Hey, I'm going to spend the afternoon working on this case. Care to grab a bite to eat tonight?"

"I can't," Mona responded, sounding sincerely disappointed. "I promised Izzy I'd go with her to the Red Sox game tonight. This time, she's the one with the tickets. Funny how things happen in batches. You were just there last night."

"Indeed," Johnny mused. "Where are your seats?"

"Green Monster seats," Mona said excitedly. "One of Izzy's relatives had a pair of tickets but there's some school activity tonight he can't get out of, so they're ours. This is the last game before the team goes on a road trip. We're pretty excited."

"For good reason," Johnny agreed. "Hey, I need to tell you a few things. Turns out the Green Monster figures into the case I'm working on. You should know more before you go. Besides, you'd hate me for not including you."

"Denovo!" Mona said, feigning exasperation. "How do you make me feel like I'm following you? First, Top of the Hub, now the Green Monster?! I don't like feeling like a stalker."

Johnny laughed. "I'll explain it later over drinks. It doesn't make perfect sense to me yet, either, but I think there's a theme. Maurice's? Five o'clock?"

"That'll work," Mona said. "OK if I bring Izzy?"

"Fine with me," Johnny replied. "See you at five."

"Bye," Mona said demurely, and they hung up.

Johnny stood up and stretched, finally letting forth the large yawn that had been pent up inside. His muscles sang with joy at being revived, the blood flow warming him from the skin in. Eyeing the clock, he noticed that his food was about to arrive. He quickly threw on the shorts, t-shirt, and baseball cap he'd worn to the game and cracked his knuckles.

With impeccable timing, there was a knock on the door. Johnny tossed the door open with brio, expecting to greet Wei. Instead, his pretty young delivery girl stood in the hall, arms cradling a bag of food. Her doe eyes pleaded with him as he lifted the bags from her cradling arms. A plaintive smile crossed her face.

Her crush on him was apparently as intense as ever.

Johnny smiled in return. Panicking, the delivery girl darted down the hall with a furtive look of fear on her face, her lithe and petite frame disappearing in a flash. Johnny's smile only widened. He was very fond of her in a fashion. Someday, he pondered, she might smile back, and then he'd be the one who'd have to flee.

Wei's cooking was excellent, as usual. Johnny paced as he ate and pondered the insights from the night's dreams. Green. Everything was green. While this was not literally true he thought as the crispy edges of the pot-stickers slid down his gullet, the salty flavors mixing with the slightly burned flavors of carmelized sugars and soy, the way his mind had unified the case suggested everything was related somehow, both metaphorically and in reality.

His limbic brain has packaged it up in a color – and color was one of the most prevalent linguistic metaphors – blue for sadness, red for anger, yellow for cowardice, black for evil.

Seating himself, Johnny clicked to check his email. The usual stream of fan mail and inquiries flooded across the screen, his macros diverting the list as it streamed in, sorting messages into buckets he could revisit later.

An email from Daniel rested in the main directory.

Johnny clicked on it. Reading it, he could almost see his friend typing it with his odd keyboarding style, elbows akimbo and concentration at maximum.

"To your request, I have some bad news. It takes about two weeks for our databases to reflect the latest claims information, so anything that happened last night or this morning won't show up for a fortnight. I'm terribly sorry to be the bearer of bad news. I will definitely pipe up if I see anything in the interim. Best regards, Daniel."

As Johnny closed Daniel's message, his email fetched another, this one from Tucker. It was a file showing a series of numbers, box score listings of plays started by the third basemen and leading to assists. It amounted to a series of short numbers starting with 5, the numerical position of third base on the field. The numbers were two or three digits in length in nearly every case. Only a botched play would generate more.

The phone rang again just as Johnny was contemplating this second email.

"Hello."

"Johnny, Tucker here," he said when Johnny answered.

"Just reading your email."

"Yes, not much there," Tucker said. "But like I alluded to earlier, I was able to push a little on that Web site you gave me yesterday. And those little numbers seem to mean something."

Johnny sat up a little more.

"You have my complete attention, sir," he said to Tucker.

"Good. Here's the story. When I got home last night, I was trying to relax, and sometimes I run little nuisance scripts to wind down, just doodles really," Tucker confided. "So, last night, I was entering the box score of the game and inserted the third-base plays into a probe script aimed at the site. I ran it, and the three plays from the game got a result. Apparently, they are short-term logins, but are combined with the game situation – score, inning – to seal the security. I needed more time this morning to verify."

"Go on," Johnny prodded anxiously. He was eager to find a way to infiltrate the group, get his hands on the beacon the site was deploying.

"Well, there were three plays last night involving third basemen, like I said," Tucker answered, assuming a teacher's voice. "Let's take one play in the fourth inning, nobody out, say 5-4-3, which I'd order as 5-4-3-4-0. Then, the next one, third to first in the eighth with two outs, would be 5-3-8-2, and the next one, third to second in the ninth with two outs, would be 5-4-9-2. If I enter all these numbers in the right order, I get a username match. Or at least, my script did last night. I just didn't know the password."

"Green," Johnny said impulsively. "Did you try 'green'?"

"Damn!" Tucker exclaimed. "Of course. That's probably it. As in 'Green Monster.' I'll try that next time. The thing is, the username isn't good anymore. I tried 5-4-3-4-0-5-3-8-2-5-4-9-2 this morning, and nothing. It seems to expire at midnight local time after a game. That's when my script stopped getting the login challenge indicating the username was right but the password was wrong."

"Really?" Johnny ruminated, a bite of Happy Family in his mouth. "Someone in our time zone must be behind it. Midnight is too powerful a choice. But tell me, doesn't that username approach lose its novelty after a while? I mean, how many combinations are there for third-base plays."

Tucker cleared his throat. "I thought the same thing, until I realized they added the innings and outs. That means it's variable length, and so situational that it's almost random. If it's only up for a couple of hours, there's little exposure for any particular one. You'd need to be inside their heads to crack it. It's virtually unbeatable otherwise. Even then, you have to be quick. But for a large group using it, it's very memorable and communicable. In fact, you can get it by just following the game online."

"Unless," Johnny considered, "the sign signals which ones to pay attention to. She signaled every time there was an assisted out from third, but maybe in other games she let one go, or only used one. That would increase the randomness."

"And," Tucker interjected, "the sign is visible on every put-out, I'd bet. They constantly sweep the Green Monster on television. She just has to hold the sign up long enough and she gets a nationwide audience."

Johnny contemplated for a moment. "OK, let's work this through. Someone has access to that site and creates a temporary username each night there's a Red Sox game, taking it down at midnight. The username is a string of numbers based on plays started by the third baseman and appended with situational numbers, outs and innings and the like. The person doing the programming can be anywhere, if that's the only moving piece. But there is another moving piece, another variable – the sign. Is it green every night? Is she always on the Green Monster? We need more information."

"Agreed," Tucker said. "Want to buy some more really expensive scalper tickets for tonight's final game of this home stand?" he asked hopefully.

Johnny chuckled. "Not in the cards, my friend. Luckily, Mona is going tonight with a girlfriend from New Hampshire. They have Green Monster seats. They can be our eyes."

"And I'll be watching the game on TV," Tucker volunteered a little deflated, the chance for another ticket denied. "That will help confirm that the chances of seeing her sign are high enough that it's reliable. I kind of recall seeing it before, but I wasn't looking for it, so who knows?"

"Perfect," Johnny said. "And I need to consult an old friend, separate fact from fiction. I'll check with you after the game. Let's hustle. The Sox leave for a road trip tomorrow. That might make our friends do something rash tonight."

Chapter 11

Dugout

Quickly showering and shaving, Johnny felt the burden of the case bearing down on him again. He knew he needed to clear his head. Chasing clues had unearthed a lot of facts. Now, he needed help thinking them through.

The case involved emotion obscuring evidence, feelings swamping facts. Jealousy. Anger. Adultery. It couldn't remain this way. He needed the bloodless plot connecting it all, stripped of emotions.

He knew who he needed to consult.

Putting the top down on his convertible, he drove out into the scattered day, graying clouds prowling overhead like a pack of restive wolves.

Speeding down Storrow Drive, Johnny weighed the risk of having his convertible open on a day like this. Then he thought of where he was headed – to visit his old friend Evan Chalmers. Given the same question, Evan would laugh, telling him the best choice was always the one that left him the most choices. If so, Johnny would stop and put his roof up. That would leave him the most choices for the rest of the day. Getting caught in a deluge would severely limit his choices. Johnny smiled at the persistent common sense Evan always exhibited.

Johnny drove across the Charles River, gazing west where the skies were clearer. He left the top down. Having won a hundred dollars from Tucker on an earlier bet, he was feeling like gambling a little more.

Turning down a quiet street in Cambridge, Johnny looked for the small parking lot he used when visiting his old mentor. The neighborhood was quaint to the extreme, seemingly protected from modernization by some strange repellant force. The miniature trees along the sidewalk were carefully protected by fluted wrought iron barricades. The sidewalks were heaved and cracked and weed-infested, but in a way that added character to the environment, a sloppy charm. The area was eerily silent, the noise from neighboring roads contrasting with the pall over this street, making it all seem polite and urbane, its neighbors rude and overbearing. It was certainly off the beaten track, a quiet oasis in the bustle of Boston. Johnny knew Evan preferred this academic hovel to a noisy office in the middle of the campus.

Parking his car, Johnny hopped out and headed into the small building housing Evan's office. He was coming unannounced, but he knew his old mentor's habits. Summer was his favorite time to cogitate and reflect, and his office was his home away from home.

Evan had been Johnny's academic mentor during a portion of his science days, a guide through the issues of evolutionary biology. He had originally known Johnny as John Novarro, but now kept secret Johnny's origins and any link to his past. When his former student John had been transformed into world-renowned detective Johnny Denovo, Evan had merely shrugged the next time they met, reflecting on the abstract nature of names in general. It had amused him more than anything else. He was an existentialist.

The small building was silent as Johnny entered. He walked softly, respectfully, as he found his way to Evan's office. Peering around the door frame, Johnny had a moment to gaze at Evan without being detected. He was surprised at what he saw amidst the piles of papers and books. While Evan was getting on in years, he had always possessed a vibrancy that belied his age. Now, however, it seemed as if Evan were on the cusp of true old age, his white hair like bunting floating freely off his head, his skin without luster, his eyes weak and watery. Johnny thought he detected a slight tremor in his hands as they moved.

Breaking the surveillance, Johnny backed up a few silent steps, and then made a few loud strides forward while clearing his throat. He knocked on the open door. Evan glanced up alertly.

"John Novarro," Evan proclaimed in a strong voice harboring only a tinge of frailty. He rose from his chair as Johnny entered his cramped office and extended his hand in greeting. "Long time, my friend."

"Yes, Evan, too long," Johnny said, shaking his old friend's hand. The skin seemed cool and more like paper than flesh. Johnny gave it a gentle squeeze. "And remember, here I'm Johnny Denovo. You know the stakes in keeping the secret."

"Of course, of course," Evan reassured him, seating himself again. "No worries here. Nobody comes down to this part of the campus anymore. Just batty old Professor Chalmers flitting about, with his crazy theories that don't require emotional investment. Just careful study, thought, and measurement. How boring!"

Johnny laughed. This kind of clear-headedness was sometimes missing in modern academics, but Evan possessed it in boatloads. While his body was receding, his mind was as sharp as ever. He knew science and served it. Too many researchers thought science served them, Johnny remembered Evan saying a few years ago.

Evan had no reservations about making his points. In the land of boundless egos, this made him more than a bit unpopular. Speaking truth to power was risky.

"Evan," Johnny interjected. "I only have a short time this visit, but I'd like to come back in a couple of days, if that's all right with you. I might have a case out of the way by then."

"Oh heavens, Johnny," Evan began, then faltered. "I have to call you Johnny, really?" Evan asked in his mild, gritty voice.

Johnny nodded.

"All right, Johnny it is, but I have to tell you, it doesn't suit you. You're much too intelligent for an infantilized name like that. But I digress. In short, what I wanted to say is that any visit from you is always welcomed."

"Thanks, Evan," Johnny said sincerely. "I always look forward to seeing you. But I am in a bit of a rush today. Let me explain why I'm here."

"Pray do," Evan encouraged, settling back into his chair.

"Evan, you keep your ear to the ground, so to speak," Johnny began, leaning against the edge of a sturdy, overloaded bookshelf. "You know there are more and more environmental groups vying for prominence, more and more egos in the environmental game, and more and more money at stake. It's not what it used to be."

"You've said quite a mouthful there, Johnny," Evan concurred. "It's lost the science in its ideology. There's no debate allowed any more. Everyone 'knows' the answers, just like they used to 'know' the Earth was the center of the universe and 'know' that overpopulation would decimate us in 20 years. Very short-sighted, a real shame. It's become a profit-driven ideology in too many cases."

"Right," Johnny agreed quickly, wanting to avoid a lecture he knew all too well. "Lots of ego, a lot of emotion. And you know my techniques, so just respond naturally when I list some words, OK? Just a little free-association."

"Fine with me," Evan replied.

"Great," Johnny said. "Now, what comes to mind when I say 'green,' 'hot,' and 'monster'?"

Evan paused for a moment. "Well, just 'green' and 'hot' suggest something, but 'monster' throws me for a loop."

"OK, let's toss that one out," Johnny interjected, losing the term that confused Evan while keeping what he felt was the real oddball term, the reference to third base as the hot corner. His limbic brain wouldn't let it go, and he trusted the instinct. Evan seemed to think it mattered, as well. "What about just 'green' and 'hot'."

"Well, they bring to mind a new group of radical environmentalists," Evan said a little abashedly. "I swore I'd stop following these groups. They just make me upset. But I keep getting their literature. They're hard to avoid. This group calls itself 'Cool & Green,' and seems trendy, stylish. They want a cooler planet and a greener planet, of course, but underneath their 'cool' exterior are some real hotheads, let me tell you. They'd set off neutron bombs if they could, just to get the cancer of humanity off the face of the Earth. Well, except for members of Cool & Green. They can stay, of course. Very little science, but plenty of opinion and apparently some money behind them."

"That's great, Evan," Johnny stated. "Do you know any members of the group?"

Evan thought for a moment, and then admitted, "No, I don't. In fact, I don't know a public face to the group other than a few tawdry brochures I threw out and rumors of their activities. Destructive, menacing. They organize protests, but don't show up themselves. Things happen, they're attributed to Cool & Green, but nobody steps forward. Cowardice. Hiding behind anonymity. That's not scientific, either, my friend."

"I agree, Evan," Johnny said. "Very strange. There has to be a ringmaster. Someone is coordinating it."

"Perhaps," said Evan. "Unless it's like fractals. Once the pattern gets started, it repeats until the energy driving it is cut off or dissipates. So, there may have been a ringleader, but now it's just energy filling and refilling the same fractal activities. You follow me?"

"I think I do," Johnny answered tentatively. "So, the implication would be that this might be an echo, activated merely by an injection of energy. That would actually fit with what I know so far."

"A lot of things in nature are like this," Evan continued. "Ice crystals, snowflakes, coastlines, earthquakes – a little energy, patterns, and repetition, and you have what looks planned but is in reality merely mimicry combined with complexity."

"That framework might explain a few things," Johnny elaborated. "So, the ringmaster might have set a pattern up, then left, but adherents are mindlessly re-energizing it, perpetuating it. It's like a nerve firing without purpose, a twitch, a seizure."

"Perfect examples," Evan beamed.

"It would also allow the ringleader to be removed from one part of a plan while executing another related to the first," Johnny considered. "It would allow a step of remove, independence."

"You always were bright," Evan said admiringly. "And, by the way, you really should go back to 'John.' It suits you much better."

Chapter 12
Bullpen

Johnny left Evan's after a few more minutes of friendly discussion, devoting some time to catching up on gossip around the university. Mostly, the conversation allowed Evan to vent his spleen at the shenanigans and power plays around him. He was a toothless lion, but a wise and watchful one.

The day had cleared, the packs of clouds dissolving into a glowing blue sky. Glancing at his watch, Johnny realized it was time to get back downtown. The choking Boston traffic would be a problem if he wasn't quick about it.

He arrived at Maurice's just after 5 o'clock, parking in a tight space out front. He whipped his car in with confidence and leaped out, feeling energized by the conversation with his old friend and the drive over on a brightening day. It promised to be a glorious evening.

He stepped inside, removed his sunglasses, and immediately caught sight of Mona. She had apparently just arrived herself. She looked lovely in the warm August shine, her skin prickling with a light sweat. Her flesh glowed beautifully into her light pink tanktop, and her legs looked stunning in shorts. Her auburn hair had lightened slightly over the summer, and her eyes were as penetrating as ever.

He could have gazed at her for half a day.

"You made it," she said as Johnny approached, rising to give him a quick kiss. Their lips met and lingered for an extra moment, both savoring the connection. In that instant, it seemed they made amends for the minor misunderstandings of the prior days while warming the passion they felt for each other.

Ivan approached from behind the bar after a discreet moment.

"Would you like the usuals?" he asked.

Mona glanced at Johnny as she sat back down. "I just arrived, so I haven't ordered."

Johnny smiled at Ivan. "A malbec for the lady, and I'll have my usual."

"Make it a merlot," Mona corrected in a cheerful tone. "Don't order for the lady, Denovo," she scolded gently.

"I'll be right back," Ivan confirmed. Mona smiled at Johnny.

"Where's Izzy?" Johnny asked, remembering they were expecting company at this rendezvous.

"She's coming along," Mona reassured him. "I thought I might be enough woman for you for half an hour, so I told her to meet us here at 5:30. She has some family in Newton she's getting together with."

Johnny smiled at Mona's subtle scheduling touch. A half-hour of privacy would make the discussion about the case much more straightforward and unguarded.

"OK, let me bring you up to speed before tonight's game," Johnny said quickly, leaning forward.

"Please do," Mona encouraged, leaning forward as well. "It sounds exciting. I didn't think I'd get involved in another case this soon."

"Well, I'll be more careful with you this time."

"Yes, yes, I'll be fine. Just fill me in."

Johnny told her about the game the night before, how they had deduced that a fringe environmental group was attacking companies, and the conversations with Evan about how Cool & Green might be involved and acting like a chicken with its head cut off, running solely on nervous energy.

"So, what does this have to do with McNaught?" Mona asked.

"Not much from what I can tell," Johnny replied. "His company is just collateral damage for this group. The blackmailing might be completely independent."

"And yet, the great detective uses the word 'might,'" Mona said, gesturing to a hypothetical jury of her peers. "One might wonder at his choice of words."

Johnny laughed at her wit. "Yes, you caught it. There is a subtext here, but I don't want to jump to any conclusions, so let's leave it alone for now. Suffice to say that McNaught has a problem of one sort or another. I'm just not sure how deep it runs, or if these things are connected."

"But you think they are," Mona observed. "You wouldn't bring them up if you didn't. You wouldn't think they *might* be connected otherwise."

Before he could respond, the door to Maurice's opened and a girlish voice shouted, "Mona!"

This must be Izzy, Johnny thought, turning to find himself face-to-face with a short vivacious redhead – electric green eyes, vivid lipstick, and cinnamon freckles gracing a petite frame and cute face, complete with a button nose. She looked like a firecracker personified.

He stood as a formality to greet the new arrival.

Mona was already out of her chair, hugging Izzy and preparing to introduce the two.

"Izzy, this is Johnny Denovo," Mona said. "Johnny, this is Isabel Chase. Everyone calls her Izzy."

"Pleased to meet you," Johnny said, shaking her hand. "Did you enjoy the Top of the Hub?"

"Oh, the view was great, but that bartender was a poopstain, I'll tell you something. Spits like a camel, too!" Izzy responded, drawing a laugh from a good portion of the bar, her voice carrying within Maurice's hushed and private interior.

Ivan approached the group, smiling as he apprised the woman the wind had just blown in.

"Can I get your friend a drink?" he inquired.

"Oh, I'll say you can, tall, dark, and dreamy," Izzy responded. "I'll take a Cosmopolitan, if you please."

Ivan clicked his heels together, smiled again at Izzy with a small bow of his head, and returned to the bar to make her drink.

"Sit down, sit down," Mona urged her friend. "Boy, you sure know how to make an entrance!"

"Oh, I don't know what it is, but the city gets me all fired up," Izzy said. "You spend as many months as I do in the notches of New Hampshire and you end up with some wild oats to sow."

Johnny watched the two – Izzy and Mona, fire and water, one burning with intensity, the other cool and sinuous.

He preferred to swim, he decided.

Izzy caught him being quiet and instinctively came after him. "So, you're the famous detective we keep reading about – good-looking, famous, wealthy, and mysterious. Don't trust those types. Usually have secrets. You'd better treat my friend right, that's all I have to say."

"Oh, I intend to," Johnny responded in a slightly restrained manner, overwhelmed by Mona's friend. "If she treats me well, I'll reciprocate."

"Fair enough," Izzy stated conclusively.

Ivan arrived with Izzy's Cosmopolitan, and their gazes locked again. Johnny and Mona shared a knowing glance.

"I guess not all bartenders are poopstains," Mona whispered to her friend after Ivan departed.

Izzy smiled broadly, and whispered back, "No, *he's* not, that's for sure. What's his name?"

Johnny interjected, "That's Ivan. He's Russian, but he's lived in Boston for a decade, a very good guy. You'd like him."

Izzy gave him a withering look. "I already do. Aren't you paying attention?"

Mona laughed and addressed Johnny. "You have to forgive Izzy. She was raised on a farm."

"And proud of it!" Izzy chimed in, raising her fluted Cosmopolitan glass in the air.

The three clinked their glasses in a toast and sipped ceremoniously.

"So, what's life like up in New Hampshire?" Johnny asked.

"Boring," Izzy replied with a huff that quickly changed into a look of mild, apologetic embarrassment. "It's beautiful, and I love it, but by the end of summer, I need a break. This trip is part of my little getaway."

"She usually has a week in the spring and one in the summer when she can take a vacation," Mona added. "Last spring, we went to Vegas together for a long weekend. That was totally cheesy."

"Totally," Izzy agreed, and both women laughed. "Remember Mr. Grossman?!" More laughter.

Mona caught Johnny's quizzical gaze. "This was a guy who was hitting on Izzy. He was straight out of central casting, I swear. Just such a New Jersey stereotype, gold chain and everything. Totally gross, so we called him Mr. Grossman. Ugh!" Both women dissolved in laughter again.

"And that cologne!" Izzy added with a peal of laughter.

Suddenly, Johnny realized he was forming a question for Izzy, but he didn't have all the information he needed to ask it. He had to fill in a blank.

"Excuse me, ladies," he interjected. "I need to make a quick phone call. Don't go anywhere. I should have a question for Izzy when I get back."

The giggles died down momentarily and Izzy gave him a ciao wave. The women erupted in a cascade of laughter again as Johnny stepped outside Maurice's to place his call.

He flipped his cell phone open and went to his contacts, pressing the number for Tom McNaught's cell phone.

McNaught answered after a few rings.

"Tom McNaught."

"McNaught, it's Johnny Denovo," Johnny indicated. "I wanted to update you and ask you a question."

"I was beginning to wonder if you were making any progress," McNaught said.

"Plenty, but I forgot to ask you something earlier."

"Go ahead," McNaught said.

"Your wife, what's her maiden name?"

"Gleason," McNaught answered. "Heather Gleason. Why do you ask?"

"Just needed to know. Also, where was she born in New Hampshire?"

"You really need to know this? You're not going to go stumbling in there and spill the beans?" McNaught said with a nervous laugh.

"Don't worry," Johnny said firmly, nearly insulted. Researchers, even those turned into CEOs, were sometimes comically earnest. "I've done this before. Where was she born?"

McNaught gave him a name of a small town in the White Mountains.

"When do you tell me what this all means?" he asked.

"I'll give you more of an update in a few days, but suffice to say this is a complicated case. Your blackmailing is part of something larger. That's all I can say for now."

McNaught sounded worried. "That's all you can say?"

"I know, but it's as much for your own safety as for anything else," Johnny responded. Besides, Johnny thought, he didn't know yet who to trust. Keeping the information to himself was the safest approach.

But he continued to soothe his client.

"If I tell you too much, I could put you in danger. I'm sure you can appreciate why that's an untenable option, and I hope you'll trust my judgment."

Johnny Denovo - The Green Monster

"Yes, certainly I do," McNaught answered, sounding deflated. "Just tell me what you can, when you can."

"Certainly. Thanks for the information. Call me if you think of anything else, or if your blackmailer contacts you."

"I will," McNaught said. "Am I in danger now? Is Heather?"

"Not at all," Johnny said, rushing now to finish the call. "Don't take this wrong, but it seems like you're a sideshow to the main event."

As Johnny reentered Maurice's, Izzy and Mona were still giggling and talking, but they quieted down as Johnny approached. Ivan was watching them from the bar with a bemused expression on his face.

"Hi, sorry about that," Johnny said as he sat down.

"No worries," Izzy said, smiling. "Must have been important to leave us here alone."

"I don't know about that, but I do have a question for you now," Johnny responded.

"Hit me," Izzy blurted out.

"You've lived in New Hampshire your entire life?"

"Right."

"Do you know a Gleason family there?" Johnny asked. "Farming family."

"Do you mean the Crazy Gleasons?" Izzy responded in a theatrical voice, her eyes shining with mischief.

"I don't know, do I?" Johnny pressed.

"You must," Izzy said, laughing. "Oh my, they are something else. Two old farts up on a farm in the hills. I think they grow marijuana, but that's just speculation based on rumor. They have some kids I think, but they never visit. I don't blame them. I wouldn't visit the Crazy Gleasons if they were my parents. Pair of nut jobs, if you ask me. Haven't heard of them in a dog's age. How did you hear about them? Do you have their personal number on that cell phone of yours?"

Johnny smiled. "No, nothing like that. I'm working on a case and the Gleason name came up along with New Hampshire. I thought I'd ask, just on the off-chance you might have heard of them."

"Oh, they're notorious up there. Reclusive old hippies, but crazy, you know?" Izzy said with a tone of inquiry. "Not just burn-outs, but something else. Some people think they're harmless, but I'm not so sure."

"I understand," Johnny said, tasting his drink. "And there are two of them?" Johnny asked.

"Oh yes, a husband and wife," Izzy moaned. "But you never see them, like I said. All I know is what the grapevine says anymore. But people still talk about them, that's for sure."

"Thanks for the information," Johnny said, taking a long swig of his drink. "Now, you two have a game to get to, and I want to ask you to look for something for me." And with that, he told them both about the woman holding up the green sign. Mona had already heard this part of the story, so she was able to help move things along.

"And you want us to see what else she does?" Mona asked as Johnny finished his description.

"That right," Johnny said. "Who does she talk with? Does she make phone calls? Does she leave her seat? If she does, where does she go? Now, you don't have to do any of this, but if you can, it would help me a lot. This is a nice coincidence, you going to the game tonight, and we should take advantage of it."

"Very cool," said Izzy, swallowing the dregs of her Cosmopolitan. "Are we deputized?"

Johnny gave her a weak smile. "No, nothing like that. In fact, you can't let anyone know what you're up to. No jokes, no stray comments, nothing. You're just there for a game."

"Gotcha!" Izzy responded. "Not a word. Tick a lock!"

Johnny looked at the loud cherry bomb of a redhead out on the loose, and worried whether she'd be able to keep her promise. Izzy's voice carried and her energy made her stand out in a crowd.

But he had no choice.

It was not an ideal situation.

The group rose as one. Johnny gave Mona a quick kiss goodbye and, as if with that tiny spark, the evening began. Johnny headed up the street, and Mona and Izzy caught a cab going the opposite direction to Fenway Park.

It had turned into a beautiful night for baseball in Boston.

Chapter 13
Road Trip

Leaving Maurice's, Johnny hopped into his car and slipped the tight parking space he'd wedged into. Accelerating onto the roads, he began driving north.

It was time for a late-night visit to New Hampshire, to see what the Gleasons were really like.

There were two of them, according to Izzy. This puzzled him. McNaught had said that his wife, Heather, had only a mother still alive in New Hampshire. Had she remarried? Was there another child, a male child, now an adult, living with her? Or was something else going on?

Fortunately, the small New England states made it possible to get from one to another quickly. Out West, the states took hours to traverse.

Gaining the outskirts of Boston, he accelerated to a dangerous speed, a warm wind gusting over the hood and filling the slipstream over his head with a pleasant turbulence.

Time was wasting.

By the time his CD player flipped to a new disc, he was in the heart of New Hampshire. The landscape had become bucolic and severely rural, small farmhouses peeking out from behind large stands of old trees and broad pastures interspersed among the low hills.

The evening was aglow with a tremulous late-summer light. Slowing now on the narrower roads, Johnny noticed the hundreds of insect carcasses littering his windshield. Peering ahead, then checking his fuel gauge, he decided it was time to delouse the windshield and refuel. He pulled into a combination mini-mart and gas station in the first small tourist town he entered. He was approaching the even smaller hamlet where Heather Gleason had been born.

The cool night air of the northern mountain dells was invigorating. It piqued his appetite. It was time to get a snack as well.

Parking in the well-lit pump bays, he shut off his car. A silence fell around him. It was the sound of no city. Only the faint hiss of a passing car intruded. In the distance, a voice called, indistinct and untroubled. A dog's bark echoed in the night. Otherwise, it was countryside quiet.

He filled his tank, then went inside the mini-mart to pay and grab something to eat. A young man behind the cash register was idly typing into a small laptop perched on the counter, a bored expression on his face. He looked like a typical slacker, scrawny and sporting a partial beard and shaggy hair.

Johnny went to the back of the store to get a soda and a peppermint patty, his favorite road trip snack.

The cashier looked up as Johnny approached.

"Is that all?" he asked from behind disinterested eyelids.

"Well, I was also wondering if you could direct me to the Gleason farm," Johnny indicated.

"The Gleason farm?" The cashier's eyes widened in sincere reaction. "Oh, you don't want to go there, dude," he told Johnny in worried tones.

"Why not?" Johnny asked.

"They're loco, man," the cashier said. "Crazy. Unbalanced. Why do you want to see them anyhow?"

"I have questions," Johnny said.

"So read a book, but don't try to talk with them, man. They shoot at people," he told Johnny.

"Really?"

"Really, dude. I'm not kidding. Dangerous. Don't you get it? What part of 'Don't go' don't you understand?"

"I get it, I understand," Johnny confirmed. "But I still want to talk with them. How do I get there?"

"OK, man, but don't say I didn't warn you," the cashier muttered, a worried expression on his face. It melted away and a look of resignation took over. "So, if you want to, go north on this road here, and at the split, turn right, by the ice cream place. Follow that past the mini-golf course on the left, and you'll see a dirt road with a dead end sign on it, and a 'No Trespassing' sign. That's the Gleason place. It's a long road back into there, and I don't know what it's like. That little hot rod of yours might not do too well."

"Well, it's a chance I'll have to take," Johnny divulged. "And it's an old married couple, right?"

"I don't know, man," the cashier answered. "Everybody just calls them the Gleasons. I've seen the lady. She's probably like sixty or eighty. I'm bad at things like that."

Johnny smiled. "Thanks very much. You've been a great help."

"Be careful, dude. Don't be a statistic."

Scrubbing bug guts from his windshield, Johnny pondered the situation. A new approach was forming in his mind. He didn't trust the cashier's age estimations at all, thinking the Gleason woman would probably be in her fifties at this point. The man was the mystery. Her first husband was supposed to be dead. But as he'd drawn nearer to the Gleasons, they'd generated uncertainty. It was the opposite of how these things were supposed to work.

He speed-dialed Tucker.

"Tucker," he said as his friend answered. "It's Johnny. Can you do me a favor?"

"Hey, Johnny! I'm watching the game, and you can see the Green Monster often enough," Tucker said, launching into a short monologue. "I've seen the sign go up once so far, but she skipped one third-base play and I could see the Monster clearly, so our theory holds with your minor modification. She can skip plays. Adds to the security. But why are you calling?"

"I wanted to see if you could lasso a satellite for me quickly," Johnny said.

"No problem," Tucker replied. "Where do you want it pointed?"

"I've found out that McNaught's wife's maiden name is Gleason. I'm up at their farm in New Hampshire, about to pay them a visit, but the cashier in the nearby town warned me they're dangerous. I want some reconnaissance," Johnny explained.

There was silence on the phone.

"Are you there, Tucker?" Johnny asked.

"I'm here," Tucker responded. "Johnny, I can't help you on this one. I'm really sorry."

It was Johnny's turn to be silent, his surprise at Tucker's reaction stealing words from his thoughts. He recovered after a moment of listening to the quiet country road.

"What do you mean?" he asked, his voice drained of color.

"You know I know about a lot of top secret projects, right? Clandestine activities?" Tucker began. "Well, all I can say is that this would create a conflict of interest, so I have to bow out. I have to recuse myself. It's that simple, and that's the only answer I can give."

"Really?" was Johnny's astonished reaction, but his brain was hard at work processing the significance of this turn of events. If Tucker knew the Gleasons were involved in something top secret, it meant they were more potent than he'd imagined.

"Tucker, at least answer one question for me. Are they on our side?" Johnny asked.

"Unclear. And I can't say any more," Tucker answered brusquely. "However, be careful. I have to end this conversation now. I'll let you know about tonight's game, but unless things change, consider me off this case for the time being."

Johnny paused again, processing the information, then said, "I understand. Let me know about the game, and after that I'll consider you off this case. But I will find a way to get you back on it, you know that."

"I'll wait for you to work that one out," Tucker responded. "Until then, hasta la vista, and be careful."

The call ended with the two childhood pals facing a gaping yaw in the midst of their friendship, a professional chasm neither could broach at the moment.

It was alien territory.

Johnny felt like he'd just lost use of a limb.

But the clock was ticking. There wasn't time to think over the situation. The light of day was fading, he had limited knowledge of what he was about to face, and he now knew the Gleasons were more formidable than suspected, probably deserving of their reputation at the very least.

But these people were not simple farmers or crazy hillbillies. They were major players in some way if Tucker knew about them. And that put Johnny on high alert.

He took a deep breath to clear his head, opened his peppermint patty, then climbed into his car and headed north, the fresh taste of peppermint and chocolate swirling in his mouth.

The low mountains of New Hampshire passed on either side as he sped northward. In just a few minutes, he reached the ice cream stand and turned right, heading up a narrow county highway full of shadowy hills, their black humps rolling like ocean waves in the fading light.

He called Mona while he still had time.

"Hello," she said loudly, compensating for the game noise about her.

"Hi, Mona, it's Johnny," he said.

"Hi, stranger. Want an update?" she asked.

"Please."

"Well, the person you described is here, and so far, she's only held it up once, a green sign," Mona said, a little more quietly.

"That's what Tucker saw watching the game," Johnny confirmed.

"Where are you?" Mona asked.

"On a little detour," Johnny said. "I'll be home by morning. I just wanted a quick first-person account."

"OK," Mona said. "It's a good game. Izzy's having a blast. Call again if you want another update."

"I will. Bye," Johnny said, closing his phone. He slowed the car. The Gleasons' road was approaching on the right, the battered sign barely discernible in the fading light, mud-spattered "dead end" and "no trespassing" panels reflecting dimly in Johnny's headlights.

A sense of foreboding stole over Johnny as he extinguished his headlights and rolled to a stop. He paused, then looked up and down the main road again. Nobody was coming.

He flipped a quick u-turn and parked off the shoulder in the high late-summer weeds next to a telephone pole, orienting his car's nose back to town, positioning it better for a quick getaway. An exit strategy would be important tonight, he thought to himself, and the best way to point his car was toward the town he just left. It was the best homing beacon he would have on these lonesome roads if things went awry.

Chapter 14
Caught Stealing

The roadway was perfectly silent, shadows from the slight embankment next to Johnny's car deepening the encroaching darkness. Johnny crept out of his car and closed the door with a soft click. He didn't lock the car. The top was down, and the flash of lights and clicks of locks might give him away. Instead, he tucked into his back pocket a flashlight from his glove box, checked the road, then crossed. He disappeared just inside the Gleasons' road, vanishing into the inky quiescence pooled beneath the dense foliage.

His eyes adjusting to the deeper darkness, he found himself on an unfinished dirt road, rutted in parts, rocky in others. He noted the uneven terrain. If he had to turn tail, he'd have to high-step it or risk a fall. Footing would be an issue.

The air was cool. The leaves around him were still, almost apprehensive. Small bugs – gnats, mosquitoes – pestered the air. Scraps of sky clutched at the fading light.

Overall, the effect was grim and suffocating.

Johnny walked alongside the dirt road, counting his paces, and stopped about a hundred yards inside the property. He scanned the area with his small halogen flashlight, making sure the beam was low to the ground, the focus tight. The trees seemed thinner here, as if he'd arrived at a boundary of some sort.

Sweeping the thin beam of light to the left, he saw that the trees along a broad path had been cut away years ago. Saplings mixed into the small trees, yet the swath was unmistakable.

As he scanned the ground, he saw a large electrical vault in the ground behind a copse of saplings, its hard, flat, green rectangular lid providing a stark geometric contrast in the mist of the chaotic underbrush. He shut the light off quickly.

A power vault in the ground was a surprising thing to see in a rural area. Power was cheaper to provide using overhead wires and telephone poles. Underground installations required laying miles of insulated power cables in trenches. The reliability was much higher, with the chances of losing power to wind damage or a car accident virtually eliminated.

You only had underground power if you weren't willing to accept downtime.

Johnny remembered parking his car next to a power pole, the cylindrical transformer hanging overhead. Underground power was not normal or necessary in this area of New Hampshire.

The Gleasons appeared to have a special supply.

These people have infrastructure, Johnny thought. They have a safer and larger power supply than their neighbors, yet they were not known to be rich, just idiosyncratic. Stuck out here in rural New Hampshire, managing to get a power installation like this was beyond unusual.

He stopped to think about what other unseen advantages they might possess, and how they might have gained their status in Tucker's realm of top-secret threats.

He instinctively swatted a mosquito on his arm, the noise of the slap breaking the silence around him. He paused, realizing that he might have just given himself away. He waited a few moments.

Nothing stirred.

Warily, he pledged not to swat again.

It was time to get off the entrance road. Beyond this boundary zone, the road was probably going to be well-protected. On the entrance lane, the Gleasons' first line of defense would be geared to deter nuisance visitors – kids on bikes, curious locals, or troublemakers. That meant lights and noise. By staying off the road, he'd probably get farther without being detected, without tripping an alarm.

Passing through the heavy undergrowth was slow going. The late-summer insects enjoyed his unprotesting blood donor status. He hadn't dressed for a nighttime excursion into the woods. He only had jeans and a short-sleeved shirt to protect himself. But the light was better off to the side of the road than along the tree-lined drive. Here, the overhead canopy was less dense and more disordered.

After another hundred paces, Johnny was able to see the silhouette of a house through the trees.

It was about a hundred yards off still. It looked small. In the dim light, he had to stare a while to discern any features. He could barely distinguish machines from yard furniture.

After peering intently and letting his eyes adjust, he identified a number of items. A satellite dish. Three all-terrain vehicles. A small out-building of some sort. The house itself seemed fairly nondescript, with a small picnic table outside. There was a tall ham radio tower behind it.

Suddenly, he startled without knowing why. On the downbeat, he recognized what had alarmed his instincts – a shadowy form walking across the yard toward him. It was hard to tell whether the silhouetted figure was approaching or receding, but Johnny's instincts had surged. He trusted them. It meant some animal part of his brain had sensed a threat, and that meant an approach.

The figure wasn't close enough to cause genuine concern.

Still, Johnny kneeled down.

It was a man. The gait and lankiness belied gender.

The man's silhouette disappeared into the settling gloom. Johnny waited, barely breathing, nerves attenuated to the slightest change. Five seconds. Ten seconds. Then, quite unexpectedly, not 50 feet in front of him, bulkhead doors swept open, blinding beams of light shining out, flooding the night. A large fake boulder lay overturned to the right.

The man stood at the entrance, arched his back in a stretch, then went down some stairs into an underground room, turning to pull the bulkhead doors closed as he went.

His face remained obscured by shadows the entire time.

The doors closed, plunging the area into darkness once more.

"An underground bunker," Johnny muttered to himself in a whisper. "Why?"

As if in response, the doors opened again, and the man emerged, this time carrying something on his shoulder. The light from the bunker illuminated him clearly as he turned to survey the grounds. Johnny's eyes, adjusted for dimmer light, registered every detail. He was older, around 50. His face was rugged, weathered, and inscrutable from this distance. A pistol was slung in a shoulder holster.

On his shoulder rested a long box, wooden and painted green, about the size you'd use for a floor lamp, but with yellow military lettering along the side. Military. It added to the impression of menace.

The man set down the box and closed the bulkhead doors, turning the fake boulder over to cover the entrance. Johnny waited until he saw the man silhouetted on the ridge once more, the box slung atop his shoulder.

He leaped to his feet and moved to leave.

Reaching his car after carefully retracing his steps in the billowing darkness, he leaned against the driver's door. He took out his cell phone and called Tucker, keeping his head down as he spoke, an instinctive effort to avoid recognition and create privacy.

"Denovo," Tucker answered. "Can't talk about this."

"Tucker, what if I have information about the Gleasons that makes me part of *your* case," Johnny said. "Then you could be part of mine, right?"

"I suppose so," Tucker said thoughtfully. "But it has to be good."

"What can I buy with a secret underground bunker and shoulder-launched missiles?" Johnny asked. "Can I get into your secret club with those?"

"You're kidding!" Tucker shouted. "You actually saw a bunker and missiles?!"

"With my own two eyes," Johnny said.

"That would explain a lot," Tucker said. "We've been trying to figure out the Gleasons, but without probable cause, we could never get a search warrant. So we could never see anything other than a simple farmhouse, tricked out for sure, but nothing too unusual. A lot of hardy souls live in New Hampshire. There were other things, but no hard evidence. We've made very little progress over the years. They seem to have a guardian angel. Are you telling me straight?"

"It's the real deal," Johnny said. "Saw it not a hundred feet in front of me. And they have a redundant underground power supply. I saw the vault in the ground."

"OK, I'm back on your case," Tucker confirmed. "It's now one and the same. Man, that was fast. I think that's going down as the shortest recusal of all time."

"I'm glad for that," Johnny said, his eyes darting upward as he spoke. "Hold it!"

A truck was coming down the Gleasons' drive, its lights bouncing along the rough road. Before he could move, the truck emerged, bright headlights painting him with light, revealing him with his phone held up to his ear.

"You!" a rough voice called from the truck's open window as the brights flashed on. Johnny couldn't make out the man's face, the dazzling highbeams preventing him from doing anything more than squinting and shielding his eyes. "What are you doing outside my property?"

"Car trouble," Johnny lied.

"Car trouble my ass," the voice shouted angrily. "You're Johnny Denovo. I know your face. Here's your car trouble!"

Johnny moved quickly, pivoting on the spot and leaping into his open convertible.

A shot was fired from the truck but missed high, its whistle cutting the air overhead as it passed. Johnny doubled over in his car, digging in his pocket for the keys. He heard the truck start to idle as the transmission shifted into park. The driver's door opened.

"You scumbag, I'll give you all the car trouble you can handle," the voice uttered, approaching. A dark silhouette moved out into the roadway.

Johnny dug out his keys. As they jingled, another shot was fired, this one exploding his driver's side headrest in a shower of white batting. Johnny shoved the key into the ignition and started the car, its headlights coming on in a brilliant display, their halogen whiteness blazing in the soupy twilight. Another shot came, again sailing high. Johnny snapped the car into gear. With a rev of the accelerator, he floored it.

His idea worked. Instead of putting the car into drive, he'd put it into reverse. By accelerating quickly, he not only avoided the shots aimed forward of his position, but also surprised his adversary. The rear of his car slammed into the gunman, knocking him down just as he lined up for another shot. Johnny popped the car into drive and peeled away, still hunched over. A shot flew over his head a moment later, but he was away.

Sitting up after rounding a corner, Johnny slipped his seatbelt on and scratched his hair, a nervous habit he'd developed over the years, one that always calmed him down. That had been a close call. His cell phone lay on the floor beneath the passenger seat. He must have closed it as he jumped in. Tucker would have heard some of the encounter and would be calling. Johnny wasn't in the mood to explain. He stretched to reach the phone. Grabbing it, he flipped it open and switched it off.

His first task was to find his way back to Boston. The only obvious casualty was his headrest. The rest of the carnage consisted of jangled nerves.

Steering down long, winding sideroads, using the tiny bright bulge in the twilight sky as a compass point, Johnny was able to backtrack. Soon, he saw the ice cream shop again and knew where he was.

He turned his phone back on and called Mona for an update from the game. He needed to touch base with someone, to recalibrate reality and settle his nerves. He'd call Tucker soon enough. Mona was his top priority after nearly being shot.

"Hi Johnny," Mona chimed as she picked up the phone. "I'm glad you called. Something strange happened here just now."

"It's been an eventful night," Johnny said mysteriously, hoping his anxious breathing wasn't discernible over the phone. "What's your news?"

"The sign lady? You remember her? Well, for no apparent reason, she just held up a red sign, and she held it up a long time. There was no play. In fact, she held it up so long that it covered two plays."

"Really?" Johnny said. "And this just happened?"

"About 5 minutes ago," Mona confirmed.

"Where is she now?" Johnny asked.

"She left," Mona told him. "She left her seat right after that and hasn't returned. Gone. We didn't follow her because she gathered up all her stuff and looked like someone who was headed home in a hurry. She took the signs with her."

Johnny was silent, lost in thought.

"Are you there?" Mona asked.

"Yep, I'm here," he affirmed. "Let me call you back. I need to find a computer, and I think I know where to go."

Chapter 15
Buzzed

Johnny pulled back into the gas station with the mini-mart, parking his car in the deep malodorous shadows near the dumpster. Gleason may be prowling for him. So far, nobody had been tailing him. He felt the confrontation was over with for now, but there was no harm in taking an extra precaution – he was outgunned, and his local knowledge was slight. The advantage was not his in this remote area of New Hampshire.

As the bell on the mini-mart's door rattled, a familiar face looked up to greet him. The same grungy cashier was on duty, still working on his laptop.

"Hi there," Johnny said, smiling at the cashier. "Remember me?"

"Dude, you're alive!" the guy crowed.

"Ha! Barely," Johnny admitted. "You were right. Crazy. I'm not going back there without a small army."

"You should have listened to me," the cashier chided in a nonchalant manner. "What's up now?"

"Can I use your computer for a minute? I just want to check one site. I'll be quick."

"Sure, man," the cashier said, turning the laptop Johnny's way. "The wireless in here is wicked fast. You'll like it."

"I bet I will," Johnny agreed, adjusting his hands to the touch-pad and keyboard. A browser was already open to a news site. Johnny cleared the URL and typed in the one McNaught had given him. The cartoon character tribute site greeted him once again. Out of the corner of his eye, he could see the cashier watching him. Johnny wished he could read minds at moments like this. Thanks to the cashier, he was sure the story of someone from Boston returning from the Gleason farm with his tail between his legs and then checking a cartoon fan site was going to make the rounds, embroidered with speculation and hilarity, refueling the lore around the Gleasons.

Fortunately, the cashier hadn't recognized him.

Johnny flipped open his cell phone and called Tucker.

"Tucker, it's me," Johnny began.

"What happened to you?" Tucker interjected, a hint of alarm in his voice.

"Unfriendly farmers, nothing major. I'll explain later."

"I was getting ready to send in the clowns," Tucker replied. "But as long as you're OK, I can wait for the story. What now?"

"Can you tell me the sequence to enter into that site as a user-name, based on tonight's sightings?"

"Sure, it's right here. 5-3-2-2-5-4-3-1-5-2-4-7-2. That should do it. Password could be green, you'll recall."

"I recall. Thanks. Hold on, let me see if this works," Johnny said to his friend, typing slowly, his cell phone cradled against his ear. He entered the string of numbers and the password, and clicked Submit. The screen flashed back a message, "Invalid username/password combination."

"Tucker, it didn't work," Johnny reported.

"Really? Let me try it here," Tucker suggested. There was a grunt as Tucker got up from his chair, and the sound of keystrokes. "You're right. Doesn't work for me, either. Maybe our password theory is wrong. It's untested until now. This is the error message the site displays if one is right, but not both. So we're not totally out of bounds. Part of this is right, and that's probably the username."

"Agreed," Johnny responded, taking a deep breath. He clicked in the password box and deleted the dots standing in for "green." He typed "red."

"I'm in, Tuck," he reported. "The password is 'red.'"

"Oh, because that chick was holding up that red sign for forever and a day just a little while ago," Tucker said sleepily, confirming that it had been visible on television. "OK, I'm in, too. And this is a little disappointing, isn't it?"

Both Johnny and Tucker were gazing at a simple white screen displaying the message, "Hold."

"What does it mean?" Tucker asked Johnny.

"I think I know," Johnny said. "Wait a second while I move somewhere else."

Johnny turned to the cashier. "Can I close the browser so my history clears from your cache?"

"Sure, man," the cashier said. "It's set to clear when it closes. I hate people seeing my browsing history, too."

"Great, and thanks very much," Johnny said, smiling at the cashier as he turned to leave. Once he was outside, he put the phone back to his ear.

"Tucker, let me get the car going and then we can talk," Johnny said. He started the engine, put the roof up, and began the drive home, bringing Tucker up to date on the events at the Gleasons' farm.

When he was done, Tucker emitted a low whistle. "Wow, you definitely took the bull by the horns there. From what I know of them, I'd want a battalion before I'd venture into their compound."

"I had a similar thought. I'm glad my lesson only cost me a headrest," Johnny admitted. "But I think that's why the lady at Fenway held up the red sign. I think Gleason's in on this, and now he knows I'm on the scent, so he called off activity for tonight. The red sign gave the password, and 'Hold' was the message."

"Makes sense," Tucker confirmed. "But now what?"

"First of all, I'm kicking myself. I blew it tonight. If I'd stayed at home, we would have been able to see how these eco-terrorists work on a normal night. We'd have had their username and password, and we would have seen what lurks on the other side. Is it a set of detailed plans? Is it a simple message? Does it let people check in somehow? Now, we don't know. We only have the word, 'Hold.' Not good."

"Don't beat yourself up about it," Tucker advised. "You didn't know the Gleasons were involved, that it would turn out this way. In any event, we can only move forward."

"You're right, Tuck," Johnny sighed. "No use crying over spilt passwords. Besides, we have other loose ends to nail down, and the Sox hit the road now, so we have some time," Johnny said. "When are they home again?"

"Next Monday," Tucker said confidently. "A crucial home stand, if this road trip doesn't go well. I swear, I should have been a sportscaster. I can do cliché with the best of them."

Johnny laughed tepidly, unease growing in his mind. "Well, then Monday's when we'll have to be ready. The Gleasons might feel pressured to move. We blew an opportunity tonight to see what that site was broadcasting, what instructions were being given. That's my fault. Now, we're in the blind and our quarry is feeling desperate. This isn't playing in our favor."

Chapter 16
Home Stand

He left his car at the dealership, dropping his keys in the overnight slot and walking the remaining few blocks home. The note he left on the seat read, "Big rock. Please replace the headrest. Call when done. Johnny D."

Arriving home after midnight, he was tired and hungry. Wei Chou's was closed, so he scrounged for some leftovers to reheat. Unsatisfied by the meager scraps he found, he went to bed bedraggled, tense, hungry, and frustrated. Leftovers and loneliness were the antithesis of what he wanted.

Mona was on his mind.

He wanted to spend a nice evening out with her over fancy food, feel her warm skin beneath his fingers, smell her neck, hear her laugh.

Sleep came to his as an anesthetic.

The next day, Johnny was late rising. Staring out his windows, he was shocked to see how dramatically the city had changed over just a few hours. A weather front had streamed in to Boston overnight, making the day cloudy and blustery, a portent of September. The flat light of autumn haunted the day, the desiccation of fall drumming impatiently on the threshold of summer.

The cloudy and turbulent sky reflected the case as it stood in Johnny's mind.

His unease had spiked overnight. Things were not going well.

Hunger stabbed at his gut, and it wasn't Chinese food he needed. It was comfort food. He found some eggs in the fridge. He scrambled a few up, soft and slightly runny, and added some white toast and a glass of orange juice. It was a grandma's breakfast, but it was what he needed – food as solace. It settled his nerves and took the hunger pangs away for the time being.

He should have eaten this last night, he thought ruefully. He might have gone to bed happier.

Last night. It only added to the confusion by cementing a new option in his brain.

Whoever was being called the Gleasons these days might not know their daughters had McNaught in common, but Johnny was betting they did, given their presence in Tucker's world of nefarious people. If so, Schwartz was no longer the only source of information about the long-lost sister connection, and the number of candidate blackmailers had doubled.

In addition to Schwartz and McNaught, there were two other people who probably knew that McNaught's wife and mistress were sisters – the radical and heavily armed Gleasons, one of whom was a cipher, an unknown.

He'd wanted new facts, but even with this new information, the maze seemed only more baffling. He needed to let his limbic brain do some work, but he needed to direct it a bit, steer it toward some options.

Other than green, what metaphors did he have in hand? With McNaught, it was the metaphor of siblings, and siblings meant chromosomes, genetics. That led to Schwartz, who was all about genetics. Genetics were sequences that coded proteins. Codes that were themselves not especially malleable, just passing information, like fractals. His old mentor Evan had suggested that perhaps this apparent plot was a pattern like a fractal, repeating itself based solely on reinjected energy. Genetics as fractals. Fractals as a pattern of self-replicating complexity. Genetics. Genomics.

There was also an abundance of duality – sisters, chromosomes, a web site that was used for both signals and blackmail. Symmetry. Balance. Complementarities. Double-helix. Genetics. Chromosomes. Pairs.

There was apparently something environmental driving the whole shebang. Johnny tried to list things in nature that were symmetrical. Wings of insects came to mind. Eyes, faces, physiques from left to right usually appeared to be symmetrical, especially in the more evolved species.

Trees were symmetrical, but vertically, not side-to-side, with their leaves above ground and root systems below. Above and below.

And trees were green. It might hang together, Johnny thought.

"Above and below" was always a powerful conceptual metaphor. The Gleasons had a house on a hill with a soaring ham radio antenna and a hidden underground bunker. There was a family tree involved, as well, with parents above and children below. Paul, the obnoxious bartender, didn't fit quite, but was high above the city at the Top of the Hub. The above-below metaphor uncovered a suggestive set of connections, and fit with the symmetry themes. The tree united it with "green."

He decided to pursue it.

The fact that Paul the bartender didn't fit became more apparent as he swiftly passed through the information in this manner.

He needed to know more about Paul.

Johnny shuffled over to his phone and called information.

"Boston, Massachusetts. Top of the Hub, please." His phone connected to his desired number, and it was answered by an operator. "Management offices, please," Johnny responded when asked.

After a few rings, a woman answered.

"Top of the Hub," she said cheerfully.

"Hello," Johnny said. "Is this the manager of the Top of the Hub?"

"Yes, this is Cynthia speaking. I'm the day manager. Can I help you?" the woman said.

"Hi, Cynthia. My name is Johnny Denovo. I'm a detective. I'm calling on business related to a case I'm handling right now," Johnny explained.

"Oh, I've heard of you, of course," Cynthia replied in a warm voice. "I'd be happy to help, assuming I can."

"Great," said Johnny. "You have a bartender named Paul. Can you tell me his last name?"

"Has he done anything wrong?" Cynthia asked, a tinge of alarm in her voice.

"Not that I know of," Johnny replied. "Unless you count being quite memorable in how he treats people."

"Oh," Cynthia laughed. "You've met him then, I see."

"Yes, I have, but I've found discretion is the better part of valor in my line of work. You can appreciate the delicacy of the matters I sometimes find myself involved in."

"Of course, but unfortunately I really can't divulge that information," Cynthia replied. "It's a privacy issue."

"I understand," Johnny said, softening his voice. "Believe me, it's a vital piece of information that can help solve a case that has to be solved in the next week. I wouldn't be asking if it weren't important. I know how careful you have to be in employee relations. I'm also on professional business. I'm seeking information. No matter what, I don't divulge how I obtain it."

There was silence.

Cynthia finally spoke, reluctance filling her words. "Robertson. Does that help?"

"That's perfect," Johnny said. "Thank you. I'll keep this conversation confidential, and I'd appreciate it if you did, as well."

"You have my word," Cynthia said. The call ended.

Paul Robertson. Paul was on a first-name basis with Schwartz, but judging by the bartender's attitude, it seemed there had to be more. As far as Johnny knew, Schwartz had never married. He might not be interested in women. What if Paul's evenings were actually spent in a relationship with Schwartz?

It was something he needed to check out. Pillow talk was often how information was transmitted without people realizing it.

Thinking of Schwartz, Johnny remembered Robert at Schwartz's office. Robert seemed discrete and knowledgeable, but also like a people pleaser. Johnny could use this to his advantage. Grabbing his phone, he called Schwartz Genetics, asking for Robert when the front desk answered. He was put through.

Robert picked up.

"Hi Robert," Johnny said. "It's Johnny Denovo. Remember me?"

"Certainly," Robert replied phlegmatically. "It was only two days ago."

"Right," Johnny responded. "I'd like to ask you a delicate question if I could, to help an investigation along. As you'll understand, I have to leave no stone unturned, even if lifting a stone may make people scurry."

"Well, I can't guarantee an answer, but I promise not to be flabbergasted by the question," Robert replied.

"That's good enough," Johnny said. "Basically, I want to know Dr. Schwartz's current romantic situation. Married? Divorced? Seeing someone? On the market? I thought you might know."

"And this matters to your investigation why, exactly?" Robert asked.

"That depends on the answer," Johnny said honestly. "But I can't know how it might matter before I know the answer."

"I see," Robert pondered. "I guess it can't hurt, assuming you'll keep this between us and not name me as the source of this information. It's just a little awkward, you see."

Johnny waited to let Robert continue.

"Well, Dr. Schwartz is away for a few days anyhow," Robert proceeded. He was obviously uncomfortable with the topic, but he kept talking. Johnny didn't speak, worried that any interruption would give Robert a moment to reassess the situation. "To tell the truth, Dr. Schwartz is gay and currently seeing someone. It's a bartender named Paul he met downtown. They've been seeing each other for a few months. Does that help?"

"How about I spare you the answer to that?" Johnny offered. "That way, you won't have a feeling about it either way."

"That sounds like a good idea to me," Robert agreed. "I'm already sorry I told you, but not knowing whether it mattered will help me get over it."

"Well, thank you, Robert. I appreciate your willingness to level with me. Either way, I know more and that will help me get to the truth of this case," Johnny concluded, thanking Robert again as he hung up the phone.

So, that was it. Schwartz and Paul were lovers. Johnny was pleased to feel his suspect pool shrinking, until he realized this wasn't necessarily the case. In fact, Schwartz was still just as likely to be innocent as guilty. If he had told Paul that he was meeting McNaught at Grand Central station, Paul could have followed Schwartz without telling him or being seen. He could have listened in on their conversation using the acoustic sweet spot at the station. Or Schwartz could have told Paul the information in confidence, and Paul was using it to blackmail McNaught. Or Paul knew nothing, and Johnny was back at square one.

But a connection was a connection, and now he knew Paul at least mattered to this tangled web of relationships and intrigues.

The question was how.

Johnny showered and shaved, then gave Mona a call on her cell phone.

"Hey, Johnny," she answered cheerfully. "I'm in a meeting right now. Can I call you back?"

"Sure," he replied. "Are you free tonight?"

"Yes, I am. I want to see you, too. I'll drop by at seven, and I'll bring pizza from that place just down the street, OK?"

"Great. See you then," Johnny said, hanging up. On a day requiring comfort food and some down time to realign his karma, pizza and Mona sounded like just the ticket.

With a substantially improved personal forecast, even the blustery, gray day couldn't dampen his spirits. Food and love were major parts of the brain's pleasure centers, and he'd been without both for a few days now. Fenway hot dogs, peppermint patties, leftovers, and scrambled eggs were pale imitations of his real needs. Pleasure centers were so vital to the brain's activity that regression in these areas undercut the rest. Without the proper stimulation, the brain atrophied. Pleasure was a matter of brain health, he knew, a way to keep the connections firing without a hitch.

Plus, it felt good.

Faith restored, he kicked back on his couch and turned up the stereo, enjoying an old favorite at high volume. He needed to let his mind relax and process all the information he'd shoved into it the past few days.

This case was complicated.

About two albums later, the phone rang.

"Johnny, it's Tucker. Have a minute?"

"What's up?" Johnny answered.

"Well, you brought the Gleasons up last night, so I decided to look into the case files again this morning, just to see if something jumped out at me. And sure enough, it did. They are investors in a company you've now become familiar with."

"Schwartz's?" Johnny guessed.

"Ack! Wrong!" Tucker said. "McNaught's."

"You're kidding!" Johnny responded, genuinely surprised. "Isn't it a family thing for Heather, investing in her hubby's bio-tech company?"

"I don't think so," Tucker concurred. "It's a pretty hefty share, and it was purchased just this spring. This isn't just play money. And the stock's not gone anywhere, so it wasn't opportunistic or a market play. That Gleason is a bad actor. He's up to something here. Johnny, this is the guy who shot your headrest last night! Man, that still gives me a chill."

"It was a close shave, but I'm fine. Also, I found out that the bartender at the Top of the Hub and Schwartz are an item. That changes things a little."

"Ooh, that's another weird one," Tucker countered. "What's the bartender's name? I can see if I can find anything on him."

"Paul Robertson," Johnny shared. "Let me know what you find."

"I will," Tucker promised. "You take it easy today. A doctor friend of mine once told me that a brush with death is worth an extra nap or two. Recalibrates your chakras or something like that."

"Was this a witch doctor?" Johnny inquired.

"Doesn't *your* HMO cover those?" Tucker parried.

"I shall heed such sage advice, no matter the source. I'll be laying low today. Call me with anything you catch on your fishing expedition. Later."

Hanging up the phone, Johnny turned up the music again. A song alluding to trees came on. It reminded him of his earlier thought about symmetry and trees, how the leaves above-ground are green but had to be fed by the roots. Roots. This case had roots aplenty, he thought. Genetics is just a modern term for roots. The Gleason girls might have craziness in their roots. And there seemed to be money involved here, the root of all evil. In fact, Johnny thought, this whole environmental angle might just be a smokescreen for something more base and predictable, like stock in McNaught's company. Greed can masquerade as green, he knew. The same roots are there, feeding it. Money, the root of all evil. Green.

His thinking stopped there, however. He needed more evidence. Motives were unclear. Metaphors were mixed and inconclusive. With the Sox out of town, the next few days were going to be quiet. And it was nearing the dinner hour, when pizza and a lovely woman would be visiting. He hoped to enjoy both completely, refueling his body and mind for the road ahead.

Chapter 17

Backstop

"This case is really eating at you," Mona said, her voice salted with concern. Johnny had just bitten into a slice of pizza. He couldn't answer, leaving the statement hanging in the air. A classic rock soundtrack droned in the background. He'd chosen it to add to the feeling of comfort and familiarity he craved.

As he chewed, he glanced at Mona and smiled weakly.

His mind was elsewhere.

Mona had arrived about 10 minutes earlier, carting along two big pizza boxes from their favorite local joint. They'd kissed passionately for a few minutes, the embrace tilting toward more, but the warm smell of freshly baked dough and hot cheese had overwhelmed them both, pulling them back from the brink of passion. Instead of indulging their carnal desires, they'd rushed to the kitchen for plates, drinks, and forks, sheepish smiles on their faces. Food came first.

"It's the tree image," Johnny muttered.

Mona cocked an eyebrow.

"What tree?"

"A metaphorical tree," Johnny confirmed. "Roots below, leaves above. Family trees. Above and below. Inheritance. It's all there, but I can't put it all together."

"Whatever are you talking about, Denovo?" Mona asked with mock disdain. "You're talking gibberish."

Johnny laughed, taking a swig of his beer.

"Probably," he confessed. "But you know my methods. There's something here. I just don't have enough information, so I'm at that point where I need more – more data, more facts, more revelations."

"I see," Mona purred. "You always want more, I can attest to that."

It was Johnny's turn to cock an eyebrow.

"Don't change the subject on me," he scolded. "Not yet. We'll get to that soon enough."

Mona smiled, a smoldering, knowing smile, her deep brown eyes taking on a dusky beauty. They suggested a dim room, shadows, intimacy. Johnny had to shake his head to focus his thoughts again.

"Let's try a little exercise," Johnny said, picking up another piece of pizza. "Let's take your family tree. Now, oddly enough, family trees can be depicted with roots at either the top or the bottom. They come in both varieties. Symmetrical. But let's pretend yours starts at the roots. What's your story? Where did you come from? Is there anything evil in your roots?"

Mona swallowed some pizza with a sip of red wine, then wiped the corner of her mouth with a napkin.

"You know some of this, but let me try it," she contemplated, tossing her hair out of her face. "My family came over in the 18th century from France, settled in Quebec initially, then came down to New England in the 19th century. If there was anything shameful in those years, it's been lost to history. My grandfather was a carpenter in Vermont, my grandmother a seamstress. He was very good at his work, and ended up working on all those fine resorts on Lake Champlain. My father was one of five boys. He met my mother at Princeton. He's retired now, but we moved around a bit when I was young, relocations for his job. He was an executive at a drug company. My mom was a homemaker. She has two sisters and a brother. We settled down in Boston when I was about 10, and I studied at Dartmouth, then at McGill in Montreal. I have no siblings. Does that do it?"

"Done," Johnny confirmed. "I didn't know some of that, I hope you realize. You've been keeping things from me."

Mona laughed contemptuously. "I don't know half of your story, Denovo," she howled. She threw a balled up napkin at him.

Johnny ducked. "It's Novarro, you know," he chided.

"Oh, I know," Mona retorted, rising from her chair and leaning over to whisper into his ear. Her voice possessed an alluring menace. "If you're not careful, I'll rip the Novarro out of you."

Johnny grasped her hips and stood. Their bodies knitted together with a pleasant firmness, the familiar physicality of compatible lovers. Their lips met, and they dissolved into a liquid embrace.

Mona pushed him away.

"Oh no you don't," she accused. "Not this time."

Johnny feigned innocence. "What?"

"You're not going to change the subject so easily," Mona replied. "I want the Novarro story now. It's long overdue."

Johnny stood silently for a minute.

"I can tell you some of it, but not all," he said softly.

"Why not all?" Mona pressed.

Johnny met her eyes with a solemn gaze. His voice was level and calm.

"Because I've made promises," he stated.

Silence hovered over the two, threatening to break into a cloudburst of emotion. But, as their gazes danced, the pall lifted.

"I understand," Mona said at last.

"I'm glad," Johnny said.

Mona approached him.

"But I will find out someday," she said. "You know I will."

Johnny put his arms around her waist. "I hope so. In the right way, at the right time. It's better that way."

They kissed, a new understanding established between them, a deeper trust, and a promise for the future. Johnny felt a bit uneasy letting himself flow into this woman so willingly, but she was irresistible.

"OK, what can I tell you?" Johnny pondered. "Born in southern Utah, nearly in northern Arizona, in the back of an Army surplus jeep. Pink. My parents had painted it pink. It had an old white cloth-top, too. It was something ugly, judging from the pictures. It vanished before I was old enough to remember seeing it in-person. My parents were mixed, Mexican and Anglo. I grew up with a foot in either culture, so my Spanish is pretty good, if a little 'street.' I was the first member of my family to go to college. I did well. I ended up coming back East for a while, but devoted a few years to the Army to help pay for it. Stayed enmeshed with them for a few projects during and after grad school. Earned a PhD for some work on certain cognitive processes. Was working in Utah again when I was summoned to help the President out of a jam. Things got messy, a reporter got confused, the government got nervous, and, bam, I'm Johnny Denovo, history obscured and erased and guarded, for all intents and purposes. And that brings us to today."

Mona had paced over to the kitchen counter during Johnny's monologue. She turned to look at him when he finished.

"Any siblings?" she asked. "Parents still alive?"

Johnny smiled. "You know I can't tell you that."

Mona smiled back. "Doesn't hurt to ask. But I know – it wouldn't be fair or safe."

"Right. That's my standard answer," Johnny confirmed. "Now, can we get back to the pizza? All this serious stuff is ruining my evening."

Mona sauntered over to him and put her arms around his neck. Her hair smelled great.

"Let's go work some off first," she suggested, leaning in for a kiss.

Chapter 18

Strike

Johnny and Mona awoke almost simultaneously, he just a handful of seconds earlier. As she stirred, he was propping himself up on his elbows. He'd not even had a chance to look over at her face in the morning light, a favorite snapshot in time. She was always lovely, sleeping peacefully in the soft early light.

"Morning, ladyfriend," Johnny said in greeting.

"Hey," Mona said groggily. "Remind me, what day is it?"

"Thursday," Johnny answered. "And a lovely day it is." Outside, he could see a clear blue sky, a sweep of cool Canadian air having cleared out the clouds and calmed the Boston skies in its chill embrace.

"OK, that's good," Mona said. "I don't have anything today until after lunch. Otherwise," she said, rolling over to face him with a smile, "I'd have to kick your ass for making me late."

Johnny kissed her on the cheek. "You almost kicked my ass last night. That was something else."

"Pretty good for a girl," Mona teased him. "You'd better start working out."

"Oh, I can keep up with you," Johnny boasted.

"Yes, but I'm gaining on you," Mona said, pushing his shoulder so hard he almost toppled over.

The phone rang as he tipped. Righting himself with a comical effort, he grabbed the phone and checked the caller ID. It was his car dealer.

"Hello," Johnny answered, then listened for a moment before replying. "Great. I'll be over to pick it up in before noon. Thanks. Bye."

"Car's fixed?" Mona asked.

"Yeah," Johnny confirmed.

"That guy really shot out your headrest?" Mona asked in disbelief. "He could have killed you."

"I think that was an eventuality he'd considered," Johnny noted with exaggerated seriousness.

"What are you going to do about them? The Gleasons?" Mona asked.

"I don't really know how they fit in yet," Johnny admitted. "They've invested in McNaught's company, and they're heavily armed and obviously prone to violence. Gleason and the lady with the sign are connected somehow, but I need to know more. Why are there still two of them in New Hampshire? McNaught told me the husband died years ago in a boating accident. Tucker's not sharing much about them, just things he believes are fair game because of what I've already discovered."

"But the daughters are involved in this, too," Mona mentioned.

"True, but indirectly," Johnny commented. "They're not on my hot list right now."

"Why not?" Mona asked, sitting up. "You've undercounted the people who might know about the long-lost sister. You didn't count the sisters themselves. What if they know, and one of them is involved in one side of this or the other, either the blackmailing of McNaught or the espionage and vandalism? Have you thought about that?"

Johnny held Mona's gaze for a moment, then turned away.

"You're right, I should include them in all this," he said. "They could have motives, means, and opportunity aplenty. Definitely an oversight, Junior Detective."

Mona pushed him again. "Well, get going, cowboy," she admonished. "Time's a-wastin'!"

Johnny laughed and kissed her on the forehead, then hopped out of bed and headed for the shower.

"The coffee maker should be ready," he called back over his shoulder as he closed the bathroom door. He started the shower water to avoid the initial cold burst when he stepped in.

He had just gotten himself under the water when there was a loud bang that shook the bathroom, vibrating the shower's water droplets in midair and nearly causing him to fall. A piercing scream followed.

Johnny jumped out of the shower, not bothering with a towel. He could smell smoke.

He flung the door open and rushed forward, struggling to keep his balance as his wet feet slipped on the hard floors beneath him.

The front door of his condo was hanging from its hinges. An acrid stench, smoke black and thick, surged through the opening. Mona clutched the kitchen counter, eyes wide and arms trembling.

Johnny ran to the door and looked out. Small fires were extinguishing themselves in the synthetic carpeting. Otherwise, the hallway was empty. Judging by the blast pattern, the explosion had originated from something deposited on the floor just in front of his door. A package bomb of some sort, he surmised. It had somehow gotten through and reached him.

Johnny turned and looked at Mona. She was still ashen but rallying quickly.

"I think it's over with," he said in a calm voice.

"And you're naked," she said with false bravado, her voice quavering noticeably.

Johnny strode toward Mona, who was wearing his bathrobe, and hugged her close, his body cold and dripping wet. Her warm arms on his back felt good. The robe's dry, absorbent sleeves stopped the chill.

"You're OK?" he asked into her hair.

"Scared shitless, but otherwise fine. A message from the Gleasons?" she speculated.

"Must be," he replied. "It fits. They aim to scare, not to kill. I think that's why the guy aimed high the other night. They're domestic terrorists, but not killers."

"And for that, I'm very grateful," Mona said, hugging him tighter. "Now, enough of this. You have a shower to finish, and I have a door to fix. I'll call Wei." She pushed him away gently and wiped her eyes on the sleeve of the robe.

Johnny pretended not to notice the tears and walked stoically back to the shower, which was still running. He heard Mona on the phone with Wei Chou, telling him about the damage. Johnny felt safe knowing Wei was on the phone with her. He would know how to tidy this all up.

When Johnny emerged from the shower, he threw on some shorts and a t-shirt, and found Mona talking with the building maintenance man, Bill, at the bombed out door. She clutched a large cup of coffee in her hands. Wrapped in the soft oversized white robe, she looked more helpless and vulnerable – somehow, even more feminine – than he could ever have imagined. Gone was the she-devil. Spending time with her had shown what a multi-faceted woman she was. He could picture her as a mother now, he thought, watching her in a bathrobe and a cup of coffee. It was a stereotype, he knew, but he couldn't refute what his mind was registering. Nature exerted a strong force on human events.

"Hi Johnny," Bill said. "What the hell happened here? You'd better call the police."

"Hi Bill," Johnny replied. "No, I think we'll keep this one to ourselves. I'm in the middle of a case and obviously making progress. You know, one death threat a case is the low average."

Bill shook his head and tsked his tongue. "You like living dangerously. I'll get a temporary solid replacement for this in about an hour, but I'll have to special order a permanent one with the proper fit and finish. That'll take a week or so. The handle and the lock from the old one still work. I'll just swap them out, so that won't be a problem. In the meantime, I'll fix up the damage to the walls and repaint the hall and ceiling. That was one smoky explosion, but all the smoke stayed low, so it didn't set off the smoke detectors. How you make smoke heavy, I'll never know."

"Takes some expertise," Johnny mused, eyeing the blast damage. "Some real expertise."

"Well, I'd better get on it," Bill concluded with a grave smile.

"Thanks, Bill. That'd be great," Johnny said. "I'll have my mail inspected for the next few weeks, even after this case ends. I might be a target for a while after this one."

"Good idea," Bill said, turning to Mona. "Sorry this happened, ma'am," he said as he retreated, bowing respectfully in Mona's direction.

"Bye, Bill," Mona said softly.

After the maintenance man left, she turned to Johnny. "OK, now you watch the door while I shower. I feel like I have an inch of smoke covering me. It got into my eyes and hair. It was low smoke but it got all over me. Yuck!"

Johnny smiled at her as she passed, amazed at her strength and resiliency in the face of a bombing. It had rattled her only momentarily. She might be cut out for the Denovo lifestyle after all. First the events in Montpellier just a month ago, and now this. She was strong, there was little doubt.

It was Johnny's turn for a cup of coffee. With Mona in the shower, he could admit to himself how the bomb had rattled him. What if Mona had been injured? Or worse? What if the Gleasons had done more? He shivered at the thought of losing her, of seeing her harmed. She was definitely getting to him in ways few women ever had.

The Gleasons were not to be trifled with. They'd reached into his world quickly, easily, and invisibly. He hadn't seen it coming. And that bothered him.

The phone rang, Mona's shower placidly spattering in the background.

"Denovo," Johnny answered. It was a private caller.

"Johnny, there's a sunset on the blackmail site," McNaught's voice, sounding urgent, reported. "The blackmailer wants another payment."

"OK, just a minute," Johnny said, putting his coffee cup down and settling himself at his computer. He typed in the now fully memorized URL and saw what McNaught was referring to. There in the right rail was a small picture of a sunset and the number 3000. If the pattern held, McNaught had 24 hours to get $3 million into the blackmailer's account.

"Can you afford it?" Johnny asked.

"That's just it," McNaught stated. "This is much more than he's ever asked for. Much, much more. It's impossible."

Johnny thought for a moment. "Apparently, something has changed."

"What do you mean?"

"Well," he continued, "you hired me. I've been investigating. Whoever's doing this has caught wind of the investigation, which means I'm on the right track. Now, I figure they're worried the game is up, so they want to score heavily while they still can. Makes sense to me."

"But I can't come up with this much without raising suspicions," McNaught whined. "It's just not possible."

"So don't pay it," Johnny suggested firmly.

"What?!" McNaught shouted. "That's crazy."

"Is it?" Johnny asked. "Play it out, McNaught. I'm on the right track. The blackmailer is about to be exposed. If you don't pay, you'll force the blackmailer's hand, and that might give me what I need to nail them sooner. When the blackmailer is caught, the story gets out, and your affair is the next thing to be exposed. I can't guarantee that won't happen. But you're still up $3 million and you go down as resisting the blackmail attempt, which gives you plausible deniability that there even was an affair. You didn't pay it, so it must have been a lie, right? Are you following me?"

"Yes, I get what you mean," McNaught said thoughtfully. "Don't pay, and I can claim the blackmail was an outrageous and false accusation, an attempt to extort money with a slander. I see how that might work. But I hired you to catch the blackmailer and to keep me out of the press."

"I know," Johnny confessed. "But given what I've found out, I'm not sure I can do both now."

McNaught's voice took on an edge. "And do you care to elucidate these facts for me? Or do I have to trust you again?" His voice dripped with derision.

"You have to trust me," Johnny replied calmly. "It's a tangled mess right now. I need to unravel it more before I start sharing findings with people involved. I'm sorry."

McNaught was silent. "I don't like it, Denovo. I don't like it. I hired you to keep me spotless."

"I know, but I think this is the best option we have right now," Johnny answered, suppressing thoughts about how McNaught might have kept himself spotless from the beginning. "Things have changed. The number of options is narrowing. This isn't something I control. I can just give you my best advice, and my advice is to stiff the blackmailer."

"Because I can say that the blackmailer was making a false accusation," McNaught confirmed.

"You keep your money and help me by forcing them to reach out to you in a new way, to break cover more than ever. It flushes them out."

"OK, I agree," McNaught sighed. "I won't pay them. Then what?"

"Call me when you hear something else. Simple."

"And you're making progress?" McNaught asked.

"Yes," Johnny confirmed. "I've almost been killed twice now for you, a good sign that I'm getting close. But I'd rather not say more. I prefer to let my clients rest easy until I achieve clarity. It works better all around." And, Johnny thought, it keeps them out of my hair.

"Your life's been at risk for this?" McNaught inquired in disbelief.

"It's typical in my line of work," Johnny reassured him. "Nothing to worry about."

"All right, fine then," McNaught said skeptically. "I'll call you if I hear more. I guess I owe you my thanks, Johnny."

"No problem." Johnny switched the phone off.

Mona had been standing in the doorway toweling her hair for the last parts of the exchange.

"How you handle this job of yours, I'll never know," she said, smiling. The shower had given her skin a soft glow. Small beads of water clung to her neck. She smelled great, warm and floral.

Johnny approached her, a salacious twinkle in his eye. "For the greater good, my dear. It's all for the greater good. Plus, there are some great side benefits," he growled, loosening the belt of the bathrobe she wore and pushing her back into the bedroom, closing the only remaining door in the condo behind them with a soft click, then turning the lock.

Chapter 19
Double Play

Bill had replaced the front door with a sturdy unfinished wooden slab by the time Mona was ready to leave for her appointment. They hadn't heard a sound as the old door had been removed and replaced. Even the work realigning the frame hadn't disturbed them.

Opening the door for Mona, Johnny kissed her one last time. She left him with a dazzling smile as she walked out. He watched her walk down the hall, through the shrapnel and patches of burned carpet, then around the corner. He heard the elevator bell ring, the doors bang open and close, and she was gone.

Johnny pressed the new door closed with a click. It didn't close as tightly as its predecessor, but it would do.

A few minutes later, the whine of a vacuum cleaner and the grind of a sander started on the other side of the door, both working quickly while men spoke in barely audible undertones. The bomb had been a smoky one. It had been more for effect than intent.

Johnny sat and gazed out at the sliver of Boston skyline he could see from his condo. The white noise from the equipment in the hall was unexpectedly soothing, and Johnny found the cliché about money serving as the root of all evil returning to his mind as he relaxed against the backdrop of aural static. If his limbic brain were sending him the right visualizations as metaphors, the environmental mask of the attacks and sabotage were just the apparent part of something with a dirty root system – feeding the tree, giving it the nutrients to grow.

Money was the root of all evil, he thought again.

But who would profit? The cast of characters so far included a few with monetary stakes in the outcome. McNaught was a for-profit biotech executive being blackmailed, and the Gleasons recently became investors in his company. Schwartz ran his own company. And the blackmailer, whoever that might be, stood to gain from the secret he or she held, but seemed about to bow out after one last, big score.

Johnny eliminated McNaught from his considerations. He was losing money in the events that were unfolding, and he was too distracted. The Gleasons wouldn't profit either if McNaught suffered. But they continued to puzzle him. They were aggressive, and had some interest in the events Johnny was now embroiled in. But they weren't the masterminds. At most, they were muscle.

That left Schwartz.

The money trail led to him, at least for now. And time was running out. He remained a key suspect.

But what was Schwartz's motivation? How could he profit? Was money truly at the root?

He had no answers. And it bothered him.

Today was Thursday. The Red Sox returned Monday. He had two weekdays and a weekend to figure things out. Ninety-six hours. The blackmailer's alarm was set to sound Saturday morning. If the blackmailer came at him hard, McNaught would be besieged.

The weekend might hold more surprises.

The money trail was vital. He needed to gain access to Schwartz Genetics' books. Robert had already helped him peer a little into the life of the CEO, and was unlikely to do so again. Plus, Johnny might need him later.

This type of infiltration was better done by a financial guru with the right skills and no compunctions.

Johnny knew who to call – a numbers jockey with no shame who owed him a favor.

"Hi, Bart," Johnny said firmly when his call was answered. "It's Johnny Denovo."

"Johnny Denovo," Bart Zeller hissed back. "I thought you'd show up again some day. To what do I owe this privilege?"

"I need a favor," Johnny replied forcefully.

"Ha!" Zeller responded. "I thought as much. Will this make us even?"

It was Johnny's turn to laugh. "I'll tell you when we're even, Zeller," Johnny stated. "Until then, keep taking my calls, and things will be just fine."

Zeller growled in response, but otherwise remained silent.

"Fine," Johnny pressed. "I need some paperwork pulled, financial records analyzed, patent filings yanked, all of it concatenated, and a report of your conclusions, done astutely and professionally, by noon tomorrow. Think you can do it?"

"Noon tomorrow?" Zeller yipped, his voice losing all trace of menace. "Are you kidding me?"

"Choke down some caffeine pills with a coffee chaser," Johnny said. "You can do it."

Again, Zeller growled. "Tell me more."

"Schwartz Genetics, here in Boston. I want to know what they're researching, what patents they've filed, what their investors are interested in. I want speculation based on facts. I want inference based on evidence. I want the Zeller magic."

"That magic is worth billions," Zeller countered. "And you want it fast and free?"

"That's right," Johnny confirmed.

Another growl.

"It'll be the lite version," Zeller muttered.

"Better taste great," Johnny retorted.

"Tomorrow noon, your time zone," Zeller spoke in low tones. "I'll call you at 11:30 and email the report when we're done, which will be by noon. 11:30. Phone. Be there." Zeller disconnected with a snap in Johnny's ear.

The sanding and vacuuming noises from the hall had subsided, replaced by the gentle scraping sound of a putty knife on the wall, rhythmically spackling the holes left by the detonation less than two hours old. Tomorrow, Johnny suspected, his condo would smell of fresh paint and floor adhesive as the traces of the blast were covered up by a few coats of latex and a new layer of carpeting.

Glancing again out the window at the beautiful day unfolding outside, Johnny remembered he needed to pick up his car, its headrest restored.

The themes echoed through his mind – roots and trees, vertical symmetry, above and below. Another visit to the Top of the Hub might be in order on his way to pick up his car from the dealer.

If anything, looking over Boston might help him see some connections that weren't yet clear. He loved gazing out upon the city. It was remarkably beautiful on clear, sunny days. The rivers sparkled while trees nested the buildings in a wonderful juxtaposition of man and nature.

Donning his baseball cap and sunglasses, Johnny picked his way past the repair crew, took the elevator down, and walked over to the Prudential Center. The day was a glorious exhibition of Boston's best. The populace was in peak late-summer form – the joggers were tan and thin, the cyclists fast and fleet, the dog walkers spritely and confident, their pets well-heeled and obedient. The women were wearing summer shorts and lightweight sweaters, and the men were in awe. All in all, spirits were high in these, the last days of summer.

Entering the Prudential Center, Johnny walked toward the elevators for the Top of the Hub, appreciating the sound of falling water coming from beside the doors, the long, deep fountain spouting about two dozen mesmerizing, translucent pillars into the air. The black onyx of the floor and fountain made the water look like an abyss, deep and unfathomable. The allure of a mystery probably attracted his gaze, Johnny surmised as he passed.

The elevator he chose was empty and went straight to the top floor without stopping. Arriving at the viewing platform, Johnny went instead to the bar. Rounding the corner, he felt a remnant of hostility well up. He remembered his last encounter at the bar here.

A friendly, relaxed bartender greeted him instead.

"Good morning," the day bartender said as Johnny entered. His hands were full of glassware. It was the shift that was mostly setup.

"Hi," Johnny replied. "How's the view today?"

"Spectacular," the bartender replied. "Take a look for yourself."

Johnny smiled and peered out the windows overlooking the harbor. The city was bright as an exhibit, bleached light illuminating every crevice, no secrets hiding in the cleansing sunshine. The broad expanse of the harbor waters reflected the flawless sky with deep azure tones, the small islands looking like toys glued to blue posterboard. The harbor was an environmental miracle these days, cleaned up by a set of scrubbers called "the Eggs" on what at one time had been a large island near the city. Johnny smiled to himself. His last case had featured eggs in abundance. These eggs, immense 12-story scrubbers, put all others to shame for sheer size. They stood clustered on Deer Island as if crated for a giant's lunch.

Johnny turned back to the bartender. "No Paul today?" he asked.

The bartender gave a pained smile. "And too bad, I suppose. He loves days like this, when the views are good. He says he feels like he's truly on top of the world, looking down at all the peons from up here. It's about as happy as I suppose I'll ever see him."

Johnny laughed at the clever way the bartender managed to be both kind and damning. This person was going somewhere in life, he thought to himself.

Johnny lingered, admiring the city from the unique vantage points at the Pru. Fenway Park looked like an empty shoebox tossed on a crowded closet floor, nestled in the midst of freeway, buildings, and signs. The academic institutions along the Charles River exuded an air of confidence and excitement, vital yet enduring, while the North End looked manic, antique, and entertaining. Back Bay remained stately and pristine from any angle.

Johnny left the privileged perch with a final wave to the friendly bartender, returning to the ground floor. He wasn't sure the visit had been worthwhile, but he felt somehow better.

As he exited the elevator, a group of small children, screaming and racing around him to press the "up" button, nearly toppled him into the fountain. He had to spin and twist to keep his balance as they darted past, the passive parents smiling apologetically but indulgently, as if such behavior were normal. Johnny had no choice but to smile back once he'd recovered his balance.

Walking a few more blocks, he arrived at the car dealership. His convertible had been washed and polished by the time he arrived. No questions were asked, but the repairman had left the twisted remains of a bullet in the cup holder between the seats.

As Johnny drove off the lot, his cell phone chimed. It was Tucker.

"Did you think I'd forgotten?" Tucker asked when Johnny answered.

"Forgotten what?" Johnny asked.

"Don't tell me you've forgotten?! Seriously, man, I do you all these favors, help you become the detective hero of song and story, and you can't even keep track of what's going on? I told you I'd see if I could dig up something on that Paul Robertson character."

"Right," Johnny said sheepishly. "Sorry, Tucker, I'd forgotten. Busy morning. Bombs and everything, you know."

"Bombs? Did you say 'bombs'?"

"Well, only one bomb," Johnny corrected. "Outside my door. Nobody was hurt, but Mona was shaken up a little. I have a new front door now and some repair work going on in the hall."

"Smoky bomb?"

"Very smoky," Johnny confirmed.

"Then it was done for effect," Tucker commented. "Do you think it was the Gleasons?"

"Seems like the best bet," Johnny replied. "They seem to be the most violent people we've encountered on this little caper. Does it fit their m.o.?"

"It does," Tucker admitted. "Do you want the FBI to investigate? They'd love more dirt on the Gleasons."

"No thanks," Johnny said quickly. "We're going to let this one slide. These people would love to think we've been scared. Involving the FBI would signal fear. We just act like nothing happened and keep after them. The capture is the best response."

"I hear you," Tucker assented. "OK, want the dirt on Paul Robertson?"

"Hit me," Johnny prompted.

"Well, he actually has quite a little criminal record," Tucker said in a satisfied manner, like a chef tasting a delicious soup. "The most relevant was armed robbery that was dismissed on a technicality or he'd still be in the hoosegow. Drug possession and vandalism as a juvenile. But the part you'll like is that you can't find this out by searching on Paul Robertson."

"What do you mean?"

"Well," Tucker exulted, pausing dramatically. "I have a little 'known aliases' routine I go through. It's kind of an anagram engine. People prefer aliases that mean something to them. Makes the alternatives easier to remember and easier to identify with, so they're easier to carry out. Anyhoo, this algorithm takes a name and rearranges it, then sends the rearranged items out in a search query to find possibly related personages. It works very well. I've really tuned it up over the years. Long story short, our friend isn't named Paul Robertson," Tucker concluded dramatically.

"So, you're now going to reveal his real name, right?" Johnny offered.

"Dramatic tension spoiled," Tucker noted. "You slay me, Denovo. Can't you see what I'm trying to achieve here? Dramatic tension!"

"OK, you've re-established it!" Johnny said in exasperation. "Just tell me!"

"His real name? You want his real name?" Tucker taunted.

"Yes, damnit!" Johnny shouted into his phone.

"Robert Paulson," Tucker revealed in a flat counterpoint. "The same name as Schwartz's assistant. They're the same person!"

"Jesus, Mary, and Joseph," Johnny said. "Are you sure of it?"

"I'd like to say that pictures don't lie, but now I'm not so sure," Tucker said. "I have Robert's security photo and his booking photos. You slick his hair back, and they're the same person. Well, at least the computer thinks so."

"What do you mean?" Johnny asked. He never would have guessed the connection.

"Well, it's the weirdest thing. Makes my brain ache because I don't see it," Tucker said. "I mean, they have the same coloring, but Robertson looks a lot different to me from Paulson. Different cheekbones, different aspects, different facial form somehow – you know, just different."

"I know what you mean. I can't recall a strong resemblance."

"Right," Tucker continued. "But humans are easily fooled because we're so subjective. When I ran the two faces through that ID program I have, the computer mathematically confirmed they are the same person. The measurements – pupil to pupil, ear to ear, chin to forehead, mouth, nostrils, all of it – they are identical."

Johnny was knocked backwards by this news. He'd met both of them and hadn't seen the resemblance or noted dramatic similarities between the two. They had completely different personalities, Robert an urbane and disassociated office lackey and Paul an angry bartender with a grudge. They dressed, spoke, and acted completely differently. Their faces didn't resemble one another's as Johnny recalled them.

"Tucker, I'm having a hard time with this one," he admitted after a moment. "I've met them both, and I didn't put it together. And I'm supposed to be pretty sharp. What gives?"

Tucker laughed. "Cut yourself some slack, oh famous one. I was in disbelief, too, so I did some digging. I read a psychological profile of Paul Robertson from his few total days in prison. The psychologist noted an amazing facility to change his voice, physical affect, facial appearance, and body habitus. Apparently, the guy is made of rubber, and can look wolfish or puckish, innocent or evil, just by thinking that way. He's a mimic, a chameleon, a shape-shifter. You saw him in completely different settings, in different clothes, with different hair, and affecting different personalities. He's fooled a lot of people in the past, from what the records show. He even robbed the same employer twice as a teenager, getting hired by HR using an alias and going unrecognized through the interview process even though the people who had fired and prosecuted him interviewed him the second time. I've never seen anything like it."

Johnny was amazed. The theme of duality Johnny had been playing with was now personified in a single individual, a duality unto himself.

"Is he a split personality?" Johnny asked.

"Apparently not if that psychologist's report is to be believed," Tucker answered. "He remains coherent, self-aware, and cogent throughout. He knows what he's doing."

Johnny thought quickly. He'd gotten information about Schwartz's relationship with Paul from Robert. That meant it was a conscious act to reveal it. Was it true? Was it a lie meant to trip him up? Was it a taunt, a laugh at the expense of the dumbfounded detective? Johnny suspected it was the latter, a true statement shared partly out of hubris, partly to be manipulative. But he couldn't be sure.

"So, Robert Paulson is his real name?" Johnny asked.

"That's what was on his birth certificate," Tucker confirmed. "He also has a degree in molecular biology and biochemistry from the University of California-San Francisco. Graduated at a very young age, so he's no dummy. Pretty bizarre, isn't it?"

"Very bizarre," Johnny concurred. "I have to think about how to use this. Tucker, this one is about to swamp me. I feel like I have discovered a knot snarled beyond redemption, a clump of seaweed I can't untangle."

"Don't fret, Johnny. You can do it. Just return to core principles," Tucker encouraged. "I have to run. Have fun untangling!" With that, he hung up.

Core principles. Johnny thought about Schwartz, who had to know that his lover was one person playing life as two or more. He visited him at the Top of the Hub at night, worked with him during the day. Johnny had to assume Schwartz knew. But Paulson had fooled an employer before.

Still, it was the better assumption.

More than the paper trail and the insider knowledge were pointing to Schwartz.

His associations were flagging him as the prime suspect, as well.

The dualities of this case were overwhelming Johnny. Here he had two sisters, long-lost and involved with the same man. He had a man acting as two men. He had a web site acting as a blackmail beacon and a communication hub for a network of eco-terrorists.

On top of it all, he was being stalked by a pushy maniac from New Hampshire and he had three days left to figure it all out.

He sighed and started his car. He needed a doctor.

Chapter 20
Hit by Pitch

Johnny knew he'd been lucky. Throughout his brief and meteoric career as a detective, he'd made friends with a few key sources he could trust, smart men and women who possessed the proper mix of idealism, knowledge, wit, and pragmatism, honorable people of substance. One of these people was Mark Linder, MD, a neurologist in Boston who still had no idea that he and Johnny had crossed paths once before – years ago over the phone, when John Novarro had needed help with a research question. Linder had proven helpful initially, and when the Case of the Creaky Gait arose, he'd been even more helpful when Johnny Denovo had called.

He could rely on Linder, who'd been willing to help an unknown young academic and an increasingly notorious detective.

Linder played fair.

While Johnny possessed the training of a neuroscientist, he was not a clinical neurologist. He was strong on theory and underlying mechanisms and physiology, but Linder brought diagnostic and clinical depth to neurological questions. These served as a reality check to Johnny's more elaborate theories. He could be blind to his limits. Linder provided counterbalance when things took a clinical turn.

Tucker's news that Robert Paulson and Paul Robertson were the same person had struck Johnny as implausible. He'd seen them both, and still could not quite bring himself to believe they were the same man. The facial expressions, not to mention their comportment and dispositions, just didn't match. How could someone deceive so effectively? He needed to know more about what was possible. Someone who saw patients day in and day out might be able to tell him.

Calling from the car, Johnny reached Linder's assistant, who said he could see Linder briefly in about 15 minutes. Fortunately, Linder's office was nearby, just down Huntington Avenue.

Linder was a lanky man in his mid-50s, impeccably mannered yet relaxed and unpretentious. He would be just as comfortable on a hike as at a white-tie dinner. His bedside manner was probably reassuring on many levels. His demeanor was approachable but did not conceal the powerful intellect of the man.

Johnny swore that if he ever acquired a neurological condition, he'd put himself in Linder's care in an instant.

He was sitting in the waiting room leafing through magazines when Linder came out, hand extended in greeting.

"Johnny, it's always a pleasure," Linder said smiling, his face relaxed and welcoming.

"Thank you, Mark, for taking time to see me," Johnny replied respectfully. "I know how busy you must be."

Linder smiled and chuckled, turning to his office manager, a thin, gray-haired woman who looked extremely fit and vital, her age a mystery. "Nola, have Nancy let me know when Mrs. Pymm is ready. I'll be in exam three for a few minutes."

Nola nodded and picked up the phone.

Linder continued as they walked into the clinic. "Neurology is a funny business," he noted. "We're like you, detectives who use mysterious methods to unravel secrets. Our patients have to be given time to reveal the clues. This means that most of what I do is wait, quite frankly. Right now, I am waiting for someone's pupils to dilate – or not."

Linder showed Johnny into a small consulting room with two clerical chairs flanking the paper-covered exam table. They each took a chair and turned to talk.

"So," Linder began, "tell me what I can do for you."

"Well, I've encountered an odd situation," Johnny ruminated. "It's about facial nerves and how finely they can be controlled. I know they're exquisitely sensitive and expressive. I know some people can consciously control them quite well. But have you ever heard of someone able to change their appearance dramatically, from one setting to another, so much so that few would recognize them? Just by using their facial muscles?"

Linder leaned forward. "And they're not using makeup or drugs like botox or anything else?" he asked.

"I don't think so," Johnny responded. "It's a man. He just messes up his slicked back hair and goes, but his face changes dramatically from point A to point B, from a passive lump of wimp to a wolfish and predatory aspect. His personality changes, as well, in the same ways, but that's less interesting to me. I want to know if something like this has ever been documented. Can it happen?"

Linder leaned back. "Well, the facial nerve can suffer from disease. Bell's palsy comes to mind. It's a strange disorder, with a face paralyzed and dramatically changed. Usually, it's caused by an infection, but truthfully we can't discern the cause in most cases. It's probably inflammation. It usually goes away in a few weeks, and our goal is to reassure patients and give them something like physical therapy to keep their minds off it and make them feel like they're beating it. It comes to mind because it can really change someone's appearance."

"But Bell's palsy is involuntary," Johnny replied. "This is voluntary."

Linder smiled. "Like those rubber-faced comedians," he said. "They can consciously rearrange their faces for extended periods, voices as well, and fool people." Linder looked at the ceiling and puffed air out between his lips. "You said he messes up his slicked back hair between his facial changes?"

"That's right," Johnny confirmed.

"Interesting," Linder mused. "The muscles of the forehead are enervated differently. Different nerves run them. In fact, in Bell's palsy, even though a side of the person's face is paralyzed, they can still wrinkle their forehead. I'll bet his normal face is the one he has when his hair's slicked back, and his transformed face is the other one, with his forehead hidden. He knows he has to hide it, since he can't control it too well. Otherwise, it might give him away if he's trying to disguise himself. But we're all born with different levels of control over our faces. Some people can raise one eyebrow voluntarily, some can't. Some can wink, some can't. Some can cross their lips or pucker them like fish, some can't. There's a wide range of normal."

"Makes sense," Johnny concurred. "But it still amazes me that this guy can fool people so well. We have records indicating that two people I thought were different are really one and the same. His appearance transforms dramatically. So my question is, can a person make his face change that much?"

"Tell me again what his normal face look like," Linder requested.

"Very passive, almost pasty."

"Well, that's a great starting point for a mimic," Linder ventured. "No expression is like a blank canvas. Any dash of color or shape on it changes it a great deal. If done right, you don't see it as a canvas anymore."

"That makes sense. So it's an additive thing in this case," Johnny mused.

Linder smiled. "Look at me," he exhorted. "If I smile, look at how far the muscles of my face move." He smiled again to demonstrate. "Now, if I try a ghoulish aspect, look at how far away from a smile the muscles in my face deviate." Linder sucked in his cheeks and made a long face. The effect was dramatic.

"I see," Johnny said. "But this guy must be holding a new pose for hours."

"It's possible," Linder said. "It would be rare, but nearly anything is possible, I've learned. People can use biofeedback – anything from formal biofeedback to just obsessive training – to change their abilities. I've known people who have been able to train muscles in many ways, just by exercising them repeatedly with their fingers. This suspect of yours, if I can call him that, must have practiced holding his face another way so intensely that it's second-nature, and all he has to do is think it into that mold, and it holds until he unthinks it. If he was born predisposed to something like that, it would feel pretty natural. He might have learned at a young age that he had this gift, then worked on it, perfecting it through some feedback or training loop. And what greater reward would there be for a child with that advantage than fooling people? What a lark!"

"Well, that could explain it," Johnny murmured. "Wouldn't holding your face differently that long have some side effects?"

Linder smiled again. "Great question."

A red-haired nurse poked her head into the doorway. "Dr. Linder, Mrs. Pymm is just about ready."

"Great, thanks Nancy," Linder responded, then turned back to Johnny. "I've got to go. But, as to side-effects, changes in facial nerve pathways can affect taste sensations, salivation, and jaw movement. I can't swear to it, but this person of yours might be battling a mouthful of spit and a hyperactive jaw. If he turns into a real talker in one mode, that might be another clue as to which is the assumed identity."

"Thanks, Mark," Johnny said, rising from the desk chair. "You've been a tremendous help. I'll let you get back to your day."

Linder was already standing, and shook Johnny's hand. "My pleasure. I'd love to study this person someday. It sounds like a case that would suit my type of detective work, too."

Johnny left Linder's office, his skepticism evaporated. He reflected on Robert and Paul in the light of Linder's smiling and sallow face demonstrations.

It could happen. It could be trained and controlled.

After a few minutes of driving and pondering, Johnny became convinced that Paul was a key to the case – spit, talkativeness, and all.

Chapter 21
Bunt

His head hurt. Johnny needed more room in his skull, more crenellations in his brain, to help him sort things out. The revelation that Paul and Robert were the same person, a modern Janus, left a part of Johnny's brain babbling in perplexity.

Crossing back over the Charles River, he wended his way through the quiet summer streets of Cambridge and its academia. With the new semester still a few weeks away, a desolate dust seemed to be settling in the curbstops. It felt like a village abandoned in time.

Evan was in his office again. It truly was his home away from home. This time, he was polishing chess pieces and humming a faint melody as Johnny knocked on the frame of his open door. Papers were cluttered around the office like nesting materials.

"John," Evan said brightly, looking up at the noise. "I mean, Mr. Denovo!" he added with a grin.

"Hi Evan," Johnny said. "Do you have a minute to help me clear my head?"

"I always have time for a friend, my boy," Evan answered, moving back to make room in the tiny office. The leafy, bright day splashed light in through the windows.

"I've hit a brick wall," Johnny started. "I have a very tangled case on my hands." He proceeded to detail the strands of blackmail, signals, Web sites, environmental sabotage, a shady geneticist, violent investors, and a person who was literally two-faced. Evan listened patiently and attentively, never interrupting, only now and again shifting position or fiddling with a chess piece in the box lying on his desk.

Finally, Johnny finished his tale, and took a deep breath. "Well, what do you think?"

Evan puffed out a bit of air, and looked Johnny straight in the eye. "You should come back to research is what I think," Evan said wryly. "However, you like danger and adrenaline, so you never will. You loved adventure when you were out West, and you still do. Accepting that fact, I then believe you need to return to core concepts, basic and less mutable principles."

"That's what another friend recommended," Johnny interjected.

Evan smiled. "Then you are fortunate enough to have more than one wise friend. In this case, I'd recommend you return to the truths your research produced for you – that language is a metaphor created by complex neural connections, all residing on a three-part, evolutionary mix of brains that provide conflicting types of consciousness, with the limbic blending emotion and judgment into instinct. Then, tell me who has the most active limbic brain in this sordid affair. I'll wager that would clarify your thinking."

Johnny smiled to himself as Evan carefully and kindly brought sense to the situation. Like any good mentor, he knew how to press the right buttons to create options while gently chiding against mistakes. Essentially, Evan was telling Johnny that he was letting himself become confused in details while losing sight of the unifying principle that had served him so well as a researcher who became a detective.

Johnny began pondering Evan's question: Who had cornered the limbic market in this case?

"Great summary. As to your question, the answer is easy," Johnny responded after a moment's repose. "Robert Paulson or Paul

Robertson. He's running purely on physical, limbic instinct, I think. He's emotional, especially as Paul, but even as Robert he's pretty icy."

"That makes sense to me," Evan offered softly. "Also, he's the most metaphorical, is he not?"

"What do you mean?" Johnny asked.

"He's living a double life," Evan stated. "He's two-faced. Symmetry, yet conflict. He's a metaphor, and he personifies the metaphors you've found elsewhere. The tension of symmetry, of pairs. He's your nexus at the center of this hall of mirrors. Much of the rest is echo, a reflection, an unavoidable bit of mimicry by those around him, subconscious design response. Monkey see, monkey do. I think if you follow him, you'll gain some clarity on this case."

Johnny nodded, gazing down at the floor between his feet. It was logical, yet intuitive. It felt right and made sense. His own limbic brain seemed to sigh in relief as Johnny agreed with Evan.

His cell phone rang.

"Thanks, Evan," Johnny said, his cell phone ringing a second time. "I'd better go. I'll let you know how things turn out." Johnny flipped his phone open to catch the call.

"Take care, John, I mean, Johnny." Evan bade him farewell, his white hair bathed in the daylight as he stood. "Be careful."

Walking out into the hall, Johnny brought the phone up to his ear. "Hello?"

"Hi Johnny, it's Mona."

"Oh, hi. Are you done with your appointments this afternoon?"

"Not yet," Mona said in a confessional tone. "I didn't schedule things very well, and I've been a bit scattered all day. Bombs have a way of lodging in the memory and distracting my thoughts, I've learned. Anyhow, I just wanted to see if you were OK. I guess the events this morning hung around with me a little longer than I thought they would, even after our little diversion down Lover's Lane. I guess I just wanted to hear your voice."

"Well, I'm just glad you weren't hurt," Johnny stated. "That's what I take away from it. The Gleasons were trying to send a message.

All right, message received. Now, I think I know how to untangle this thing, so I need to search for slack. I'll call you tonight to check in."

"That would be great. In the meantime, be careful. Someone's obviously on your tail," Mona said. "Bye."

Johnny closed his phone with a click, pushed open the heavy door leading from the dim hallways of Evan's academic enclave, and walked to his car.

The relationship with Mona was deepening, it was clear. She had called out of concern for him but also because they shared a rich emotional bond, one that was developing rapidly and finding no limits as it blossomed. It was one of the best starts to a relationship he'd ever experienced. It made him happy, but also raised the stakes in his life. As a careless Lothario, he'd felt cavalier and immortal, as if his jaunty lifestyle protected him from the dangers in his line of work. Now, he felt more vulnerable. Something could happen to her, and that would be unacceptable. People would pay.

Putting his key in his car's ignition, he glanced down and noticed that the bullet the dealer had left in his cupholder was gone.

Gone.

He pulled his hand away from the ignition as if electrocuted and hopped quickly out of the car. Thinking fast, he recovered his cool demeanor and walked at a modest pace back toward the building. Slipping inside, the chill shadows reinforced the sense of protection the building afforded.

He flipped open his cell phone and dialed Rodney Sullivan, an old friend on the police force.

"Rod," Johnny said when his friend answered. "Got a bomb squad you can lend me? I think my car's been booby trapped. No, I haven't checked for wires. I think it might be wireless anyhow. How do I know? I've had a little experience lately with an advanced practitioner of your trade, let's just say. You will? Great. Let me give you the address."

Johnny had to wait 20 minutes inside the building, watching his car from afar. As he waited, he was able to appreciate how lonely

Evan's office was, how isolated and yet how conducive to concentration this neighborhood could be. Barely any cars drove down this backwater road awkwardly placed in the sprawling campus, convenient to nothing, linking nothing. It was the kind of road you only traveled if you were lost.

A gray van arrived on the street and pulled into the small parking lot. Three men in dark police uniforms emerged, each wearing a Kevlar vest and eye protection. They were retrieving long-handled mirrors from the back of the van as Johnny approached. The senior officer acknowledged Johnny.

"Johnny Denovo, I'm Sergeant Polich," the officer said, stepping forward with an extended hand. The two shook hands, and the sergeant looked into the open-top car. "Chief Sullivan asked us to stop by on the QT. Do you usually leave your keys in the ignition?"

"Only when I jump out thinking my car might explode," Johnny replied evenly.

"I understand," Polich said. "Just need to assess the situation. These two boys here will give your car a thorough inspection for any tampering. In the meantime, I'd suggest you move to the other side of the van. It's been reinforced. It'll put a heavy-duty wall between you and any trouble here."

Johnny nodded and walked around the nondescript gray van, leaning against the far side. It was shaded and cool. The chill of the van panels felt good in the warm afternoon temperatures. Johnny listened to the men's footsteps as they circled his car. He began to lose himself in thought again, the level of preoccupation with this case edging toward obsession. Every spare moment was spent considering it. Working this fast on a case carried risks, and obsession was definitely one of them. He would need a vacation after this one.

Judging from the sounds, there was a sudden centralizing of activity, the footsteps and voices gathering at the rear corner of his car.

"Mr. Denovo?" Sgt. Polich's voice rose, summoning him.

Johnny stepped out from behind the van and saw two of the men kneeling down near his tailpipe, flashlights pointed at the side.

"Do you recognize this?" Polich asked, pointing to a long tube placed directly against the tailpipe.

"It's not an after-market add-on, if that's what you mean," Johnny responded. "What is it?"

"Now we find out," Sgt. Polich said reflectively. "If you could move back behind the van, I'd feel better. Boys, let's suit up and bag this thing."

Johnny stood listening for about 15 minutes as the men donned safety clothing and equipment, removed the device, and put it in a container for transport. Then, he heard his car start. Nothing abnormal occurred.

"All clear," Sgt. Polich's voice announced. Johnny once again strode around from behind the van.

"What was it?" Johnny asked.

"It looks like a bomb. Possibly a smoke bomb, but it could be more" Sgt. Polich explained. "We need to test the contents to be sure, but in any event, it's a clever one. The heat of your tailpipe would have activated it by melting a thin plastic wrap around detonation materials, causing two catalysts to mix. No wires, and all evidence of the bomb would have been incinerated. If it's more than a smoke-bomb, the explosion would have looked like a terrible accident, a leak from your fuel line or something like that."

"Pretty sophisticated?" Johnny asked.

"Very," Polich responded. "Getting the mix done alone is tough. This is clever and well-made. But I won't take any more of your time. You seem to be in the clear. We gave your car a thorough going-over. Nothing else out of the ordinary. Have a good day."

"Thanks, Sergeant," Johnny said, hopping back into his idling car and putting it in gear. "Please keep this out of the papers if you can."

"Oh, I will, Mr. Denovo," Polich answered. "Chief Sullivan was very clear on that issue. Thank you."

Johnny drove away, thoughtful and concerned. He'd been targeted twice in the same day. Mona was right – obviously the Gleasons were in the area, following him. He checked his rearview mirror, but saw nothing unusual. He drew no reassurance from that fact.

If they'd been in his car, they could be tracking him in other ways.

He ground his teeth. He had an active adversary, but it looked like he'd have to wait for his opportunity to turn the tables. At the moment, he had no leverage.

He kept driving. His thoughts turned again to symmetry, as much to distract himself from the feelings of threat, vulnerability, and retaliation as to work on the case.

Most conceptual metaphors dealt with dualities, dialectics: inside-outside, over-under, higher-lower, home-away. Which one fit this case? Some of the most emotional ones were higher-lower and over-under. They connoted superiority and inferiority, strength and weakness, power and dependence. If Robert/Paul were at the center of this, the higher-lower metaphor resonated. Paul worked at the Top of the Hub, Robert worked as an assistant to a CEO, a servile position in many respects. Paul was high, Robert was low; Paul was angry and arrogant; Robert was whiny and aloof. It was as if Robert Paulson were living his metaphor.

The higher-lower metaphor also fit Johnny's image of the tree, leaves reaching high into the sky while beneath hungry roots dug into the dirt for nutrients. The signs at Fenway were high on the Green Monster, yet . . . suddenly, with an almost blinding flash, Johnny realized something he hadn't to this point – every attack Daniel had listed for him had occurred at ground level. The photos they'd browsed had ground-level camera angles in every case. There wasn't an act of sabotage or vandalism that had occurred above that level. Reports of broken windows noted they were ground floor windows. Whether it was a fence cut open at the bottom, slashed tires or brake cables, electric meters destroyed, or any of the hundreds of things listed on the reports, everything occurred at ground level.

While it was logical that most vandalism would occur this way, for everything to have done so across the country and throughout a network of people who likely never met, except through a web site conveying instructions, struck Johnny as significant.

Extend the metaphor, he thought to himself. Higher-lower also relates to over-under. You could go overland, underground. You can go underwater, Johnny thought.

Water.

His limbic brain lingered over the word, his well-trained sense of instinct giving him a quick wink of recognition. Somehow, water had been factoring into his world recently. Whether it was gazing out at the harbor and its scrubbers and the Charles River from the Top of the Hub or watching the fountain at Prudential Center, water had been a theme.

It was worth a look.

Johnny flipped open his phone and called Tucker.

"Denovo, is this important?" Tucker growled. "Did it ever occur to you I might be busy?"

"Never," Johnny retorted. "Hey, I do need another favor, though. Remember that data from Daniel about the vandalism? Did he give you addresses?"

Tucker grunted, and there was a loud bang. He's been training again, Johnny thought.

"He did," Tucker said, breathing heavily. "But nothing was linked up, if you remember. All I have is addresses, but I don't know which attack occurred where," Tucker stated.

"That's fine," Johnny said somewhat dismissively. He was in a hurry. "Can you run an analysis of the addresses? Basically, I'd like to find the closest above-ground water source for each. I want to know the maximum distance for the entire set."

Tucker cleared his throat. "Let me get this straight. You want to know if everything reported in the database occurred close to an above-ground water source. And if so, what's the farthest distance away."

"Right," Johnny confirmed.

"That's not an easy one, you know," Tucker grumbled. "When do you need it?"

"The sooner the better," Johnny answered. "Saturday would be too late."

"Wow, you are crazy, Denovo. Are you trying to kill me?"

"Not yet," Johnny answered. "Besides, if this works out, you'll be able to afford a new kilt for your he-man games. That should be motivation enough."

Chapter 22

Pop-Up

Friday at 11:30, Bart Zeller called Johnny right on schedule. Johnny had set aside the afternoon to read Zeller's report but knew the phone call would be the most revealing part of their interaction. Bart had an amazing mind, obsessed with nuances and subtleties and able to notice and elicit them from data in a truly remarkable way. He was one of the richest, most secretive people in the world because of it, and he owed Johnny many favors. This would draw them closer to even, but not quite square the books.

"Denovo," Zeller barked when Johnny answered the phone. "You remembered."

"As if you had any doubt," Johnny parried. "What have you been able to find out?"

"Nothing too bizarre, but some suggestive things. Want me to just spill it?"

"Spill it, Bart," Johnny urged.

"Fine," Zeller said, taking a deep breath. "Schwartz was CEO of the company just over eight years ago when it went public. It was founded two years earlier, but that's where my records start. There are a few major investors, most of whom hold investments in other biotech or genetics companies. One is Tom McNaught, the big biotech mogul you have there in Boston. He has a 10 percent share.

A Paul Robertson owns 10 percent. Schwartz has kept about 60 percent for himself with a shadow account I couldn't get a look into in the time given, so that leaves 20 percent to divvy up between the remaining few hundred shareholders, most holding a few dozen shares each max. It's a pretty high-priced stock, not many shares out there, but it's been volatile lately. There seems to be some impatience for therapeutic outcomes, based on my reading of the annual reports and analysts' statements. The marketability of genetic tests and probes will only take revenues so far. Treatment's the Holy Grail of genetics. And, as you know, enzymes and proteins might be the real actors, not the genes. So, with all the activity in proteomics, Schwartz's little venture is looking a bit shaky. But his patent filings have come at a rapid pace lately, apparently in response to the pressure to move toward therapies. He's patented some novel ways to suspend genetic materials in an aqueous state, preserving their ability to replicate by creating hydrophilic, virus-like sheaths synthetically. Seems like a targeting approach maybe, moving therapeutics, timing them for ingestion. I don't know. There are a few patent filings that comprise this R&D direction. I could only give these a cursory review, there are so many. He's careful to parse the applications so as to not give away his endgame strategy, and I'm inferring, but that's what it looks like to me. It's pretty heady stuff, but it hasn't moved beyond the hypothetical as far as I can tell. Just proof of concept stuff in these patents, it looks like. And he's carrying a load of debt to keep it all afloat."

Johnny was listening intently.

"Is that it?" he asked Zeller.

"You know, I hate to disappoint you, but this isn't a very interesting company," Zeller observed. "He's keeping his head above water with investors, some significant debt coming due in the near future, and some minor league products in genetic screening and testing technologies, pursuing the big game of therapies with some interesting but unproven technologies, and keeping his ring of investors small and close-knit. He has the standard insurances and whatnot in case things go sour. I'll send over the patent filings, financials, annual reports, and other documents in a compressed file after we hang up. Some of the scientists seem to be worth following, based on the patents, but overall, it's a snoozer."

"That's great, Bart," Johnny noted.

"So, we're even?" Zeller asked.

"Not yet," Johnny answered. "But this brings us closer. Thanks very much."

Zeller laughed. "I knew that would be your answer. I accept it. Take care, Denovo."

Robertson owns 10 percent. Paul again. The association had even more layers to it.

And water again, Johnny thought to himself. He let his mind wander. He'd noted the aqueous suspension and sheathing patents Zeller had mentioned. Water feeds trees. If money is the root of all evil, and water feeds roots, then turning water into gold instead of wine would be the alchemy Schwartz was after. But how would you do that? Especially if your genetics company was on the verge of drowning in debt.

Sitting at his desk, he clicked an icon to check his email.

A large file downloaded speedily. It was a compressed file from Bart Zeller.

Johnny opened it and scanned down to the "Patents" folder. Opening this, he sorted the files by date, then clicked on the latest filing. It was a very detailed description of a way to safely transport unstable virus in water, having it release only when the water was removed and the protective sheath dried out. It was described as a technique for shipping and handling viruses in research environments. The scientific jargon and technical specifications were laid on thick for the sake of the patent office, but the essential idea was straightforward. How it might be turned into a therapeutic application Johnny couldn't divine.

Scanning to the end of the application, arriving at the last page, Johnny found a link to a much older patent from Schwartz Genetics, possibly the first the company had filed.

He went back out to the file system and located the referenced patent.

The file was in an outdated word processing format, so it had to be converted. When it finally opened, Johnny scanned through it. He nearly slipped off his chair.

The inventor was listed as Robert Paulson, not James Schwartz. Johnny was stunned.

Robert Paulson couldn't possibly be a scientist as well. Too much trouble in his life. Too much of a record.

Or was he so driven he managed to pull it off? His school records indicated a high performer with the right credentials.

The most recent patent issued had been submitted two years ago. Paul had been a bartender at the Top of the Hub for three years, Robert an assistant at Schwartz's for eight. The older patent went back 10 years.

Was the older patent filing in Paulson's name for another reason? Perhaps he had extorted it from Schwartz? Or perhaps Schwartz was disassociating himself from certain inventions to cover his tracks? Paulson might not even know his name was on the patent.

Johnny squared his mindset to this reality, sure that it was significant but unsure why.

Scratching his hair, he read the Paulson patent. It described a method for neutralizing adenoviruses outside an aqueous suspension. These were the same viruses used in the more recent patent's proof of concept drawings, data, and schematics. Apparently, the same experiments had yielded two complementary findings. That was nothing unusual, Johnny knew from his years in the lab, but having these techniques come years apart, and to have the older one attributed to a person who wasn't known as a scientist – these could be more mysterious facts not quite touching Schwartz.

Proximity without contact.

And this patent had never been turned into a commercial application.

Perhaps it didn't work outside the lab.

Once again, Johnny felt stymied by Schwartz. Was he an innocent scientist with a devious boyfriend and secret accomplice? Or was he a mastermind so adept at covering his tracks and creating misdirection that even documentary evidence was unable to attach itself to him?

Either way, this patent was a fulcrum.

Chapter 23
Stretch

To blackmail, long-lost sisters, and a two-faced neurological freak, he could now add a virus.

What a case.

The adenovirus added a worrisome dimension. Johnny needed to learn why this virus in particular had been used in the two patents filed 10 years apart.

He knew a little. He'd done some animal research years ago, so the adenoviruses were somewhat familiar. But his information was old, and viruses mutated unpredictably, so detailed information on their potential effects on humans was the order of the day.

He needed more medical advice, this time from a master of bugs and drugs.

While you couldn't swing a dead cat in Boston without hitting a doctor, Johnny thought morbidly, this particular cat corpse would now smack into the side of a massive mega-lab devoted to studying emerging infectious diseases. It had just opened at a local university amid predictable protests and fear-mongering. Yet the scientists and economists had prevailed, and now a gleaming edifice stood on the outskirts of Boston, providing research and jobs.

He knew where to call. He just didn't know who to call.

It was time to dial for doctors.

The center's automated system was annoying but typical. He was able to reach a disinterested operator by pressing just a few commands. After being passed to and from a few desks, his call was finally answered by a young research physician named Stan Deresinski, a specialist in infectious diseases who turned out to also be a fan of Johnny's style and work.

"Mr. Denovo, I'm very glad they put you through to me," Deresinski said, his deep voice resonating very clearly over the phone. "I follow your cases whenever I can, at least what little I learn about them through the news. I think your work's fascinating. I'm not sure how you do it, but you get it done. I'm sure there's more than meets the eye."

"I could repeat the same compliments for you, Dr. Deresinski," Johnny answered deferentially. "I think if I knew half the emerging diseases you have there, I'd duct tape myself into my bedroom."

Deresinski laughed. "Tape yourself into the bathroom. Trust me, it will work out better," he replied. "Actually, don't make me think about them. I only cope because I've been trained to. If I started to think I'm not invincible in the pressurized suits we wear, I'd never stop washing my hands. But why are you calling? Certainly not to make the acquaintance of your friendly neighborhood germ doc."

It was Johnny's turn to chuckle. "No, I'm working on a case. I've come across some information suggesting that someone is toying with an adenovirus. There's a chance for malign intentions, but I'm not sure yet."

There was silence on the other end of the line. "Are you talking bio-terrorism?" Deresinski asked guardedly.

"I'm not sure," Johnny answered, his own shields going up. Bringing his questions to one of the nation's fortresses of disease research might have been a mistake. He'd have to think quickly.

Deresinski sounded grave in response. "We're trained here to assess biological threats as well as analyze emerging infectious diseases. I served in the Air Force to pay off my medical school bills, and have some intelligence training on top of it. I still have a clearance. This sounds like something the FBI or Homeland Security should be involved in."

Johnny had a live one here. "Well, Dr. Deresinski, I understand your concerns. To reassure you, let me tell you that I'm working with one of the most highly placed experts in the intelligence field," Johnny responded, referring obliquely and truthfully to Tucker. "If and when this case becomes more clearly about bio-terrorism, we will involve the right people," Johnny reassured. "Until then, I'm trying to assess whether this is benign, a ruse, or something we have to take seriously. You know the damage a false alarm could cause, so I want to tread carefully here. Your expertise will be vital in helping me avoid a mistake. Also," Johnny continued in a more confidential tone, "there are complications that I can't go into now, but the initial reason I was hired has nothing to do with this. I owe it to my client to resolve the case with some discretion."

Deresinski seemed assuaged. "I'll take you at your word, Mr. Denovo. After all, you're good at what you do."

"Thank you," Johnny responded. "And, please call me Johnny."

"Great," Deresinski said, sounding more relaxed and chipper. "So, you said you wanted information about an adenovirus, right? Let's see, depending on the strain, adenoviruses usually cause things like upper respiratory infections, conjunctivitis or pink eye, the stomach flu or gastroenteritis as we call it, and croup in infants. Onset occurs 24-36 hours after exposure, but it's pretty mild. I can't imagine it being seen as a threat, unless it's the new serotype 14, which I doubt."

"What is serotype 14?" Johnny asked, zeroing in. He recalled seeing mention of that particular virus in the latest patent filing. Novelty was vital to patents, so he'd thought they'd mentioned a new strain to differentiate their filing. Now, he saw, there might have been another reason.

"Serotype 14," Deresinski said dreamily, as if recalling a lost love. "That's a very interesting little bug, a new and emergent strain we call Ad-14. It's sprung up here and there around the globe over the past few years, and it's much more virulent. People die from it, from pneumonia and respiratory infection. It's a nasty one."

"Can it be weaponized?" Johnny asked.

Deresinski sucked in his breath. "Now, you know, I can't really answer that without knowing your security clearance. Do you have one?"

"No, I don't," Johnny admitted, careful not to add the word "anymore." He once did, and at a level that probably would have floored Deresinski.

"Well, then, I can't go there," Deresinski stated baldly. "Does that tell you what you need to know?"

"Yes, it does," Johnny answered, playing along. "And adenovirus likes water, as I recall."

Deresinski gave a snort. "That's where it lives most of the time, either water outside humans or water inside humans," he exclaimed. "It's a non-enveloped virus, a naked virus, and it can live in all sorts of conditions. It's very stable. It can survive water of various pH levels, and can live for a long time out of water, too. Why do you ask?"

"Just curious," Johnny mused. "If it's so stable, would anyone have a reason for protecting it more?"

"You mean like sheltering it in a liposomal sheath?" Deresinski asked.

"I guess that's what I mean," Johnny confirmed with a little uncertainty in his voice, while noting the extra information Deresinski had inadvertently added.

Deresinski fell silent for a long moment. Johnny could hear him breathing, almost humming a little to himself. Finally, he answered. "I told you, I can't talk with you about whether this virus can be weaponized," he said in a monotone voice.

Johnny smiled on his end of the call. "Thank you, Dr. Deresinski. You've been an incredible help."

"Good luck," Deresinski said. "And Johnny, I know you're an independent private detective, but don't forget to call the calvary *before* you need it."

Chapter 24
Slide

Johnny felt the lens of possibilities tightening its focus, a good sign for the detective in him. But given the fact that he had fewer and fewer hours to act, the pressure to have a real breakthrough was ratcheting up.

The worst-case scenario was that there was a weaponized deployment of adenovirus-14, or Ad-14, in the cards, and sometime soon. All the signs pointed to an approaching crisis – third base, the pending home game, the end of the season, the breadth and intensity of attacks. And Boston was the epicenter. The plotters were here. The network had emanated from a Boston landmark. How widespread the worst-case scenario could be, Johnny shuddered to think. If the entire network were leveraged, it could be nationwide, with weaponized infectious organisms poised to release on a massive and unpredictable scale.

The best case scenario was a mild adenovirus and a limited release. That didn't seem likely. Again, the image of a tree, its leafy height counterweighted by its deep roots, flashed in Johnny's mind. Money fed this plan in some way. There had to be a money angle. He had to find that now.

Water was the other major variable. Water fed root systems. Water and money.

Above and below.

Johnny felt a tingle of an idea, but the ring of his cell phone interrupted his thought process. He reached across his table and picked it up, chasing it a little as it vibrated away from him.

"Johnny, for this one I'll need a signed baseball from you know who, mounted and under glass," Tucker said as soon as Johnny answered. "You owe me big time."

"I'll be the judge of that, but let's assume you're right," Johnny said.

"Fine," Tucker grumbled. "You won't believe how creative I am. Now, your request, m'lord, was to see how close these acts of vandalism, theft, and property destruction were to above-ground water sources. Man, just hearing that makes me feel so clever knowing what I'm going to tell you," Tucker gloated.

Johnny laughed, delighting in his friend's brilliance and enthusiasm.

"I'm waiting with baited breath," Johnny admitted.

"And I'm going to draw this one out, really enjoy it," Tucker said whimsically. "You ruined the dramatic arc last time. Not this time. And it's so worth it. So worth it."

Tucker paused to catch his breath. Johnny didn't dare interrupt his flow.

"OK," Tucker continued, "So I geo-located all the records in Daniel's database, and then used a vector map overlay of rivers, ponds, oceans, streams, lakes, and reservoirs. I did some fancy programming, and found that the greatest distance between one of these damage reports and an above-ground water source as listed was about 1.2 miles. The mean was 0.4 miles, and the median was 0.69 miles. If proximity was what you were after, this exercise wasn't very fruitful."

Johnny knew Tucker's style. It was time to ask for the other shoe to drop.

"But this isn't where the best fruit was. Am I right?" Johnny asked.

"You are right!" Tucker exclaimed in a big voice. "I went out for a walk after crunching all these calculations, just to clear my head and broaden my mind, when I saw another source of above-ground water. In fact, I almost tripped over it. When I mapped sources like this to the data, the numbers tightened a great deal."

"What source? How much?"

"Ah, the dramatic structure of this presentation is working much better!" Tucker bragged. "All right, a few doses of reality, a few cautions. First, geo-location against addresses has major problems. Very imprecise. Luckily, about 30 percent of the reports used GPS-enabled cameras to photograph the damage, so I dived into those photo files, and used only those data for this analysis. That makes it much more robust. But GPS cameras have an error of about plus or minus 40 feet. That means anything less than 80 feet is meaningful, but it still leaves a lot to be desired. That's in theory. In practice, however, these GPS cameras usually do much better than advertised, and because there are multiple pictures taken of damage, the aggregate data smoothes out the errors, adding to the accuracy. So, let's just say for argument's sake that something less than 40 feet, so half the inherent error rate, would be meaningful. And when I calculated for this new source of above-ground water, I got a maximum distance from damage, vandalism, or theft of 12 feet. I kid you not, Denovo. Twelve feet! It was a pretty amazing data run. On that final command, it was like striking oil by merely pressing Enter!"

Johnny felt a surge of excitement light his mind. Tucker had hit paydirt. But he kept his voice calm and somewhat disinterested, leaving room for logic in the face of Tucker's excitement. He needed to counterbalance Tucker's enthusiasm, make sure there wasn't a blind spot somewhere in his approach or interpretation.

"So, what was the magic water source you panned the gold from?" Johnny asked.

"Fire hydrants!" Tucker almost shouted. "Freaking fire hydrants! I grabbed the municipal sewer schematics for all these towns, plotted them against the data, and in every case for the GPS-enabled reports, the damage photographed was 12 feet or less from a fire hydrant."

In a flash, Johnny's view of the case tilted definitively to the worst-case scenario. Fire hydrants connected to municipal water supplies. Weaponized adenovirus released in municipal water supplies would be a terrifying scenario.

Tucker's finding was so sensible that any of Johnny's skepticism immediately vanished. It had to be true. Johnny trusted Tucker's math, and it made complete sense based on what they'd discovered thus far, even the metaphors. Above and below. Fire hydrants fit perfectly, the above-ground extensions of the water supply buried beneath every town and city in the country. Schwartz, Paulson, the Gleasons, or all of them were after municipal water supplies, and two of them shared patents that made sense together in a twisted manner – one to deliver virus, the other to eradicate it.

"Amazing, Tucker. Absolutely amazing," Johnny exulted. "That is one of the best breakthroughs you've ever delivered."

"I told you man," Tucker bragged. "I told you. It was like magic. It is definitely baseball-worthy."

""I agree. When we're done. When we're done, my friend," Johnny said. "Tucker, I think I know what's going on." Taking a deep breath, he described the patents he'd discovered with Zeller's help and how those findings dovetailed with Tucker's discovery.

"Apparently, they can protect the virus in a weaponized form using a hydrophilic sheath. It releases when it dries. But they haven't released it yet."

"So that's the reason for your fixation on water," Tucker murmured.

"Exactly," Johnny answered. "I'd been noticing it subconsciously. My brain was making a connection, pointing something out to me. That's why I asked you to look into it. I was only afterwards that I found out about the patents and the virus. But I'm still missing something," Johnny heard himself saying, despite the fact that his limbic brain was purring happily in the midst of the conversation, still intuiting the sense of Tucker's findings. But Johnny's cerebrum was dissatisfied. It needed logic and answers. "Why not just insert containers of virus into fire hydrants and not do the damage? Why risk the trail?"

"That's an easy one," Tucker answered. "Cover. If they're caught in the act, they only get busted for slashing tires, cutting fencing, stealing computers, or burning loading dock doors. Their true purpose would remain secret, the larger plan would remain intact. The vandalism is a misdirection, a diversion in case something goes wrong. It's a classic technique."

Yes, that was the answer, Johnny knew. The vandalism had to be a way of managing risk to the overall operation. Tucker's years of unraveling situations in the intelligence service had proven valuable yet again.

"Let me get this straight," Johnny interjected. "They've been putting the virus in all along, for months now. Yet it hasn't been released."

"It's their time bomb," Tucker groaned. "I did a bit of research, and the hell of it is that I think it's easily done. If it were me, I'd just seal a Petri dish with enough liquid in it to preserve the virus. It would fit perfectly into a fire hydrant's outlet. Since most hydrants are full-on or full-off, I'd be safe inserting it into the outlet. Then, once the hydrant was turned on, the pressure would blow the Petri dish apart. Bam, virus everywhere."

Tucker paused so profoundly Johnny held his breath.

"It's a doomsday scenario,"

"What do you mean?" Johnny pressed.

"We've had entire teams working to protect our municipal water supplies from terrorists," Tucker muttered. "Everyone thinks they aren't secured, but I can tell you, they are very secure. At least the filtration plants, the reservoirs, and all that. But here you have a brilliant approach, one that gets us in a blind spot, frankly. There are relatively few reservoirs servicing the municipal water supplies, but there are hundreds of thousands of fire hydrants. We can't protect all of those. And if they've planted viruses in hydrophilic sheaths that releases when exposed to air, it would work. If we open the fire hydrants, the virus floods out. Nobody can contain it all. And if it goes the other way, people wash their hands and faces, splash water, fill pools, wash cars. Some virus dries and goes airborne. I'm going to assume it's a virus that we wouldn't want people taking in, like hanta or smallpox or something else. Schwartz is a genetic engineer. It might be a boutique virus."

Johnny was deep in thought, listening to Tucker.

"I think it's an emerging infectious disease," he said at last. "I talked with an infectious disease expert. Something called adenovirus-14 might be our candidate. Schwartz and Paulson both hold patents that use an adenovirus as the core virus."

"We'd better call Homeland," Tucker stated.

"Not yet."

"Johnny, we've got a plausible bio-terror threat to our nation," Tucker argued. "We need to involve law enforcement. We can't do this on our own."

"Not yet," Johnny repeated. "There's something else going on here, some larger force involved. And given the hack to your systems last month and the insider who turned on us in France, I'm not giving the authorities the benefit of the doubt. Someone's still dirty in there."

"But not everyone, Denovo," Tucker rebuked. "Don't go painting with that brush. This isn't a 'one bad apple' situation. We need their help."

"Then explain the Gleasons," Johnny retorted. "Explain why I found another bomb, this time on my car."

"When?"

"The same day as the bombing of my condo," Johnny explained. "It might have been just another scare tactic, but they know what they're doing. There's something else going on here, and I'm not bringing the feds in until I'm further along. Something feels wrong."

Tucker sighed. "It's your call. I'll play along. But I think it's the bad move."

"Understood. Just a few days more," Johnny requested. "Someone's trying to create fear. The virus can't have been released yet. Otherwise, where's the terror? And who's the terrorist? The Gleasons seem like terrorists. They didn't kill me with the bomb at my apartment, and they removed the bullet from my cupholder to scare me into looking for the bomb they'd planted. Killing me wasn't within their capacity. They stopped short."

Tucker picked up on Johnny's train of thought. "So the virus has to be contained somehow, ready to be released if they need it but under control. So what's their plan?"

Johnny kept talking it through. "The patent for the hydrophilic sheath was in Schwartz's name, but the patent on a potential reversal mechanism was in Paulson's name," he said colorlessly, lost in thought. "Terror is usually a means to an end, either political or otherwise. I've been thinking this is actually all about money. Money is the root of all evil."

"What are you talking about, Denovo?" Tucker asked, confused.

"I've had this image in my mind for the last few days of a diagrammatic silhouette of a tree, like from a botany text, with the branch and leaf system above ground and the root system symmetrically positioned below ground like a reflection of the tree," Johnny elaborated. "The case seemed like that, like the environmental attacks and sabotage are the visible part but something else has been feeding the system. Using the old maxim that money is the root of all evil, I've been trying to figure out how someone would profit from this. And now I think I see it!"

"Do tell, Denovo, because I still don't get it," Tucker confessed.

"If Paulson is the two-faced front of the terror aspect of the plan, and he holds the patent on the most important part of the terrorist plot, he's positioned to be the underling at Schwartz Genetics who can sell the government the solution to the crisis," Johnny said. "He'll make hundreds of millions in government contracts when clean-up and prevention and monitoring activities kick in, and Schwartz Genetics will become the first genetics firm to thwart a terrorist plot. A possibly frustrated research agenda will be redeemed, and he'll be rich. Meanwhile, Schwartz will be off the hook, just an innocent CEO with some important patents that were abused by a bio-terror group. No fingerprints. He never leaves them, I've found. Paulson and Schwartz are the masterminds in this. Both are two-faced. Just for one, it's also visible, observable."

Tucker remained silent for a moment. "By Jove," he finally uttered, "I think you've got it. So the blackmail with McNaught has nothing to do with this, then."

"Oh no, it's part of the same plan," Johnny exclaimed. "I didn't see it before, but if Paulson wants to be the hero, he can't have competition. McNaught is a biotech wunderkind, one of the stars of the field. The government would likely turn to him to help once they learned of the terror plot. The blackmail is meant to paralyze McNaught, make him unwilling to respond because he's in a compromising situation. He'd want to avoid the spotlight. That's why the blackmailer asked for more. He wanted to put McNaught in an even tougher situation, raise the anxiety level and really shut him down. It fits. And it means we're almost at the end-game."

"And Fenway?" Tucker asked.

"Part of mobilizing a network of radical environmentalists, to conduct the war and make Paulson and Schwartz war profiteers," Johnny concluded. "What a plan!"

Tucker was treading carefully with the next question. "And the Gleasons?"

Johnny felt his enthusiasm deflate. "I have no idea. They perplex me. I can't tell. They have a soaring antenna above their house, a bunker below. The man comes from the same metaphorical batch. But something tells me it's different somehow. They really perplex me."

"Welcome to the club," Tucker chimed. "They've stumped us for years." Tucker hummed a single note, low and pleasant, then spoke. "You know what's next, don't you?"

"What?" Johnny asked.

"It's Terrorism 101, especially if they're going to extort money," Tucker offered. "They stage a demonstration."

Chapter 25
High Heat

If Tucker was right, a potent virus would be released soon to demonstrate the capabilities of a bio-terror network, but a wagonload of questions remained. Where would it occur? When would it happen? And who was going to make it happen? Johnny felt the pressure of the case intensify again as he faced a deadline that might be more literal than figurative for hundreds if not thousands of people.

His antagonists were working against the same clock, though. Time was immutable, a constant he could work from. He tried to deduce the timeline.

It was now Friday.

Red Sox home games were the key to the network's communications. The team was on a road trip until Monday, three days from now. This created a viable window to sow seeds of fear. It also gave him a fixed point in time. It could be part of their schedule. They could have some public panic well underway by the time the next home game began. The blackmailer was playing with fire. The crisis was looming, final bets were being made. Once the Red Sox returned, the ringleaders would want to strike soon, while the anxiety and fear was fresh and growing.

Whatever was going to happen next, fear seemed like the missing ingredient, and they now had a few days to plant it.

Fenway Park was being exploited to broadcast a message to dozens, hundreds, or thousands of sympathetic souls who were following instructions posted on a web site. But for a demonstration of viral capabilities alone, there was no need to leverage the entire network.

Instead, the mastermind could work alone.

It would only take one attack.

In Johnny's estimation, this could mean any time between this moment and Monday morning. He needed to narrow. He needed to think about the victims. They were keys to creating fear.

It would take a while for victims to appear.

First, a virus would need time to blossom and show an effect for any threat to be plausible and convincing. The way Schwartz's patent read, the hydrophilic coating would dissolve if dried, leaving the virus free to become airborne as soon as that happened and would need about a day for symptoms to develop.

To have an effective demonstration by Monday morning, that meant that the attack had to occur either tonight or Saturday morning. There just wasn't time for enough people to get sick and upset and on the news otherwise. The media would have to broadcast the fear.

Now Johnny felt he had a tentative solution to the question of when, and even a hint about what could happen. But he needed to put himself into his adversary's mind even more, reshaping his thoughts as best he could to reflect a reality he could only glimpse indirectly and incompletely. He settled deeper into a trance-like state and gave himself over to the fundamental processes of his limbic brain.

What did they want? The demonstration was meant to elicit fear, but it couldn't kill. So they wouldn't use Ad-14. The goal was terror, not death. But creating a hundred cases of the sniffles wouldn't be sufficient to generate fear on a widespread basis. The demonstration illness would have to be something dramatic – a fever, pustules, a lung disease. It had to make an impact on television, Johnny thought again cynically.

And it had to happen somewhere a lot of people went, a place people would know by name so that fear could take root.

Where would it be? And who would set it off?

Paulson would set it off. The thought leapt unbidden to his mind. Paulson would want to handle this himself. He'd feel the same way if he were in their shoes – the first step was always the hardest. He wouldn't leave it to chance. Neither would Paulson. And since Paulson was one of the masterminds, Paul would be the best disguise to assume while lighting this fuse. And he worked at a landmark.

Assuming Paul was the trigger man, an above-ground water source would have to be nearby and accessible. Paul was a bartender. He could use ice, bar equipment, or a number of other means to deliver water, but the water had to dry. The bar wasn't a suitable place. Besides, Paul wouldn't want to sicken himself. Infecting himself would be beneath him, Johnny thought, a rueful smile playing across his countenance.

Beneath him. Johnny lingered over the phrase. Paul's coworker had referred to the fact that Paul liked working at the Top of the Hub because he felt he was on top of the world, looking down on the peons below. He certainly acted like a haughty, arrogant jerk in his Paul mode. If he were indeed a terrorist, this arrogance would have transformed into aggression and hatred, a deep and true disdain for others.

And suddenly he had his answer. Johnny had seen an above-ground water source near Paul, but definitely beneath him – the fountain in the Prudential Center.

The fountain would make practical, logistical sense. Not only would its dark onyx basin and bubbling waters provide a perfect hiding place for a load of hydrophilic virus, it was in a populated and well-known area. When emptied and dried, it could cause illness in hundreds or thousands, all of whom could corroborate the fact that they had been at the Prudential Center at a designated day and time. The terrorist's claim would have credence. The demonstration would be effective.

But for the plan to work, the fountains would have to be shut off and drained after the virus was planted.

Suddenly, Johnny saw the possible chain of events clearly. Paul worked the night shift. Leaving the bar in the wee hours, he would somehow drain and shut off the fountain. By morning, it would be dry, releasing a virus that would propagate throughout the day. When he returned to work Saturday night, the fountain would have been turned back on, the virus delivered, and the air likely cleared sufficiently for him to avoid illness.

But Paul would want some guarantee that the fountain wouldn't be turned back on prematurely. He had to be sure it would dry, that some attentive and enterprising maintenance person wouldn't thwart his plan with the twist of a valve. He would need to damage it, vandalize it well enough that a minor repair would be required. Damage like that would be easy to accomplish – pull off the handle or strip some threads on a bolt hole, a two-minute job at most.

Paul only needed a few hours of morning foot traffic along the shopping mall connected to the Prudential Center for his demonstration to work.

As Johnny pondered this, he realized he had no time left for speculation. If this road trip was their window, the hours were few.

It was time to move.

Chapter 26
Night Game

Johnny sat with his hands in the pockets of his lightweight jacket, his cell phone cradled in his palm and set to vibrate. He wanted to be discrete, not draw any attention to himself. He needed to look innocuous. The crowds in the shopping mall were sparse this time of night, mainly theater-goers returning to parked cars, tourists wandering between restaurants or bars and their hotels, and the occasional teens goofing around. He wore his baseball cap to provide some level of anonymity. His shock of black hair was often the first clue people used to identify him.

As he sat on the edge of the fountain, he tried to pick the best time for his move. It was getting later and later. The halls were empty more often than not at this hour. The bar at the Top of the Hub was edging toward its own closing time.

Upstairs, Mona and Izzy sat at the bar, lookouts to ensure that Paul remained on the job and presumably oblivious to his plan. They had agreed to call if they lost sight of him for more than a minute.

As Johnny waited for the opportune time – a burst of activity followed by a noiseless lull – he pondered the steps he'd have to take.

And he knew this was only interference. It wouldn't stop the perpetrators, just frustrate them. But throwing off plans helped tilt the table in his favor.

Finding the virus in the first place had been tricky. He'd assumed it would be in a disk like those he'd pictured going into fire hydrants – flat, thin, like a Petri dish, sealed but easily opened when the time came.

It helped that he'd handled many of these himself over the years.

Only by peering furtively into the splashing waters of the fountain behind him with a small, powerful flashlight had he been able to detect a small plastic disk at the bottom, barely discernible in the lighted waters playing over it. A few coins had landed on it, camouflaging it further.

Handling the dangerous material at the bottom of the fountain would require care.

The fountain was only two feet deep, so he could reach down and retrieve the disk. The trick would be to fish it out in a plastic bag, seal the bag underwater, and bring it up without being noticed. He didn't want any of the virus to splash out as he lifted it. The disk seemed to have a cover on it, but he wasn't willing to bet that it provided adequate protection against what lurked inside.

Moving the disk recklessly could jar the lid loose, so he wanted to bag it as close to the bottom as possible. The last thing he wanted was to make a mistake. His hands felt clammy in his jacket pockets.

At last, a group of three couples came down the hallway, their boisterous, inebriated laughter echoing through the mall's empty kiosks and gated storefronts. As they passed to his left down another long hallway, the men's ties askew and one lady carrying her high-heeled shoes by the straps, Johnny noted the wake of silence following them.

The moment was right.

Johnny took his hands out of his pockets, revealing blue latex gloves. With a quick sweep of his shoulders, he shrugged the jacket off and retrieved a clear bag from the inside pocket. He opened the bag and thrust it down into the splashing fountain, the spray from the jets dappling his face as he bent close to the surface.

By the time he heard the footsteps, it was too late for him to react. From behind, three light, rapid steps fell. Reluctant to disengage from the underwater bag, Johnny didn't dare turn. He maintained his concentration, dreading the disk at the bottom of the fountain more than any human being in the surrounding mall.

Without warning, his head was wrenched into a full-nelson grip, his neck locked tight and pushed forward, his skull immobilized. He couldn't see anything except the black-clad arms of his assailant and the water-filled basin of black onyx.

"Don't do it," the man's voice hissed. "Leave it there."

Johnny's neck was so compressed he could barely speak. "What do you care?"

The man laughed. "You are definitely a Johnny-come-lately. I've been working on this for years."

Johnny struggled against the man's hold, but he couldn't budge his assailant. The grip was iron, and the man had leverage, leaning his full weight into Johnny's back.

"What do you mean?" was all Johnny could gasp.

"I want to catch Paulson, too," the man whispered, his breath hot on Johnny's ear. "But this isn't the endgame. This is nothing. I know what's in the dish. It'll be an inconvenience, but nobody will die. Trust me. This needs to happen."

Again, Johnny instinctively struggled, but to little effect. He tried to screw up his eyes to see if he could catch a reflection of his adversary. He glanced into the waters, at the windows, at the onyx. Only shadows.

"Why should I trust you?" Johnny rasped, the pain of the headlock starting to register.

"Because I've let you live twice now," the man said. "Two smoke bombs when it could have been much more, and I left you a big clue about the last one, a clue you caught, to your credit. Besides, I could kill you here and now. But we need you to continue what you're doing. You weren't part of the plan at first, but you fit right in. This step, just skip this step, and keep going. Save your hero instincts for another day. We'll meet again."

Johnny felt the pressure on his back release, the headlock slacken, but before he could recover and turn to face his assailant, his legs were lifted high in the air and he was dumped into the fountain face-first, the cold water filling his eyes and mouth, pushing up his nose and shocking his system.

Coming to the surface in a burst, Johnny looked around frantically, spitting water from his face and wiping it from his eyes. The empty halls echoed the fountain's waters. He reached for his jacket heaped at the edge of the fountain and grabbed his cell phone.

He flipped it open and pressed a few buttons, his body chilling from the water and the air conditioning. He needed to know what was happening upstairs.

"Mona," he said quietly, lifting his legs up on the ledge of the fountain as he extricated himself. "It's Johnny."

"Hi," Mona said guardedly.

"Paul's right there, isn't he?" Johnny asked.

"Yes, that's right," Mona answered.

"You two can come down whenever you want," Johnny said. "I'm done."

"Great, I'll see you in a little bit," Mona responded brightly. "You have the children?"

Johnny raised an eyebrow, but played along. "All twelve of them," he answered. "The au pair has the night off."

"Bye, honey," Mona said in closing, and the call ended.

Johnny's stepped out of the fountain and stood on the ledge, drawing quizzical looks from a group of slightly inebriated businesswomen walking warily around him, giving the fountain a wide berth. He stripped off the latex gloves he was wearing.

Standing there dripping, he felt cold and self-conscious, but had little time to indulge the feelings. He had another call to make while he waited for Mona and Izzy.

Dialing Tucker, Johnny was grateful when his friend picked up, the noise from the televised Red Sox game competing with Tucker's lazy voice.

"Tucker here," his friend answered gruffly.

"Tucker, it's Johnny. This is urgent," Johnny began. "I need to know if your people track the Gleasons."

"We can't. That's part of the problem," Tucker said sleepily.

"Tuck, did you fall asleep watching the game?" Johnny asked.

"Yeah," Tucker said. "I've been doing a lot of favors for friends lately. It makes for late nights," Tucker responded pointedly.

"Great, then you're in training in more ways than one right now," Johnny answered without a hint of sympathy. He knew his friend was as passionate about solving cases as he was. Fatigue was not a real issue for either of them. "Gleason just threw me into the fountain at the Pru."

Tucker stirred, clearing his throat. "What?!" he exclaimed. "You saw him?"

Johnny felt his face warm in embarrassment. "Not exactly," he confessed. "He was too quick and caught me off-guard."

"Then how do you know it was him?" Tucker asked.

"He told me that he'd let me live twice this week," Johnny replied. "Sounds like something only Gleason could say."

"Really?" Tucker responded, then cleared his throat. "If it were anybody else, I'd scoff. For you, I'll bite. Let's assume it was him. First off, don't feel bad about being caught unawares. Nobody's seen him up close in years. Your brush with him in New Hampshire is the closest I've heard of. He's very elusive. And every time we think we're getting close, it's like a force field goes up. They have extra-sensory perception or something."

"Well, it seems he's after Paulson, too," Johnny submitted.

"Huh?" Tucker responded. "How do you know that?"

"Gleason told me."

"Now why would one bad guy be after another?" Tucker mused.

Johnny paused before replying. "Maybe they're not both bad," he speculated.

A silence fell upon the two friends as they pondered this hypothesis.

"That would mean that the Gleasons are good guys," Tucker finally said, breaking the stillness. "Paulson's fingerprints are all over this. But the Gleasons as good guys doesn't make sense," he concluded.

"Why not?" Johnny asked.

"Well, we have them dead to rights in too many situations," Tucker answered, then caught himself. "I can't tell you any of this. It's classified. I can only help a little with what's happening now, not delve into their history."

Johnny glanced up. Mona and Izzy were approaching from down the hall behind him. He must have recognized Mona's footfalls from afar, he thought to himself, another sign that they were becoming increasingly intertwined. He recognized her instinctually.

"OK," Johnny agreed, backing down. "But do me a favor. Think about what you know. What if there were a different explanation? What if they were good guys, just misread, accidentally or purposely? It's like the story of the cop who's always surrounded by criminals. It's true, but he's associated with criminals because his job is to bring them to justice. Associating with criminals in that case doesn't make him a criminal."

Johnny waved weakly as Mona and Izzy approached, both pointing at his dripping clothes and expressing a mixture of concern and laughter.

Tucker remained silent.

"Does that make any sense at all?" Johnny asked.

"It does make some sense," Tucker finally responded. "That's why I'm mum. It might make a lot of sense."

"In any event," Johnny continued, "he made me leave the item in the fountain. He said it needs to go off, that it would only give people the sniffles, and that Paulson was up to something much bigger. I don't know if he knows about Schwartz, though. Didn't mention him."

Mona and Izzy were now standing at Johnny's feet, his position on the fountain's ledge allowing him to lord over them. He glanced down. They were listening attentively, realization dawning fastest on Mona's face, Izzy trying to pick up cues by looking from one to the other.

"What if he's lying?" Tucker asked. "What if he's in league with Schwartz?"

"He could have just snuffed me out, three times now," Johnny replied. "No, he was clear and direct in his speech. No metaphors, obfuscations, uncertainty. His actions and words jibe."

By now, Izzy was becoming more agitated in her confusion. Johnny ignored her body language, locking eyes with Mona. Tucker sounded cautious in his reply.

"Johnny, no matter what we end up finding out about the Gleasons, they are formidable. They leave collateral damage. You need to stay out of their way."

"Great," Johnny groaned. "And he said I'm integral now. That doesn't seem possible."

Mona's eyes flicked with concern.

"Well, I guess the next move comes Monday," Tucker concluded. "The Sox just lost. They play tomorrow, a day game, then come home for Monday's home stand. That will be when we can find out more."

"Right," Johnny said. "By the way, the virus is in a sealed disk here, like a Petri dish. Might be big enough to fit in a standard municipal pipe. They'd only need to open the disks for things to start happening. That would mean going back to the hydrants to make the plan go."

"Makes sense," Tucker said. "I hate it, but it makes sense."

"Talk tomorrow," Johnny said with finality. He closed his phone with a snap.

"Are you OK?" Mona said.

Johnny glanced down at his dripping clothes, his arms out to his sides in an attempt to emphasize his pitiful plight.

Out of the corner of his eye, he saw two clear plastic disks bobbing atop the splashing waters – one was clearly a lid. Apparently, he'd dislodged it with his tumble into the fountain.

He could feel his skin drying in the air conditioning.

A chill of realization washed over him, and a surge of panic flooded his body.

"Get out of here," he barked at Mona and Izzy. "Get out fast. Run! Don't wait for me! A virus is about to release!"

Johnny stood in the fountain, angry and frustrated, the echoes of high heeled shoes reverberating as two women fled into the night.

Chapter 27
Foul Ball

Saturday morning, Johnny's automated window shades opened gradually, spilling the soft, filtered August light across the room like slow honey. He groaned in pain. His head was throbbing and his eyes stung. He felt feverish, achy, and nauseous.

Groggily, he thought at first that the dip in the cold water the night before had affected him. At least, that's what the grandmother's voice in his head said. Then his rational, scientific side took over, and he realized that you don't get a cold from being cold and wet – you get a cold from a virus.

He remembered.

He must have picked up a load of the adenovirus when Gleason dumped him in the pool. It had gotten in his eyes, nose, and mouth. It had clung to his clothing, drying and releasing as he slept.

And now he was ill.

This was a fast-acting virus. It had been less than 12 hours since he'd been exposed to it.

He was relieved Mona and Izzy had turned heel and fled. They were likely unaffected.

Last night, he'd thought about throwing his clothes away immediately or washing them, but no matter what he'd done, they would have infected someone – through the water released by his washing machine, through the air from his clothes dryer.

Better that he took the bullet. It was his case.

He shifted his weight. Moving was agony. His joints felt rusted in place. The light hurt his eyes. His mouth was dry and sour. His fever had him sweating profusely. If this was the virus Paulson had unleashed, there would be plenty of people at the emergency room later today, dehydrated and worried. Johnny was young and healthy. Others – older people, people with medical conditions, children – they would be more severely affected. If the demonstration had indeed gone off as planned, a message would be forthcoming, placed in the media to instill fear and uncertainty.

The physical aches were distracting him from thinking properly. Myalgias like these reminded him of influenza. His stomach churned. His head pulsed. An adenovirus had been released, one that would penetrate the exposed population, creating enough of a caseload to validate the terrorists' claims.

Johnny needed to relieve some of the symptoms so he could concentrate. He struggled out of bed to the bathroom and from there over to his kitchen, downing some pain relievers with water.

A ripple of nausea crawled up his spine. He shut off his coffee maker. The smell was repugnant.

It was Saturday, a bad day to get things done from home. People were not at work. They'd be hard to reach. He wasn't sure what to do.

He decided to see if there was anything in the media about a terror plot yet.

He slid gingerly into his computer chair. Even moving his arms to enter his logins and passwords was painful. First, he checked the blackmailer's site to see if the message to McNaught had changed or a new one had been posted. The site appeared untouched, the celebrated cartoon characters grinning at him in bright, saturated colors.

Next, Johnny checked his email, but no messages other than fan mail filtered in.

Finally, he returned to his browser and loaded his news sites.

Paulson's plot was in high gear.

The first headline to meet his eyes read, "Bio-terror Claims Backed by ER Visits." The story reported that a number of individuals had been admitted to emergency rooms in downtown Boston complaining of fever, aches, breathing difficulty, and eye infections. An email sent to the mayor by a group called Cool & Green claimed a virus had been released into the air at the Prudential Center, part of a demonstration of what would happen if the United States did not curtail use of fossil fuels, cut back on carbon dioxide emissions, cease over-fishing the oceans, and the like. Nature was potent and dangerous, the claim stated, requiring our humility. It was classic eco-babble, Johnny thought. To think there was a place where nature ended and mankind began was a complete fallacy. The bacteria in his stomach would laugh at the idea – if they were up to laughing, considering how they were under siege at the moment.

Reading deeper into related stories, Johnny found that each victim showed signs of an adenovirus infection, and each had been at the Prudential Center overnight or very early in the morning – security guards, janitors, the homeless.

To add to the sense of fear, reporters had discovered that the security cameras had been offline during the evening. Officials claimed it was due to routine maintenance, but the reporter implied that this was doublespeak for sabotage. Johnny agreed. Somebody had knocked them out of commission. Air travel into and out of Boston was slowed to a crawl by heightened security. The empty, broken fountain at the Pru had been implicated in the outbreak. Now, all the public fountains around the city had been drained and inspected. There were being left dry until the crisis passed.

One public health official appealed to guests checking out of adjoining hotels, asking them to report symptoms in case this wasn't a terrorist act but actually something akin to Legionnaire's Disease, a conventioneer's plague.

Johnny knew it wasn't Legionnaire's Disease.

Paulson had executed his demonstration.

He had the attention of the country now.

Johnny shivered with chills but continued to read.

In its email to the mayor, the group also claimed that this attack would be the first of many around the nation if immediate policy changes were not forthcoming, an impossible demand. Johnny knew Paulson had no intention of making reasonable demands. His goal was being accomplished with every breathless headline and screaming news graphic.

It all fit with what Johnny had discovered thus far. Cool & Green wouldn't be asking for any ransom. Paulson would make his money by selling the solution to the dilemma he was creating. Paulson wanted Cool & Green to continue on their trajectory of eco- and bio-terrorism. The media was playing right into his hands. In fact, if Evan's theory of an energized fractal were accurate, Cool & Green could be using an outdated playbook, Paulson manipulating them into doing his bidding, without their knowledge but with their complicity.

Dogma was hard to change, easy to exploit.

A deep fatigue overwhelmed Johnny as he sat shivering and sweating. He must have gotten a mega-dose of the adenovirus. With a shiver he recalled the rush of cold water going up into his eyes, nose, and mouth. For a fleeting instant, the emergency room seemed to beckon. But he couldn't give in – he had a case coming down around him.

Rising painfully, he walked slowly back to bed, chills wracking his body. Instinctively, he assumed a fetal position, shivering helplessly. As he closed his eyes, he thought of the Cool & Green connection and the woman in the stands. They had yet to identify her. She was a crucial link, but a mystery. Her disguise had thwarted Tucker, her face was unknown, her identity a secret. Who was she? Where had she been last night?

Johnny quickly fell into a feverish sleep.

He was awakened many hours later by a ringing phone. It was his cell phone, lying on a table across the room. He almost tipped out of bed and onto the floor as he struggled to rise, his body resisting efforts to unfold and stand. Flipping his phone open, he answered, "Denovo." His voice sounded like wet sandpaper.

"Johnny, it's Tom," McNaught said. "Are you OK?"

"I'm fine," Johnny replied, trying to steel his voice but coughing instead.

"You sound ill," McNaught stated. "You've heard about the virus that was released at the Pru, haven't you?"

"Yeah, I've heard about it," Johnny responded.

"Well, I hope you don't get that," McNaught said, laughing slightly. "Anyhow," he continued, sounding grim suddenly, "the blackmailer's back. My deadline came and went. He called."

"Did you get a number?" Johnny asked.

"No, it was a private caller," McNaught said. "He's threatening to go to the media."

Johnny chuckled, starting a rumbling coughing fit. "Let him go."

"What do you mean?" McNaught flared. "I don't want this in the press."

Johnny tried to take a deep breath, but failed. He coughed some more. "You're not thinking clearly. Do you really think a salacious blackmail story is going to make the news this weekend? There's been a bio-terrorism attack, and there are more threatened. It's not a slow news cycle. It's a bluff." Johnny coughed again, a dry, hollow hack.

McNaught was silent for a moment. "I see what you mean. You're much better at this than I am. I get it. It's an empty threat."

"Right," Johnny confirmed. "He's powerless. The media's in a feeding frenzy."

"OK," McNaught said. "Sorry. I panicked. I should have remembered, should have realized. I'll let you go, then. I hope you feel better."

"Thanks," Johnny replied. "Did you get anything else from the call? Recognize a voice? Anything at all?"

"Nothing," McNaught said. "He sounded angry, but I didn't recognize the voice. Sorry."

"That's OK. By the way, do you have a picture of your wife and one of your mistress? I don't even know what they look like."

McNaught cleared his throat. "I do, but I'd rather not pass those along."

"Get over it," Johnny said abruptly. "Did I mention how many times I've been in jeopardy for this case? You can share a couple of pictures. Go to a public computer if you have to, but get me one of each. I need to know what they look like."

"All right, I will," McNaught pledged, sounding overwhelmed. "I have to run an errand anyhow. I'll send one of each soon."

"Great. I've got to go," Johnny concluded, closing the phone as another coughing fit beset him. He tossed the phone back on the glasstop table and crawled into bed, his body feeling like an empty ketchup packet, limp and bled, ready to be thrown away.

He had just pulled the covers over his shoulders when his cell phone rang again. Johnny poured out of bed with lassitude and weariness. Flipping open the phone, he sighed, "Denovo."

"Johnny, it's Dr. Deresinski," the voice said. "We spoke the other day. I'm on official business. I've been put on an emergency task force based on the events unfolding today. We're checking every angle. Do you know anything about this outbreak?"

Johnny groaned inwardly, but managed to maintain his well-practiced façade of cool nonchalance.

"Just enough to feel confident that it's not terribly dangerous," Johnny mumbled.

"You sound sick," Deresinski countered. "Did you contract it, too?"

"Yes," Johnny confirmed. "But it's an annoyance. The bigger fish is still out there."

"And you've alerted the authorities?" Deresinski pressed. "You're involving the authorities, right?"

"As much as I need to," Johnny said evasively. "Have you cultured it?"

"We've analyzed it," Deresinski confirmed. "It's a standard adenovirus, but weaponized and sheathed in an unusual manner. That's what has us worried. Now that I know you're sick, I'm going to have to call Homeland."

Johnny paused, hovering on the edge of annoyance and collaboration. Deresinski was a potential ally, but he didn't know all the details. Involving Homeland would slow things down, take his investigation off the rails. This was getting a bit out of hand.

"If you could hold off, I'd appreciate it," Johnny said at last. "I have connections into the agencies, and I'll use them when I need to. I'm very close to asking Homeland for help myself. But I have a client I need to protect, who has nothing to do with this. I need some time to line things up a little better. Then I'll call them. I know who to contact."

Deresinski cleared his throat. "I'm not comfortable with this," he stated. "This is big. I'm going to have to let them know at least that you have a related investigation. How they handle it from there is up to them. But I can't just let this go. It puts too much on my shoulders."

Johnny coughed.

"I understand," he managed at last. "That's fair. But I'm going to keep running an independent investigation."

"Fine," Deresinski replied in obvious relief. "I'll call them now. And feel free to call me if you need help or treatment."

"Thanks," Johnny finished quickly, another coughing spell coming on him. He closed his phone with a snap. He didn't want bureaucratic entanglements, but Deresinski was in a tough spot. This would complicate things, but he'd dealt with worse. He'd manage.

His coughing subsiding, he slid the phone back on the glasstop table and tumbled sideways into bed, pulling the covers over his entire body in a desperate effort to fend off the chills that had started climbing out of his ribs.

Falling asleep quickly, he missed the silent vibration of his phone as a text message came across: "Sorry UR sick. G."

Chapter 28
Squeeze Play

When Johnny finally awoke, the sun was low in the sky. His muscles protested every movement, rebelling against their owner, seeking stillness in which to recover. He wanted to ignore the pain, get back into the case, mix things up. He knew it wasn't his muscles that were protesting but his nerves. They were agonizing over the pressure from the inflamed tissues wrapping them. They transmitted their displeasure with each flex, each step. The sickness was baking into him. He couldn't overcome it through sheer willpower.

Food. Johnny needed something. He felt lightheaded. He rose slowly, sitting first, a bout of shivers rattling his bones. He stood as it subsided, walking hesitantly to the kitchen.

Glancing reflexively at his cell phone as he passed, he noticed a text message awaiting him. He stopped, peering closely at the words, his watery eyes making it difficult to focus and causing him to blink rapidly as he tried.

"Signed 'G,' huh? And how did you know?" he wondered aloud, studying the message again to make sure. His immediate reaction was to assume the message was from Gleason. But why? Why would the person who dumped him in the infected fountain send him a sympathy text message? And how did he get his unlisted cell number? Deresinski had caller ID, but Gleason? Maybe he'd picked up the number when Johnny was in New Hampshire. He had infrastructure.

There were too many puzzles for him right now – he was weary, sick, and hungry. He shuffled onward, his empty stomach propelling him to his regular phone.

He dialed Wei Chou, who heard Johnny's voice and immediately intuited that won-ton soup was the order of the day. And lots of it.

"By the way, Johnny," Wei whispered into the earpiece, "you have company down here. Suits, earpieces, black car. They look like Homeland stiffs."

"How many?" Johnny asked, a pulse of defensive anger rising in his sternum. As promised, Deresinski had called up the chain, and now Johnny had to deal with these potholes.

"Two," Wei said more clearly. "What do you want to do?"

"Nothing for now, but thanks for letting me know. I was expecting them, but not this quickly," Johnny replied. "I might need to use the back way soon, though. Think you can have everything ready?"

Wei chuckled to himself. "Sure, just give me a few minutes notice. I'll have it all set."

Probably because of the surveillance surrounding the building, Wei delivered the soup himself, his sincere nursemaid personality coming forth in all its apron-clad glory. He was an excellent father, Johnny knew. It was good to have him on his side.

Leaving the condo, Wei reminded Johnny, "Just give me five minutes notice if you need me."

"I'll call you on your cell," Johnny replied, opening the lid on the large tureen of soup Wei had brought up. Wei closed the door with a wink.

The soup tasted tremendously good. The salt, warmth, and liquid were absorbed ravenously by his depleted body.

He began to feel better almost immediately. Glancing around his condo with heightened awareness, his eyes lingered on his still-damaged front door, a vivid reminder of the high stakes in the game he was now a part of. If Homeland made their way up here, they'd have no problem prying the door open or breaking it down. He wished he had Tucker's security system full of secret snares.

Studying the door also reminded him of Gleason and the recent text message. Revived by Wei's soup, Johnny's mind was feeling sharper. Some strength had returned to his muscles. He stretched cautiously.

Gleason's text message was short and sympathetic, but how he knew to send it was a mystery. Yet, the motivation was more puzzling to Johnny. Taken at face value, it could be sincere. After all, Gleason had acknowledged that Johnny played a role, was part of the plan now – whatever that plan was.

However, Johnny thought perhaps the message had a more pragmatic subtext, with Gleason wanting to communicate that he could reach Johnny in yet another way, through his private cell phone number.

This triggered a thought. Johnny rose slowly to retrieve his cell phone. Opening it, he scrolled to the text message Gleason had sent and reviewed the details.

As he'd hoped, Gleason's cell phone number had registered as well.

Now, Johnny had an important piece of the Gleason puzzle, something Tucker would probably want. Johnny would have to hold it as a bargaining chip in case he needed to coax his friend into more work in a hurry.

He texted a quick reply: "Thx. J."

The connection was now mutual.

Quickening his pace as best he could under the circumstances, Johnny finished his soup and went over to his computer.

He still needed to figure out Gleason.

What kind of idea was he?

The metaphors around Gleason confused him. At his compound in New Hampshire, the wires overhead had been buried underground, and Gleason had entered an underground bunker.

Yet his attacks had relied on smoke.

He was hiding. It suddenly occurred to Johnny that Gleason was underground in more senses than one – hoping to conceal the electricity going to his house, both from attack and from observation, hoping to conceal his stash of weapons and other goods, and hoping to conceal himself.

Gleason was undercover. His metaphor was about concealing and revealing. Taking the bullet from Johnny's cupholder had been an act of revealing to Johnny that he was only attempting to scare him off. This text message was revealing Gleason's true self, while concealing his location and motives.

It all made sense now. Gleason was on their side, but hiding.

The question was, from what?

And why had the government been after him for years?

Rousing himself from his reverie, Johnny noticed that evening was creeping in, the light around failing as dusk approached. His eyes were still light-sensitive but he forced himself to turn on a lamp, if only to modulate the glare from his computer monitor. Having a full stomach now made everything a little easier to bear. Now, the gentle glow of a lamp added to the homey comforts he always sought when he was ill. It was a primordial need.

He clicked on his email.

McNaught had been true to his word, having sent an email two hours ago, two attachments included. One was named Heather, the other Ivy. Johnny opened both pictures immediately.

Despite being taken from different angles, one indoors with a flash, the other outdoors, he could see clearly that both women shared similar facial features. Heather's face was slightly more rounded in jawline and cheekbones. Her hair was longer than Ivy's and lighter in color. Her eyes were blue. Heather looked wise and a little weary in the photo.

Ivy had angular features, almost athletic in their overall effect. She looked more intense, both traits probably alluring for a middle-aged man seeking some excitement, Johnny thought. Her hair was cropped very short and tight to her head. She looked a little unhappy in the picture.

Now, there was one other woman Johnny wanted to take a look at, and that was the woman from the Green Monster. Tucker had sent over the video clip after analyzing it. Johnny had saved the email but hadn't watched the video. There hadn't been time. He'd seen the woman, so the video had seemed superfluous.

Now, he opened the file and played it.

It was her.

While a computer might be baffled by blowing hair strands, Johnny wasn't. Even the blowing hair and bad lighting couldn't conceal the true identity of the woman in the stands.

It was Ivy Thomson.

She was the signal caller, the sign girl.

She was the one on top of the Green Monster.

His limbs still complaining, but less so now, Johnny reached for the phone and dialed McNaught's cell phone.

"McNaught," Johnny rasped when he answered. "I need to ask you a question."

"Not a good time," McNaught said with false cheer in his voice. The sounds of a social event were in the background. "Can I call you back?"

"No time," Johnny barked. "What does Ivy do for a living?"

"Environmental advocacy of some sort," McNaught replied, his voice maintaining false social levity. "We don't really talk about it."

"Know who she works for?" Johnny asked.

"Some group with 'green' in the name, don't know the specifics. Look, sorry, if I have more, I'll call you back, but I need to go now," McNaught said, and the line went dead.

Fine, Johnny thought. I have my answer. Ivy Thomson is part of the plot. The long-lost daughter of the Gleasons, the mistress of his client, and now the signal caller for Paulson's plan. This complicated matters. It complicated matters a great deal.

Johnny quickly searched online for Ivy Thomson and environmentalism, hoping to find some hits. He was kicking himself for not having investigated the wife and mistress sooner. Mona's instincts a few days earlier had beaten his.

His search hit the mark. There were blogs, sites, and screeds aplenty, some written by Ivy herself. She was apparently one of the more extreme members of the environmental movement. An incendiary and restless voice emanated from her writings. Reading a few of her posts, Johnny found her voice strong and convincing, despite many strange leaps of logic and factual errors. She was a true believer, a leader in the movement.

He'd seen enough.

Johnny shuffled back to bed, weariness overwhelming him yet again. Now, he thought, the question was whether Ivy was another pawn in Paulson's plan or a willing participant.

As he lay down and closed his eyes, an image of Ivy raising a green sign high in the air over Fenway filled his mind, her hair blowing proudly. He felt angry.

No matter Ivy's willing involvement or innocent exploitation, Schwartz and Paulson and their sociopathic, money-driven plan had to be stopped.

Chapter 29
Against the Wall

Monday arrived with Johnny still ensconced in his condo, his illness imposing a quarantine of chills, weakness, and lassitude. And while the isolation allowed him time to contemplate the case, untangling threads, during his waking hours he yearned to claw his way back into the case. To add insult to injury, it was another glorious late-summer day. A cool breeze brought a distant whisper of fall to the air, but it was easily overpowered by the warm sun.

Johnny's symptoms were abating slightly. His joints were still afire and his lungs full. Breathing was extremely difficult at times as the illness waxed and waned. His stomach problems had ended, and doses of Wei's won-ton soup had given him renewed vitality.

Whatever Schwartz and Paulson had unleashed, it was bad enough. If they had something worse in store, Johnny could see how the plan would quickly come to fruition. The government would be willing to pay a very high price for some way to prevent the social panic that was already beginning to seep through Boston's spirit. People were worried. Threat levels were at their highest. The demonstration had installed a substrate of fear that could be exploited further.

Fortunately for the residents of Boston, the local medical establishment was among the greatest in the world, and physicians were readily available to treat the ill and reassure them via the media that the symptoms would pass in a few days. Already, the virus had been identified as a simple adenovirus, and the public alarm quieted as reporters began to understand and communicate that the situation was self-limited. Quickly, however, the alarm regenerated with questions like, "What Next?" and "Was This a Prelude?" as news commentators ratcheted up the dramatic music and creepy graphics. The interviews with victims only added to the mounting sense of a populace one step shy of hysteria.

Watching the local morning news, Johnny contemplated the panic a more virulent attack would bring. So far, because the first attack had occurred late at night and into the early hours, no children were affected, and few senior citizens. Most of the victims were not the kind to elicit worldwide sympathy or family-wide panic. But if the larger attack occurred, children and grandparents would be affected. The fright could quickly spiral out of control.

The fire hydrants served the plot to an extent, Johnny thought, but they were the slowburn part of the plan – a problem Paulson could promise to solve, thereby securing a lucrative government contract. Schwartz and Paulson still needed a big splash, a release of the new virus that would showcase its dangers. They needed to demonstrate that Cool & Green was capable of much more, that their claims were not just a bluff or a bad cold.

And they needed to do it soon, before the restless media spotlight moved on.

But how would they carry it off? He knew they could activate the network in the same way, most likely using the sign atop the Green Monster and the same web site. But where would they make their signature move? Where would they stage the major attack that would cement their plan, catalyze the exploitation?

They'd want to see to it themselves, Johnny thought. Paulson had seen to the attack at the Pru personally. There was precedence. And there was pride of invention here, a vanity that often led criminals to make predictable choices.

And Paulson was vain.

First, though, he needed to know what means Schwartz and Paulson possessed. He lifted his arm to reach for the phone, grimacing slightly as the body aches crept up his torso and through his limbs.

"Daniel," Johnny said in a dry voice when his call was answered. "It's Johnny."

"You sound awful," Daniel said in reply. "Are you all right?"

"You've heard of that virus that's going around, the one the environmental group is claiming they planted as evidence of the ills wrought by our industrialized society? I got it," Johnny whispered, finding it difficult to speak in long sentences, his lungs hungry for air.

"Oh dear," Daniel said. "I do hope you'll be better soon."

"Another couple of days," Johnny replied, keeping his sentences short and closing his eyes against the painful brightness of daylight. He felt dizzy without the horizon line to balance his senses. "Need a quick favor. James Schwartz. Geneticist. Owns Schwartz Genetics, Incorporated. What does he have insured? What property does he own?"

"A suspect of yours?" Daniel replied. "Am I right?"

"A person of interest," Johnny confirmed over the sounds of Daniel's two-fingered typing.

"I see," Daniel said distractedly. "Just a moment. Owns Schwartz Genetics, you say? Well, he's the owner of record, but the founder was a Robert Paulson. The insurance is still under his name. Says here that a James Schwartz is the CEO of Schwartz Genetics, but the insured is Robert Paulson. So, which one do you want the property report to cover?"

Johnny was getting used to this dyad. But even in his compromised state, he felt his adrenal glands kick in. A rush of wellness surged through his body. Paulson was the founder of Schwartz Genetics and still listed as the insured? Zeller hadn't found this in his study of the company. It wouldn't jump out to anybody on the public side. Daniel had the insurance angle. The fact that Paulson was insured changed Johnny's thinking dramatically.

"Daniel," Johnny said in a stronger voice, pushing himself into a more upright sitting position. "How long ago did Paulson found Schwartz Genetics?"

More typing from the other end of the phone. "It was incorporated 10 years ago, but as a private entity. It's not unusual for an owner to turn the keys over to a CEO when a company goes public, you know, transfer operational control. Happens all the time. Some founders are notoriously secretive, so having a name swept under the rug would be trivial, beneath notice."

"Beneath notice," Johnny echoed, carefully maintaining his composure as his mind raced. "Can I get personal property reports for both of them?"

"Certainly," Daniel replied. "They have different personal insurers, so it will take a while. Can I have until the end of the day?"

"How about by three o'clock?" Johnny countered. "The more time I have before the evening, the better things will be."

"Three o'clock," Daniel confirmed. "I'll email you the information by then. You will let me know what happens, won't you?"

"I'll tell you when I bring the gift by," Johnny replied. "You and your wife will like this one, I'll make certain. I'll use a disinfectant before I wrap it."

Daniel laughed. "Feel better."

"Thanks. Three o'clock."

"Three o'clock," Daniel confirmed, the phone disconnecting.

After hanging up with Daniel, Johnny sank back, the aches and pains returning as the adrenaline rush abated. Paulson was an enigma. Not only was he two-faced in the literal sense, using a rare nervous system physiology to alter his appearance at will, but he was an assistant at the company he owned.

Above and below, simultaneously.

An idea suddenly occurred to Johnny. The circle was closing. He felt another surge of adrenaline liberate him from his symptoms briefly.

He dialed McNaught's cell phone.

"Tom McNaught."

"Tom, it's Johnny Denovo," Johnny said in a voice that sounded surprisingly normal after two days of croaking like a frog. "I have a question for you."

"Give me a minute," McNaught said. "I have to close the door." There was a pause, the sound of a firm click, and McNaught returned. "Go ahead."

"Does the name Robert Paulson mean anything to you?" Johnny asked.

"Can't say that it does," McNaught replied. "Why do you ask?"

"Did you ever employ anybody by that name?" Johnny pressed.

"Might have. Let me check. We have thousands of employees, especially when you count those who have moved on," McNaught reflected. "I don't use the HR database often, so this might get ugly. Let me see what I can find." There was the sound of typing, then silence. McNaught spoke again after a long pause. "We did employ a Robert Paulson for about six months," McNaught confirmed. "It was in the early days of the company. He was a bench rat. Worked on a project Schwartz was heading when he was in a different role in the company. Then Paulson left. Looks like he gave notice. No personnel reviews, he wasn't here long enough, but no disciplinary actions, nothing really stellar or bothersome either way. Just a lab rat who moved on. We have boatloads of those, as you might imagine."

"And what was the project he and Schwartz worked on together?" Johnny asked.

"Minor thing," McNaught replied. "Synthetic lipid sheaths for inserting viruses into bacteria. It's a futile effort, real Don Quixote work. We keep tilting at some of these windmills, but haven't had a breakthrough yet. It's a shame, really. Paulson must have grown frustrated. He wouldn't be the first, believe me. I know Schwartz asked to work on other things a long time ago, too. That's when I made him the company physician. He felt this one couldn't be cracked."

So there was the answer. Paulson had cracked it, and the patent Zeller had discovered linked to the one he used to found the company, drawing Schwartz in as the CEO so they both could exploit the breakthrough. Paulson needed Schwartz to have enough patents in play at his new company that the key one would be concealed in an intellectual property snowstorm. It would look just like a reference patent, but it had been the breakthrough patent. Paulson was hiding not only his talents as a geneticist, but his breakthroughs, role, and power over Schwartz.

Johnny thanked McNaught and reassured him that the blackmailer would still be stymied, with the media attention fixed squarely on the crisis the virus had generated.

Hanging up the phone, he sank back, another infusion of adrenaline exhausted, leaving him feeling even more ill and fatigued.

He closed his eyes again and began to think about trees once more.

There was more than one tree here. He needed to study the forest.

The blackmail still bothered him. While it was clearly meant to sideline McNaught, who actually carried it out? He had no evidence that it was Paulson or Schwartz. Neither of them seemed to be on that flightplan. They were headed somewhere else.

Johnny thought back to the scene he'd imagined at Grand Central station, the acoustic sweet spot. The term "earshot" bubbled up in his mind again, surfaced by his insistent limbic brain. It still mattered. Why? Who would be listening on the other end?

There was a third person involved.

The woman in the stands, Ivy Thomson, the Gleasons' long-lost daughter. She could have been the third person, another pawn in Paulson's game.

Another scenario played out in his mind. Ivy was sleeping with McNaught, but, through her blind anger about environmental degradation, found herself truly in league with Schwartz and Paulson. She was the environmentalist link to all this. By keeping an eye on McNaught and gaining access to information from his sphere of the bio-tech realm, she had been doing her part. But she'd grown disenchanted and wanted out, and with more than just her liberty restored. She wanted to make McNaught pay. In her mind, he was part of the problem. She'd been listening in on the conversation at Grand Central station, wanting to know for certain that Schwartz had delivered the news that she was the sister of McNaught's wife, that the affair was about to be exposed. Then, it would be time to turn the tables.

Ivy Thomson was carrying out the blackmail, he tried to conclude.

His cerebrum didn't like the answer. There wasn't enough of a logical framework to support it. Why sideline him in such a relatively gentle way? Why not hamstring him more certainly?

There was something almost polite about the approach.

Maybe there were extenuating circumstances?

His limbic brain purred happily, indicating a direct hit.

But these circumstances weren't clear. Was she freelancing? Was she collaborating with Schwartz and Paulson? Or did she have feelings for McNaught?

And who was providing the male voice for the phone contact with McNaught?

Then it occurred to him – it didn't matter to the task at hand. The blackmail was a diversion. While he had an inherent compulsion to figure everything out, understand each piece of a crime, this one he had to let go. It was immaterial. It was meant to paralyze McNaught, distract him from being aware and available. It was an insurance policy of some sort. A sideshow, a feint, a bit of misdirection.

He needed to ignore it for now.

He felt his body relax, his mind slow. Sleep crept through his bones and he reverted to unconsciousness, an immobile pile in the chair, dozing.

Hours later, Johnny awoke grudgingly, a faint ringing sound disrupting his nap. As consciousness resumed, the ringing became louder, and Johnny realized it came from the phone he'd let drop at his side. He picked it up and glanced at the caller ID. It was Daniel.

His mouth was dry and neck sore as he accepted the call.

"Hello." His voice sounded disembodied.

"Hello Johnny, it's Daniel. I've emailed you the file you wanted. Very interesting property situation. Paulson may own the company, but Schwartz owns more property," Daniel related. "And I mean a lot more. Boats, cars, houses, a small plane. Paulson owns almost nothing, or at least insures almost nothing, other than the company."

"Really?" Johnny said, limiting his conversation as much as possible. "Off-shore, too?"

"Ah, I see," Daniel replied. "Well, he could be hiding stuff in some of those well-known safe-havens in the Caribbean," Daniel mused. "I can't list everything. In any event, you have the file. It's an unusual ownership-to-property ratio. Take a look. You sound terrible, so I'll let you go now. Call if you need more, and good luck."

"Thanks," Johnny rasped, and hung up. More strangeness emanating from this little den of iniquity, Johnny thought, struggling to his feet. The analgesics had worn off, leaving the aches and pains free to plague his mind as he moved to his computer. He seated himself with a groan.

The file Daniel had sent over indeed showed Schwartz as owner of a small plane in Connecticut, a large boat harbored in Boston, and a number of cars and houses.

The houses were scattered around. Most were out West – vacation destinations or, in the event of a waterborne infection being let loose and transmitted through the densely populated Eastern seaboard, a retreat. Literally.

Johnny noticed the clock. Daniel had beaten his deadline. But another deadline was looming – the Red Sox returned home tonight, and Johnny sensed the crescendo was coming.

Chapter 30
Home Run

As evening approached, Johnny forced himself to eat again. Wei brought up more won-ton soup and even dared Johnny to add some fried rice to his diet, worrying over him like a lonely aunt.

"Eat, eat, you'll feel better," Wei said waving his hand at Johnny imploringly as he left. He'd delivered the meal and arranged it all on the table. "Eat it all. Call if you need more. I don't mind. It's on your tab anyhow," Wei finished, laughing. "Remember, the Homeland suits are still downstairs. It's Day Three for them. They're working in shifts, and this pair is really ugly. We can still use the back way with just a few minutes' notice."

Johnny smiled and raised his spoon in a happy gesture, his mouth full of soup. It would take a while to digest all of it, but he was finding his appetite again. He felt the upswing of a recovery coming. But the pain from interminable body aches still distracted him.

In the midst of his slow meal, he consumed more pain relievers and anti-inflammatories, trying to time things so that the small relief they provided lasted the bulk of the evening. He didn't know what would happen tonight, but he needed to be ready for anything.

Finishing his meal, he sat for a while, letting his stomach settle and the nutrients suffuse his bones. After an hour or so, he showered and changed, setting his jacket and baseball cap near the front door.

Through text messages, he and Tucker had agreed to watch the game on television from Tucker's condo. Text messages weren't likely to be monitored by Homeland Security's surveillance monkeys, but they had coded their short phrases a little just to be sure.

Tonight, they would watch more views than just the edited broadcast would provide. Tucker had called in a favor at the local sports network and was now set up to tap into the video feeds from the truck. Johnny wanted to see every possible angle.

Now, the challenge was to get to Tucker's undetected, with two Homeland goons downstairs surveying his condo and watching his building's main entrance. He not only had to leave, but he had to make the sentinels think he was still in his condo, too sick to travel anywhere.

Johnny knew the phones would be tapped, his as well as Wei's. He couldn't call Wei using his own phone without being overheard. He needed another way to communicate with him, and since text-messaging was forbidden in the Chou household, that option didn't exist.

It was time for a little subterfuge.

Walking over to his computer, he clicked on one of the internet telephone applications he kept on-hand for emergencies. These communication channels were much harder to monitor, and he doubted Homeland was competent with these new technologies yet. Homeland consisted of retreaded FBI flatfoots and paper-pushers, for the most part. They tended to be old-fashioned, by-the-book types.

But Wei's phone would still be monitored.

The first trick was to call Wei without letting anyone know who was calling. To the tracers, he would make it look like a blocked caller ID on an internet phone call. The next trick would be controlling what they said.

Johnny dialed Wei's number. Wei picked up on the second ring.

"Wei Chou's, where the food's way good. Can I help you?"

"Mr. Chou, it's Mister Lyman from around the corner," Johnny said in his best mixed-European accent. "Do you remember me? We go way back."

"Ah, Mr. Lyman, such a pleasure to have your call. Yes, way back indeed."

"I'd like a delivery for one, please."

"Of course, Mr. Lyman. What would you like?"

"Something quick. I'm in a hurry. Maybe the Pad Thai?"

"Pad Thai it will be, Mr. Lyman," Wei said courteously. "I will have your delivery to you as soon as possible. I'll make the normal substitutions. I know you're watching your health. And don't worry, I know the destination."

"See you soon, then," Johnny said in his quasi-Swiss accent, clicking the phone application off.

He only had a few minutes now. His muscles ached as he strode around his condo. He walked slowly, wanting to look incapacitated. As he roamed, he slipped his cell phone in the jacket lying near the door. He wrapped the jacket around his baseball cap. He also nonchalantly opened the deadbolt on his front door.

He'd have to grab and go when Wei did his magic.

It was only a minute or so before Johnny could smell smoke. Shortly, he'd hear the sirens. He turned on his television and lay down on the couch, making sure his trademark thatch of black hair was visible over the top of the pillow.

The sirens were approaching, their faint wail coming closer by the moment. They must have sent a battalion, judging from the din.

As the sirens blared below, Johnny waited patiently for the right moment.

The sirens stopped, but the lights still flashed on the adjacent buildings.

It was only a matter of time. He'd have to move quickly.

The lights went out. Dim emergency floods clicked on. Johnny knew these lights showed next to nothing through his condo's tinted windows.

Still, he wanted to be sure.

He rolled off the couch and crawled across his pale tile floor, the coolness threatening to set off another bout of chills. Standing up in the shadows by his front door, he grabbed his jacket off the small table he'd set it on, then moved to the door.

At that moment, the door opened, and a scrawny teenager – Wei's nephew – entered, leaving the door ajar for Johnny, who stood up and slipped through.

"Hi, Zach. I was lying on the couch over there. Keep your hair showing over the top of the pillow to start. Watch TV. Act sick. Eat whatever you want. Thanks, Z," Johnny whispered to the young man, their eyes meeting. They were the same height, and the teen's thick black hair was similar enough. Homeland should bite.

His door closing behind him with a click, Johnny donned his jacket and baseball cap. He had to wait for a wave of dizziness to pass. Standing quickly was still too much for him.

After a moment, the lights in the building flickered on.

It was a quirk of the place, but to reset the fire alarm, the main power switch had to be thrown so the system would reset. Twenty years ago, it might have seemed a good idea, but now it was just an oddity Johnny could exploit when he needed to disappear.

Darting down the hall, his weak legs complaining, he pushed open the storeroom door at the back of the hall.

He pressed the down button on the service elevator.

The contrast between the posh décor of the hall – damaged as it was by the recent bombing – and the stark service area was extreme. Property values like his were only skin deep, Johnny mused as he waited for the elevator.

The bell dinged as the elevator arrived. The doors opened. Empty. He turned as he entered and pressed "B" at the same time as the Close Door button. Speed was still required.

The elevator lurched as it reached bottom.

Stepping out in the much larger main service area, Johnny glanced to his left. The exit's bright warning stickers beckoned. He opened the door, setting off a wailing alarm. He didn't pause.

Outside, a sleek red sport bike idled, its tiny driver dressed in shiny leathers, a black helmet completing the outfit. Only the high heels revealed his driver was a woman.

Wei had sent a racing bike.

The motorcyclist nodded tersely at the seat behind her. Johnny turned his baseball cap backwards and mounted the bike, placing his hands on the driver's hips. The engine revved, and they sped off, turning quickly down a narrow alley, weaving side to side to avoid dumpsters and debris.

Johnny felt the motorcyclist give a satisfied sigh as he clung to her, his hands now wrapped about her thin waist, the speed and tight cornering requiring a firmer grip.

He smiled to himself. Apparently, Wei's shy delivery girl was also a speed demon who could fearlessly handle a crotch rocket at high speeds. He gave her a little squeeze of recognition and their bodies relaxed together as the speed increased.

In a matter of seconds, Johnny and his driver were blasting along the wharf, the low buildings hunkered down against the waterlines like beached whales. Boston's waterfront was quiet. Autumn's slumber had started and heightened threat levels were keeping people indoors. The city was tense.

The noise of the motorcycle's engine reverberated through the empty streets, trailing off behind them like a wild animal's guttural howl of longing.

Stopping abruptly, the bike nearly threw him off to the side as the driver tipped it toward the curb. Johnny responded with quick reflexes, landing on the sidewalk with both feet. A tire squealed, and the bike was away, the black rider disappearing into the night.

Johnny didn't bother to dust himself off. He turned and quickly made for Tucker's building, afraid he might be seen.

By the time Johnny arrived, Tucker had arrayed his computer monitors and a number of televisions of various sizes across a wall of his den, making the longest wall look like part video-editing studio, part unfinished puzzle game. More than a dozen images of Fenway Park competed for Johnny's attention as camera operators adjusted and toyed with their equipment, checking focal lengths, angles, and lighting, even before the first pitch was thrown.

"Man, you look awful," Tucker said as Johnny shuffled into the room, putting his hat and jacket on a table near the open door. "Are you sure you're not contagious anymore?"

"No, I'm not sure, but you're just going to have to take your chances," Johnny replied. "And thanks for the support."

"Sorry, Johnny," Tucker apologized. "You know I hate being sick, and you look like Typhoid Johnny, all rheumy and sloppy like that. It just sets me on edge."

"I'll sit way over here," Johnny replied, indicating a chair across the room from Tucker. "Will that help?"

"That'll help," Tucker answered happily. Johnny knew his friend hated disease, hated being ill. It slowed him down, and Tucker disliked anything that slowed him down. The two had this in common, but because he was healthy, Tucker deserved a respectful distance.

The illness issue put to rest, Tucker continued. "OK, here's the deal. The four monitors in the middle are the replay monitors. Those are the ones the truck cycles through to pick and edit replays. The others are live camera shots, and the monitor over here," he said, gesturing to a television set apart from the others on a small end table, "is what the viewers at home are seeing. You like?"

"I like," Johnny confirmed. Having watched for a minute or two, he'd begun to understand what he was seeing, started to sense a flow inherent in the information. It felt rational now, not chaotic but multifaceted. His head no longer rebelled against the onslaught.

"Is Mona there yet?" Johnny asked, motioning to the bank of monitors, indicating Fenway with his gesture.

"She says so. She called about 10 minutes ago," Tucker answered. "That was a good idea, getting her those tickets. I was able to find a scalper pretty quickly tonight. The Sox did well on the road trip, so the fans are taking a breather. Plus, on a Monday night with school back in session, supply was plentiful. She and her two companions are down the third base line. They have a good view of the Green Monster."

"Great. Now, to the surveillance," Johnny said with weak bravado, his illness still sapping his vitality.

"Are you sure you're up to this?" Tucker asked.

Johnny smiled weakly. "Don't mother me, Thiesen," he said with some menace in his voice. "I can still break you."

Tucker scoffed. "You couldn't break wind in the state you're in, Denovo. Just sit back and watch the pretty lights," he said with a flourish toward the wall of televisions facing them both.

The game was beginning. The starting lineups were being introduced with a lot of fancy graphics appearing on the television tuned to the finished broadcast. Yanking his eyes away, Johnny forced himself to scan the other monitors, with their panning cameras, lack of graphics, and multiple unreconciled angles. The edited version with the slick graphics and dazzling transitions was much more familiar than the raw feeds from the production truck. Images bounced, went in and out of focus, and wandered as cameramen responded to commands from the director and changes in their surroundings.

As the game got underway, the cameras settled into some level of synchronization, but the raw images were still distracting, making Johnny a little nauseous. He settled his stomach by watching solely for the Green Monster and focusing on any image featuring it. Soon, he began to sense habits and pace in the camera work, allowing him to routinely predict when a camera would shoot the landmark.

"You want something to drink?" Tucker asked, peering over his computers at Johnny.

"Do you have any sparkling water?" Johnny asked.

"One sparkling water, one beer," Tucker confirmed, jumping up and heading into his kitchen. Johnny glanced out of habit at the large artwork on the wall, the blocks still filled with little lightning bolts. He hoped his illness didn't change his biological profile somehow and trigger the system. Those little designs portended something painful.

Tucker returned a moment later, a bottle of beer in his left hand, a tall glass of fizzing water in his other.

"Let me know if you want more," he urged Johnny, handing him the glass and turning to watch the monitors. "Ain't this cool? I'm thinking I'm going to leave this up for the playoffs. Should have thought of this earlier, you know?"

"It doesn't drive you crazy, watching all the feeds?" Johnny asked, cradling the cold glass in his hands.

"A little," Tucker confided. "But it's also like being there. You get to glance around. There's more freedom. I like it."

Johnny could see his friend's point. It was a little liberating to have so many perspectives on the game and the setting. Stealing a glance over at the the network's finished version, he realized how impoverished the unified broadcast was, now that he'd seen all the options. He might join Tucker to watch more games this way.

He sipped at his cool mineral water as the first few outs were recorded. There weren't many fielding opportunities – a pitching duel was being staged in the early innings as the cool autumn temperatures gave the ball life. It was diving and sliding away from hitters.

It was hard to stay awake. The adenovirus had sapped his energy and his eyes felt soggy, heavy. He had almost drained his drink. He set the glass down on a side table, his hands relaxing at his sides. The low, monotonous voices of the announcers, themselves bored by the late-season pitcher's duel, added to his sonorous state. Soon, despite Tucker's enthusiastic responses to the great curveballs and borderline pitches, Johnny nodded off.

He awoke with a start, Tucker's loud war whoop shattering his sleep.

"Home run!" Tucker shouted. "Bottom of the eighth! Just what we needed!"

Johnny's eyes roamed wildly in the mental disarray following the rude awakening. The room seemed to waver in front of him. He blinked hard and stared straight ahead to focus and steady his gaze, the bank of television monitors providing hard rectangles and edges that helped him stabilize his eyesight. He blinked again, and this time he saw on a monitor a shot of the Green Monster, a large green sign held aloft atop it. He glanced at the network coverage off to the side, and the shot was replicated there, clarifying his scattered attention even more. Judging by how some fans to the side were scrambling for a ball at their feet, the home run had gone up into the Monster seats.

"What did you say?" Johnny croaked, his throat dry.

"Home run, my man!" Tucker bellowed again pointing at the televisions, his eyes transfixed on the replay monitors, apparently trying to anticipate the angle they would choose for the highlight. "Don't tell me you missed it?"

"I fell asleep," Johnny confessed. "Tucker, look at the Green Monster."

Tucker's disposition became instantly serious as he scrutinized the shot from the network. "The green sign's up. Why's that? It wasn't a third-base play. It was a home run."

"It's the progression, Tucker!" Johnny shouted hoarsely, standing up suddenly and swaying a bit, unsteady with illness and torpor, sleep still clawing at his consciousness. "Third base was three-quarters of the way through the plan. Tonight, they're completing it! This is the signal for the end-game! This is it!"

Tucker stared at Johnny, then back at the monitor, then back to Johnny.

"Damn, I think you're right," he said loudly, almost bellowing. "First things first. We need to shut down the fire hydrant angle. That's the biggest issue."

Tucker moved swiftly and nimbly to the other side of his computer workstations, disappearing amidst the machines, donning a headset and frantically typing. He began speaking into the microphone arcing down his jawline.

"Netter, it's Thiesen," he said crisply. "I'm uploading a file. We have a code red. Local units should apprehend anyone near fire hydrants at these locations. We'll file charges later. Apprehension and detainment are the keys. This is not a drill. This is a code red, biological. Mobilize police and fire personnel. Get the ERs ready. We need bio-hazard units wherever possible. If water is spilled, contain and decontaminate. I repeat, this is not a drill. This is a code red, biological!"

There was more frantic typing from Tucker. Johnny glanced back at the game, his head clearing, sleep receding as adrenaline pumped into his arteries. A camera off the main broadcast showed a close-up of the counters along the top of the Green Monster. The seat where the woman had perched was empty. She was gone.

"Definitely the end-game," he muttered to himself over the sound of Tucker's typing.

There was a loud, definitive keystroke, and Tucker fell silent. His breathing was audible, but controlled.

"That should give them what they need," he finally uttered. "Virus type, GPS coordinates, case profile, suspect profile. It should lock down pretty well. I did prepare a little, you know. But they have a few thousand locations to secure. Now what?"

"Water," Johnny said, bringing his voice under control. "They're going to take the virus to the water. But where?"

"I sent those hydrant coordinates, too," Tucker reassured him.

"What about the rivers? The harbor?" Johnny pressed. "We're at the epicenter. The bad guys are here. They don't need to rely on the network. They can foul the waters themselves."

"What, just drop it in the water?" Tucker scoffed.

"Why not?" Johnny asked. "It would only spread it farther. They want an outbreak. The hydrants are the slow burn, but they want a catalyzing event, a kick-start. This city is the epicenter, and it's surrounded by water."

"If it's the end-game," Tucker said pensively, "they want the biggest distribution they can get. So we ignore the rivers. Too slow-moving. Plus, they want things to dry, not stay wet. Rivers at this time of year are receding and there aren't many people in them. No vessels except near where the harbor ends."

"Right," Johnny agreed. "You want things that dry, a lot of churn, a wide distribution."

"It's got to be the harbor," Tucker stated. "Would they just throw it in?"

"No, there's something more," Johnny murmured. "But you're right, the harbor makes sense. You'd want the boat traffic. The virus clings to the hulls, the ropes, the decks. It gets into the Charles from the harbor, gets the sailboats, the sculls. It travels around the world in some cases. The outbreak is magnified. In fact, the harbor would be key to their plan. The fire hydrants are for America, the harbor is for the rest of the world."

Tucker leaned back. "Damn, that's devious," he said admiringly. "I hope you never go to the dark side, Denovo. I've been telling you that for years. We'd all be dead."

"Thanks, I think," Johnny responded. "But what's the best way to spill virus into the harbor?"

"Hard to say," Tucker said thoughtfully. "It's got a lot of cross currents, and the Charles' flow is good but limited. Could be the Charles, I suppose. Maybe we shouldn't write off the rivers just yet."

"I suppose," Johnny answered. "But I don't think so. What about the scrubbers on Deer Island?"

"The scrubbers?" Tucker asked. "Oh, you mean the Eggs?"

"The Eggs," Johnny confirmed, the dozen 150-foot tall egg-shaped processing plants appearing in his mind. "They process millions of gallons of water a day. They distribute it throughout the harbor. The Eggs were *designed* to diffuse the water over a large area."

"The Eggs," Tucker repeated, this time not as a question. "Wouldn't the scrubbers eliminate the virus? They use chlorine to decontaminate the water, I think. The chlorine would kill them."

"Not viruses," Johnny said. "Chlorine doesn't kill viruses. Besides, these viruses are protected by a synthetic sheath, remember? They'll endure until they dry out."

"The scrubbers and filters?" Tucker asked hopefully.

"A virus is too small. It'll go right through."

"The Eggs," Tucker said for a third time. "I can't beat that. They churn the water all the time, day and night." Tucker leaned forward in his chair. "And you told me Schwartz owns a boat."

"That's right," Johnny confirmed.

"Then let's find it," Tucker bellowed, diving into his computer nest again, his keystrokes sounding like popcorn. "Got it. It's at the wharf just around the corner. Should we check it out?"

Johnny began to struggle up. "You stay here, keep your fingers on the pulse with the APB you've just issued. We need to make sure that piece doesn't get botched or shift beneath our feet," Johnny said, rising weakly to his feet. "I'll go check out Schwartz's boat."

"You're not up to it," Tucker insisted. "You're sick as a dog, weak as a kitten. Let me call in some muscle from Homeland."

"I'm up to it," Johnny responded, shrugging his jacket on while concealing a grimace as his muscles complained. "I just need to get going again. No time to argue." Johnny checked for his phone and scratched his head. "Don't call Homeland. We might be wrong. This could be a wild goose chase. Let me check it out first. I'll call you."

Chapter 31
Triple Play

In the depths of the night, the wharf was deserted, its silence broken only by the sounds of clanging buoys and waves slapping at hulls. Sulfur lights shimmered off the currents. Johnny's footfalls were barely audible on the soft, thick wooden planks.

Schwartz's boat was supposed to be tied up near the end, a large flying-bridge vessel. It had a name only Schwartz could muster – "The Codon."

Paulson wasn't the only vain one, Johnny mused. Leave it to a body-builder to also be vain about his boat's name.

As he approached the end of the dock, Johnny treaded more lightly and became aware of a spectrum of maladies he'd been able to ignore before – his persistent sniffles, sore throat, and cough, gifts from the adenovirus. He tried not to sniff, afraid that the noise would betray him. He also swore not to clear his throat, even as the secretions from his illness built up. The tickle from his cough had subsided. He could only hope it didn't return.

It was a very unpleasant set of problems to have when you needed to be clandestine.

Approaching the water, Johnny slowed his pace and began to plan his approach. There were some small outbuildings nestled up away from the water, the dock ambling around them to the boats. He headed for the cover they'd provide.

Peering around the edge of a storage shed, Johnny saw a row of fine boats, mostly sailboats but some larger pleasure craft, all moored and bobbing in the gentle waves created by the harbor breezes. Near the end of the pier, a short, muscular man was loading boxes onto a fishing boat with a flying bridge. It was Schwartz. Johnny knew his profile and physique. He could also make out the name of the boat, even as it swayed slightly in the water as the boxes were being loaded aboard, its gold letters reflecting the ambient light. The Codon. It all matched.

It was impossible from a distance to know what was in the boxes. Suppressing a sniffle, Johnny thought bitterly that he had a pretty good idea by this time. If he'd guessed right, the boxes contained loads of sheathed adenovirus, ready to slip into the waters just below the churning Eggs on Deer Island.

From there, the scrubbers would suck the water out of the harbor, process it, and pump it back into the bay, all day and night, the intact virus shunted out in the effluvium.

The scrubbers had done a magnificent job cleaning up a polluted harbor in the decade since they started. The waters were clear and blue again, not the sludgy gray they'd been.

Now, the Eggs would be appropriated to pollute it again, this time with a biological substance, invisible to the naked eye, one intended to paralyze the world with fear over the next few weeks, months, and years as boats traversed the seas and the virus released unpredictably in harbors and towns far from the point where it was injected.

Paulson would become a billionaire, the founder and the owner of the only company that could stop it, Johnny thought bitterly. And Schwartz would share in the winnings.

They only had to complete this final step, then wait.

But where was Paulson? Johnny glanced around, listening carefully. There was nobody else on the docks, only Schwartz grunting slightly as he lifted box after box onto his boat.

Paulson was nowhere to be seen.

Schwartz must have been sent out to do the dirty work. He was the muscle in all of this, Johnny thought, seeming enigmatic because he was merely a tool. Paulson was really orchestrating everything.

Schwartz placed the last box on the deck of the boat, hopping aboard with a sense of urgency that hinted at a schedule. Hustling amidships, he propped open a door and began moving the boxes onto the lower deck, the muffled grunts coming again as he hoisted the crates down into the hold.

Johnny's throat felt full, his eyes watery, and his nose threatened to drip. Wiping his nostrils with his jacket sleeve, he felt small, like a helpless little boy watching something bad happening but unable to do anything about it. He couldn't confront Schwartz physically in the shape he was in. Schwartz would easily overpower him. Johnny hadn't brought a weapon along. He only had his phone.

Suddenly conscious of another point of vulnerability, he reached into his pocket and muted the device.

As he did so, his phone vibrated. He pulled it out of his jacket pocket and glanced at the small display in the cover. A text message read, "Here 2. G." Johnny glanced around, but saw nothing. The dock looked deserted.

Nevertheless, he believed he had an ally nearby.

The stillness of the pier, the rhythmic lapping of waves, and the gentle dinging of buoys was beginning to lull Johnny, the deep fatigue of illness pouring over his tendons like a sauce, heavy and warm. His eyes fluttered closed briefly and his shoulder sagged against the frame of the small building.

Suddenly, the stillness was broken by the roar of a powerful engine starting. Johnny glanced back around the corner of the shed again, his alertness returning in a frenzied rush. Schwartz was preparing to depart.

A sense of panic gripped Johnny. He had to do something. Even in his weakened state, he couldn't allow himself to stand by and let

Schwartz have a free ticket to Deer Island to inject the Eggs with virus. He had to present some resistance, attempt to thwart the plan, or at least create enough of a stir that the plan fell apart under its own weight.

He thought fleetingly of calling in Homeland Security, but it was already too late – they were too slow and procedure-driven, and the decision point had arrived. He'd waited too long.

Now, he needed the benefits of speed and independence.

He moved to leave his hiding place behind the shed when a voice whispered behind him, "Going somewhere, dirtbag?"

He froze. He knew that voice, the venom in it, the formless anger. Without turning, Johnny responded.

"Hi, Paul."

The voice behind him chuckled and its owner spat onto the dock. "Very good. Or," the voice said, now taking on a vacuous quality, "you could call me Robert. Either way, it doesn't bode well for your future good health that I found you here."

As Johnny began to turn to face Paulson, he felt a gun press into the small of his back. He stopped, half twisted around. He could barely see his adversary. His whole body ached with illness.

It was Robert's face that greeted him, but atop it was Paul's tousled and manic hair, creating a strange hybrid of the two personas mixed together like a failed experiment.

"We know what you're up to," Johnny said calmly, sniffling for the first time in many minutes. It didn't matter if he made noise now. The relief was immediate, his head clearing even as he craned around to face Paulson. "You're going to fail."

"You think so, eh? You underestimate me, Denovo," Paulson said in Robert's more phlegmatic voice. "Even if we're caught, I'll be fine. Remember, I can be the innocent assistant, a victim of a power-mad scheme, as much a victim as anyone. I'm not taking the fall."

"What do you mean?" Johnny asked.

"If we insert the virus tonight, I get rich," Paulson said flatly. "If our plans are thwarted, Schwartz gets arrested, our corporate malfeasance insurance kicks in, and I still get rich. He's a fool."

Johnny's breath hissed from between his clenched teeth.

"Sociopath," he whispered.

Paulson growled in response. "Schwartz is just a plaything, a guy with a degree and polished manners but ultimately of no consequence to me. Not a real scientist, no business sense, no ability to go for the jugular. I do all that. He's just my hedonistic outlet and conspirator. He's disposable. No matter how things turn out tonight, I'll be set."

Johnny heard the Codon's engines rev to speed. The boat was pulling away from the dock. Out of the corner of his left eye and around the edge of the shed, he could just see the prow gliding ahead into the harbor.

"The only thing I have left to do is eliminate one or two loose ends," Paulson hissed, the gun digging into Johnny's back. "You and your friends will have to vanish. Yes, I know about them. I'll deal with them later. Now, it's your turn, you vainglorious prick. And I don't think you're strong enough to swim tonight. Am I right?"

Johnny watched the boat pull away, disheartened. Paulson had created a fallback position. He'd anticipated failure and set himself up to win despite it. In fact, he might even prefer perceived failure because then any suspicion of him would evaporate. Schwartz was not so lucky.

As the Codon pulled into full view, its stern rotating around until it was perpendicular with the pier, a dark figure appeared on the rear ladder, hunched down, with a strange load on its back. Paulson was too far behind the edge of the shed to see. Johnny concealed his eye movements as best he could, not wishing to give away his ally's advance.

He was convinced it was Gleason climbing aboard the Codon, the bulge on his back a scuba tank.

Gleason thought he was thwarting the plan, but he was playing right into it, Johnny thought despondently. He felt his cell phone vibrate.

"What was that?" Paulson demanded, leaning in toward the faint buzzing noise Johnny's vibrating cell phone had emitted.

Johnny sensed imbalance in Paulson's stance and pushed down and back with a violent jerk of his shoulder, his head striking Paulson's hard on the downstroke, his shoulder shuddering Paulson's jaw on the upstroke. With lightning speed, he spun and thrust his hands up into Paulson's eyes, his fingers feeling the damp squish of soft tissues and fluids, gouging mercilessly. Paulson shouted in pain and anger, grabbing for his eyes, his gun forgotten but still hooked over his index finger.

Johnny pushed away, his adrenaline flowing easily now, his dulled senses flooding away in the pain from knocking skulls. Paulson had turned, his head in his left hand while his right hand held the gun limply. Johnny struck his arm, and the gun fell on to the dock with a clatter.

Johnny kicked Paulson's gun away and heard it fall into the harbor with a splash. In that instant, Paulson lashed out, his eyes streaming and red, catching Johnny across the face with a solid right hook.

Recoiling from the force of the punch, Johnny staggered to regain his balance but failed, his weakened legs unable to muster the speed and strength necessary. Knocked to his knees, he raised his hands defensively, blocking the sole of Paulson's shoe as a hard level kick came for his head. He reached out instinctively, catching Paulson's foot in his hands. He twisted with all his might.

Paulson torqued in the air and fell to the dock with a slam, swearing as the air gusted out of his lungs.

Johnny had to release Paulson's foot. His strength was waning. The surge of adrenaline had allowed him to react normally for a couple of short bursts, but his sick muscles protested and collapsed of their own accord. He couldn't get them to respond. Feeling weaker by the moment, he stood unsteadily, Paulson rising quickly and with a vital menace Johnny couldn't match.

It was time for a strategic retreat.

Johnny backed as quickly as he could toward one of the pylons surrounding the dock, reaching a little desperately for the solid support it would provide, his bones feeling as soft as caramels.

Paulson rushed at him, his fury reflected in his red eyes, his pliable face twisted in a visage of rage unlike any Johnny had ever seen. The amazing nervous control Paulson possessed amplified and tightened his facial expression, stretching it into an animalistic and evil mask of primal fury.

Johnny was running out of options. Weak, tired, and pushed into the proverbial corner, he clung to the pylon on the side of the pier, watching as Paulson charged. Their eyes locked. But as Paulson neared, he lowered his head, breaking the connection.

He was running blind.

Johnny worked to time his next move perfectly. It was his only chance. If it failed, he'd be thrown into the harbor to drown and Paulson would prevail.

His adversary's breath was just beginning to warm his face when Johnny braced his back against the pylon and raised his left foot straight out, locking his knee, aiming his toes directly at Paulson's left knee. At the same time, he bent his upper body away from the pylon with all the strength he could muster in his arms, clinging by his fingers as his back strained against the twist. He needed the pylon free as a target for this to work.

Paulson's momentum was too great as it met Johnny's inertia. His knee struck Johnny's foot awkwardly and buckled with a pop. Out of control, Paulson tumbled into the pylon head-first, smacking it with a sickening puree of cartilage, flesh, and bone. A shine of blood coated his face immediately as streams erupted on impact. The repercussion from the collision with the pylon was so great that it snapped Paulson nearly upright. But he struggled on, thrashing and dislodging Johnny from his precarious hold on the pylon.

Johnny was falling, his ankle screaming in pain from the blow he'd delivered to his opponent's knee. He hit the dock hard, his phone clattering out in front of him.

He could only watch what happened next.

Stunned, Paulson flailed blindly, one leg useless, seeking his bearings, reeling in pain, his consciousness dimmed. His feet slipped on the edge of the dock just as his eyes rolled back in his head. Then Paulson fell into the murky waters like a dead weight, no sound from his throat, only a single splash marking his disappearance.

The splash was subdued, and soon the night was eerily silent once more, the stillness broken only by the low rumble of the Codon's engines in the distance.

His aching body protested mightily as Johnny extended an arm forward to retrieve his phone. He flipped it open. There was the text message that had distracted Paulson. It was from Gleason. He hadn't signed it, but Johnny recognized the number by now. "Beneath. Beacon. Fire. Trust me."

Gathering his resolve with a huff of exhale, Johnny flipped over on his back and began to get up, tucking his phone into the front pocket of his jeans. His ankle buckled slightly as he stood, the pain shooting up the center of his leg like an injection of acid.

The sound of the Codon's engine was directly ahead now, but growing fainter. He glanced out on the waters where he could just make out the spotty outline of the boat, its silhouette barely illuminated in the dappled and watery light.

Johnny stood at the edge of the dock. If he'd interpreted Gleason's message correctly, he knew he'd find something hidden underneath. Gleason shared the above/below metaphor with Paulson, but only in a tactical, pragmatic sense, not in a base, survival sense. The bunker in New Hampshire had shown him that much. The coincidence had confused him for a time, but no longer.

It was the same metaphor Paulson exhibited, but Gleason used it differently. For him, it was practical, not primal. Gleason was about concealment.

Johnny lowered himself to the ground again and knelt on the dock. He bent over the edge, peering below.

He was looking for a box. If he was right, he'd seen it once before.

After sweeping his eyes left to right a few times, he saw it – a long box resting on a bed of strapping running between a set of pylons, its wooden case green, its contents described with painted yellow letters and numbers.

The trick was how to get it out. It would be heavy, and Johnny had no leverage from above. Even with his full strength, he couldn't have lifted it. But sick and weak, he had no hope.

Only one option remained. Moving fast, he removed his jacket and kicked off his shoes, his left ankle slicing splinters of pain up his leg as he struggled to remove the shoe on that foot. Stifling a groan, he shed his jacket and dove into the water.

The cold penetrated his clothing immediately. He treaded water and made his way over to the bed of straps beneath the dock. Reaching up and grasping the straps with one hand, he was able to wiggle the box out slowly, pulling and shifting it while keeping his head above water. The effort became easier as he found a rhythm, but his congested lungs were struggling to keep up with the oxygen debt he was incurring.

At last, the box tipped out and fell with a gentle splash into the water. It floated innocuously, the unsecured lid tossed askew by the impact. It hadn't been sealed, probably intentionally. Gleason had anticipated things would have to happen in a hurry.

Johnny reached into the box and felt the heft and cold metal inside. Clinging to part of the strap webbing for support, he lifted the shoulder launcher from the box. Out of its buoyant container, the weight of the weapon threatened to drown him on the spot.

Johnny hoisted the launcher onto his shoulder as he pulled on the straps to balance himself. He tried to check the controls. The controls were set to a pre-programmed sequence. It didn't matter – bobbing in the waves made it impossible to contemplate using both hands to change settings or freelance it. He'd have to assume that

Gleason had envisioned the situation and placed a beacon onboard the Codon as the text message suggested. It was the only way now to stop Schwartz from releasing the virus. Johnny's aim alone wouldn't get this done.

Johnny turned toward the Codon, the shoulder launcher flopping forward and backward and side to side on his shoulder as he rose and sank in the water, his finger grasping for the right balance point while his body was tossed to and fro by the small but relentless waves. His other arm ached from clinging to the straps just above.

All around him, the night was silent. No cavalry was coming. He should have called for help. He'd overestimated his ability to handle this. The illness was leeching his energy bit by bit. He felt like an overturned bottle being emptied, helpless to stop the flow and quickly getting down to the bitter dregs.

A sense of desperation swept over him, a final push of adrenaline or a cry of survival, he couldn't discern, but it gave him a small surge of strength. His head cleared and his vision brightened. He had to make this work.

He had to level the weapon, stabilize it.

Bobbing in the waves, he didn't know how he could. Then he glanced up at the strapping Gleason had rigged beneath the dock, his fingers still grasping the nearest corner of it for support. In its entirety, it was almost the size of a small bed, and the weave of the straps was fairly tight. The clearance it provided between itself and the bottom of the dock was about two feet, Johnny judged.

It wasn't just a place to store a rocket launcher. It could also be a platform, he realized.

With a grunt, he heaved the launcher onto the bed of strapping, pushing himself beneath the waves with the effort. Spitting out a mouthful of seawater, he tried to lift his weight up, but his wet clothes added twenty pounds, and his cold, sick arms were too weak for the extra burden.

The first attempt failed. Johnny splashed back into the harbor with a groan.

Battling back to the surface and over to the platform, he looked out at the receding boat again. Without leverage in the water, Johnny felt defeated.

He couldn't do it. He was too weak.

Mustering one last desperate effort, he lifted himself up to the edge of the strap platform, then clawed forward from strap to strap, never letting go, spit forming at the corners of his mouth, his teeth gritting, his arms pleading for relief, his back straining until finally, with a great scream of effort, he pulled himself up and over, the launcher rolling into his side with a dull smack as his weight deformed the bed of nylon.

Orienting himself back toward the distant outline and lights of the Codon, Johnny reached into his front jeans pocket to retrieve his cell phone. Luckily, it hadn't fallen out or floated away.

The launcher pressed against his arm, limiting his movement and contributing to a claustrophobic feeling in the small space.

The wet phone was still working. The seawater had not yet done its inevitable, corrosive damage.

Somewhere off to his right, Johnny heard a small but distinct rush of water. Overhead, quick, worried footsteps circled. He tried to listen, but his aching head, sick and battered, was struggling with too many thoughts and sensations. He had to concentrate, shut out anything else except the rocket launcher and the Codon.

Opening his cell phone, Johnny found Gleason's last text message. He hit Reply, and then quickly texted, "Now." He pressed Send and wedged the phone, still open, into the webbing.

The footsteps overhead changed. There was another set of heavy, irregular footsteps. A man's voice shouted something Johnny couldn't make out. It was muffled by the waves and the dock. A woman's voice answered. It sounded familiar but angry.

He had to concentrate. He shut out the noises from above.

Johnny twisted his body and lowered his shoulder beneath the launcher, leveling the weapon and finding its balance point. He set the sighting on what he assumed in the darkness must be the horizon.

Above him on the dock, there was a scream and a pop, like a muffled gunshot or a small heavy object falling hard. Then there was another thump on the dock above. He fought to focus on the task at hand.

Something was happening overhead.

Johnny took a deep breath and pressed the trigger.

The missile exploded from the launcher with incredible force and bright yellow smoke, rocketing Johnny backward and upward with its violent repercussion. His head struck the underside of the dock, pain enveloping his skull.

The world turned black.

Above, Mona heard the pop and hiss of the rocket's launch and watched the contrail originating below her describe a straight line out into the murky night. In less than a breath, the missile found its target.

A vessel exploded in a fiery ball, lighting the harbor with a brilliant display of heat and light.

The flash illuminated the scene around Mona – a soaking wet dead man, a gun-toting double-agent, Johnny's jacket and shoes, and a visitor from New Hampshire who shook with fear while a bartender clutched her around the shoulders.

In the roar from the explosion, Mona barely heard the splash Johnny made tumbling into the dark waters below.

Chapter 32
Walk Off

His mind was processing the experience as if it were a dream, the boundary of the real and imagined unclear and tantalizingly fantastic. The pain – from his ankle, his head, and his ribs – was the only indication that it had all happened and that something was terribly amiss.

In his dream, Mona straddled him, pumping his chest with her hands, her hair dripping into his face. She was crying and speaking his name in a voice that was alternating between sad and angry. He couldn't make out the words. She was desperate and growing weary.

She was beautiful.

The dream resolved in a flicker of consciousness. Johnny coughed sharply, water spilling from his mouth, spraying upwards.

"I think he's back," Mona yelled breathlessly, straightening up, her arms limp and expended at her sides. A woman holding a pistol approached from behind. Johnny recognized her, the wild hair unforgettable.

"Mona," he groaned in what he hoped was a tone of warning. "Behind you."

The woman with the pistol drew closer, peering at Johnny.

"He'll be OK," she murmured. "That was close. Too close."

Mona pushed her wet hair back, her light summer blouse soaked and clinging, water running down her shoulders and arms.

She turned to Johnny and started to stand up, pushing on his chest to brace herself as she rose from her straddling position. Johnny coughed again and wiped his mouth with the back of his hand. His skin felt clammy.

"Damn, you are heavy, Denovo," she said. "It took three of us to yank you out of the water. I'm glad Ivy was here to stand guard while we fished you out."

The wild-haired woman smiled gently at Johnny.

"Ivy," he said, propping himself up on his elbows. His clothes were soaked and his head throbbed. "Ivy Thomson."

"One and the same," she said, just as the sound of something large emerging from the water arose behind her. She turned to look, the pistol tensing noticeably in her hand.

"Gleason," she said with a sigh of relief and recognition, her grip relaxing. A shadowy figure approached from dockside, feet flapping against the boards, a regulator dangling like a third arm.

He stopped to examine the corpse on the dock, using his flippered right foot to turn the man's head to the side.

Johnny recognized the corpse's clothes and wild hair.

Paulson.

His body lay like a lump on the boards.

"Thomson," Gleason replied in a business-like tone, tossing a diving mask aside. "We stopped them."

Ivy Thomson holstered her gun behind her back and hugged the man in the wet suit.

"A summer well-spent," she smiled at him.

"A summer and a lot of baseball games," Gleason replied. Stepping into a brighter area of the dock, Johnny could make out the same rugged man in his 50s he'd encountered in New Hampshire less than a week ago, the face weathered and craggy but possessing a youthful vitality and intelligence he found immediately appealing and reassuring. Up close, the man looked wholesome, sincere, and entirely trustworthy.

Gleason turned toward Johnny. "Nice to meet you, Mr. Denovo," he said, extending a hand to help Johnny to his feet. "I'm Special Agent Gleason. Art Gleason. And this is Special Agent Thomson."

Johnny heaved to his feet with Gleason's strong hand doing most of the lifting. The icy waters had dulled the pain from his injured ankle. It throbbed as he placed weight on it, but it held. "So, you're Gleason," Johnny marveled. "And you are alive. Would somebody mind telling me what I've missed?"

Gleason snorted, and Thomson laughed in a manner that wasn't quite humorous.

"Why don't you get rid of that awful wig?" Gleason said in an aside to Thomson as he shrugged the scuba tank off his back. She smiled, yanking the wild hair from her head and throwing it to the dock in disgust. "I hope I never see that thing again," she spat, stomping on the wig with evident relish. Without it, Ivy was revealed to be a beautiful young woman with lovely bone structure and cropped, stylish hair.

Johnny glanced around. Mona stood to one side, observing the scene. On a nearby bench next to the storage sheds, Izzy and Ivan sat in a gentle embrace, watching the proceedings. Ivan was dripping wet. He must have been the third rescuer, along with Mona and Gleason.

In the harbor, a small fire still burned, the wreckage of the Codon. Far away, the faint wail of a siren could be heard.

"How did you all get here?" Johnny asked.

Mona motioned over to Ivan and Izzy. "After the game, Izzy, Ivan, and I headed toward Maurice's. But we got to talking about the case on the way there, and they thought it would be fun to see you in action. I knew you were going to try to get to Tucker's, so we walked over here instead. When we saw Ivy ahead of us, we began to follow her. And then we got swept up in events."

Johnny reached over and squeezed Mona's forearm affectionately.

"You're OK?" he asked quietly.

"I'm OK," she smiled, placing her hand atop his.

"She almost wasn't," Ivy interjected, having overheard the exchange. "For some reason, Paulson was in the water. Your friends were following me. I knew that. But when I got here, I heard something come out of the water. I turned. It was Paulson, and he was coming at them. I shouted for him to freeze, but he ignored me. I had to take him out."

"So that's the gunshot I heard," Johnny murmured.

"You heard that?" Mona asked.

"I'm the one who put Paulson in the water. He got the drop on me, but I had the last laugh," Johnny explained, glancing down at his foot. "Cost me an ankle, though. After Paulson went into the water, Gleason signaled about the launcher and the beacon. I had to dive in to get to the launcher. I was below, getting ready to fire on Schwartz's boat, when I heard the shout and the gunshot. I didn't know what was going on, but I couldn't do anything about it."

Ivy had a soulless gleam in her eye. "He got what he deserved."

Gleason looked at his colleague sternly, as if she'd said something they'd discuss later. But she showed no remorse.

"And you were the blackmailers?" Johnny asked. "Blackmailing McNaught?"

Ivy and Gleason exchanged a glance.

"We were acting as double-agents," Gleason said, taking the lead. "Schwartz and Paulson thought I was a radical environmentalist from New Hampshire, part of Cool & Green. Having the reputation I do up there only helped. We started the affair and the blackmail with McNaught once we sniffed out a bio-terror threat because he was the most likely bio-tech suspect in Boston. We had to get close, see if distracting him would slow the plan. It didn't. He was clean. But it threw a light on Schwartz, then Paulson. They became our prime suspects. And the blackmail proved useful in a different way. From Paulson's perspective, it antagonized McNaught while also providing his plan with a small, independent cash flow. We had to keep it up."

"And then the fact that Ivy and Heather are sisters entered into the blackmail," Johnny commented.

"That happened later. Schwartz discovered the connection," Ivy offered. "Once he knew, Paulson had Gleason follow McNaught to New York, where Schwartz had agreed to share the information. Paulson wanted us to receive the information in a way that nobody could trace back to Schwartz. He had Schwartz tell Gleason using a foyer in Grand Central station. It lets someone on the opposite side overhear a conversation. It's something architects call a whisper gallery. After the sister connection became part of the blackmail, we increased our demands. It still served the same purposes, so there was no problem really. Satisfied?"

"I'm not finished," Johnny said, looking hard at Gleason and Thomson. "Please tell me how a father and daughter blackmail and special agent team came into being?"

Gleason smiled as he kicked off his flippers and removed his dive belt. "You figured that out, did you?" he said jovially, as if Johnny had solved a child's riddle. Then his voice took on a tone of utter solemnity. "All right, I'll tell you, but you are all sworn to utter secrecy. This means even to your good friend Tucker Thiesen, Mr. Denovo. Especially to him, actually. If you break this pledge, we'll know, and there will be repercussions. Does everyone agree?" he said, casting a level gaze at the assembled group.

Everyone nodded.

Gleason took a few steps over toward Izzy and Ivan, the others following. "Let's gather into a smaller circle," he urged. "I need to speak quietly."

Johnny struggled to move, his body aching, his energy sapped. He hobbled forward on his lame ankle. As his strength ebbed, the night seemed to stretch thin around him. Ivy handed him his jacket and shoes. He slipped the jacket on, it's dry warmth bolstering him in the night's chill.

Once everyone was in a tight cluster, Gleason spoke.

"First of all, you have just been part of one of the most important intelligence operations of the past decade," he murmured appreciatively. "Mr. Denovo, you should be proud of the part you played in this. It has taken us years of careful planning to infiltrate this organization and accomplish what we finally did tonight."

Johnny nodded. "Please, call me Johnny."

Gleason smiled his reassuring smile again. "And you can call me Gleason," he said. "It's how I'm known in the agency."

"Fine," Johnny replied. "But answer my question about you and Ivy."

Gleason shot a glance at Ivy. He spoke rapidly, the sirens in the distance now clearly headed in their direction. "Like I said, Thomson is a special agent, one of our best. She and I met when she was recruited out of Yale. I merely saw a talented intelligence recruit. But we talked and soon discovered our connection ran much deeper. As you've learned, Johnny, we're father and daughter. I 'died' before she was born. I was forced to. I'd become entangled in a situation where my entire family would have been jeopardized if I'd lived. The nearest we can figure, she was conceived the night before I went into hiding. I had to leave to protect my children, and I've remained hidden ever since, even though the threat ultimately passed. When Heather left home for good, I returned to New Hampshire and reunited with my wife. But I remained estranged from my daughters. I had to. I couldn't contact Heather, and I had no idea where the other had gone after my wife gave her up. Even if I'd known, there was no way to explain the gap to them, to return to the world of the living without blowing my cover. It was part of what I signed up for, even though I never imagined the agony it would create for me and my wife." Gleason cast a glance toward Ivy, his eyes softening as they appraised her face.

"But I have to give you credit, Johnny," Gleason continued, "The night I confronted you outside my farm, I was uncertain whether I should scare you off or include you. I asked Ivy to put up the red sign to give you a clue that we were connected. But a very safe clue, one that not everybody would have understood was actually a signal with two potential purposes, since it also helped maintain our cover as part of Paulson's plan to have you believe we were working together. If you figured more out from there, fine. If you didn't, then I knew you weren't up to the task. The next day, orders came down – I was to drive you off. Our superiors were worried. Your reputation precedes you. Hence, the smoke bombs. But within a couple of days, even my superiors changed their minds. And here we are."

Mona looked from Ivy to Gleason and back again, assessing the family resemblance. Izzy pushed close against Ivan. His clothing was soaked, but Izzy didn't seem to notice or mind.

"And you were also Tom McNaught's mistress?" Johnny said to Ivy, turning to face the short-haired double-agent.

"Yes, but that'll end now," she replied. "It was part of the job. The operation's over as of tonight. From the start, we wanted some-one close to him. He was a key connection initially, with the bio-ter-ror angle emerging early in the investigation. I knew he'd married my biological sister, but we thought we could keep that fact under wraps. And the people who calculate these things believed the biological attraction he'd feel toward me would increase my odds of success. They certainly were right on that last point. Then McNaught became someone we wanted to neutralize with the blackmail. We wanted him confused and distracted. He's too smart otherwise. He might have caught on. It wasn't an easy job," she concluded, her eyes downcast.

"We make a good team," Gleason interjected quickly, deflecting the awkward moment. "These are not easy missions. We are the elite, Thomson. We set the standard."

Thomson glanced up, her eyes steely. "I know that," she said in a chill voice.

Gleason shrugged it off. "We're like shadows, Johnny. We come, we go, depending on the light. Thiesen has to remain convinced that our affiliations are, at best, unclear. We can't be found out. There's too much at stake, for us and for the country."

"I understand," Johnny said. Motioning to the group, he added, "We understand." His friends nodded in assent. The sirens were drawing near.

"All right," Gleason said. "Our people will clean this up. Your story is that you came across me with Paulson and Schwartz. You were battered about by us, outnumbered. We left in the boat, and it exploded. Got it?"

"Fine with me," Johnny said.

"And don't worry," Gleason said, noting the question in Johnny's eyes. "The virus is destroyed. I added some accelerant to the boxes without Schwartz seeing me. They burned first. There is no way there was any virus left to get in the water once anything ignited."

"And Tucker took care of the fire hydrants," Johnny mentioned off-handedly.

Gleason's head snapped around, his eyes fixed on Johnny.

"What fire hydrants?"

Johnny smiled. "I wondered if you knew. Apparently, Paulson wasn't sharing everything with his sign-caller or his angry farmer. Paulson's network was planting the virus in fire hydrants when they vandalized the companies. Containers of it were distributed all across the country. They were going to release it tonight as well."

Gleason looked shocked. He turned to Ivy.

"Did you know about this?" he asked with alarm in his voice.

"I had no idea," Ivy replied, her face pale. "Months of working with these creeps, and I had no idea. I thought we were just trigger-ing vandalism. And I thought we were insiders." She glanced at Paulson with poison in her eyes.

Gleason turned to face Johnny and was about the say some-thing, but the sirens were too close now for more conversation. He closed his mouth.

Mona cleared her throat. "What about Johnny's fees?" she said.

Gleason's gaze was angry. "McNaught will have to pay those," he said hastily. "The blackmailing will stop now, his mistress will vanish, and Johnny can take all the credit. We don't pay," he finished with a growl.

Mona was not intimidated, the flames from the harbor flickering in her eyes. "Fine. But remember, he has an equal moral claim to solving your case, and he did it in a fraction of the time."

A twinkle came into Gleason's eye as well. He liked the banter, Johnny could tell.

"We were the clues. He solved us," Gleason noted. "Without us, this would have gone off without a whisper, Johnny Denovo or no Johnny Denovo."

Mona folded her arms across her chest. "That's a load of crap, and you know it," she said. "He discovered things you didn't even know about. You can tell your superiors you figured the fire hydrants out, I don't care. We just want to get paid for our work. The government can afford it. And we wouldn't want any secrets to get out, now would we?"

"I'll think about it," Gleason agreed, still smiling, but now with a glinty edge. He'd been out-negotiated and knew it. "I'll review the logs to confirm the fire hydrants when we get back. Thomson, let's go. Trash the wig. I've called the clean-up crew. They're running interference now, slowing down the constabulary, and they'll deal with the local authorities. Now, scatter!"

Chapter 33
Safe

Tucker was asleep in his armchair when Johnny and Mona entered.

Mona had been reintegrated into Tucker's security system after it was compromised during the last case. She strode in with confidence.

The bank of televisions was mostly black, with one lonely monitor playing an old situation comedy to its unconscious audience.

"What should we do?" Mona whispered, her bedraggled hair slithering over her shoulders like slender vines.

Johnny smiled slyly. "Give me a minute," he said quietly, limping over toward the kitchen. He had only moved a few halting steps when he was stopped by a deep voice.

"Don't even think about it, Denovo."

Johnny froze. Tucker opened his eyes, glaring up and over his shoulder at Johnny.

"What were you thinking? Ice cubes?" Tucker asked.

"Pudding," Johnny confessed. "Different sense experience, much more alarming."

Tucker huffed in mock disgust. "Gross, Denovo. Hey, why are you both wet?" he asked, looking from Johnny to Mona and back again. "And why are you limping?"

The two looked at each other, weighing the moment. Mona was the first to respond.

"Didn't you hear the explosion?" she asked. "The gunshot?"

Tucker leaped up out of the chair. "What explosion? What gunshot? What happened? I was in here dealing with the APB and the virus squad roundup. That wrapped, then I guess I dozed. What happened down there?"

Johnny squeezed Mona's arm, indicating he'd take over. "Tucker, we did it. Paulson and Schwartz are dead, and Gleason might be, too. The virus was destroyed. Homeland's cleaning it all up now."

Tucker sat back down hard in his chair again, a whoosh of air escaping the leather cushion as he collapsed it. "And you did this how?" Tucker asked, his eyes wide.

Johnny described the scene at the dock with Paulson, but modified some facts, putting Gleason on the boat and attributing the explosion to him, while claiming that a fight between the woman on the Green Monster and Paulson had led to the shot that killed Paulson.

"She got away after I was knocked unconscious by Paulson. I must have fallen in the water. Mona fished me out. She saved my life."

"I had a little help," Mona chimed in shyly, playing along. "Izzy and Ivan were with me. We had to drag him out together. He's heavy when he's wet."

Tucker looked at them both. "Wow, what a night! And Gleason got away again. Or he died in the explosion. I guess we'll never know. Again!" Tucker punched the armchair. "The guy is a phantom."

Johnny tensed. Having used the word "phantom," he worried that the truth might occur to Tucker – that Gleason was a phantom indeed, an official ghost in the machine. But if the idea occurred to him, he never expressed it.

"So the APB worked?" Johnny asked, rapidly changing the subject.

"Like a charm," Tucker replied. "Most of the people were arrested on trespassing charges, enough to put a scare into them and get them a police record. It should be sufficient to keep most of them on the straight and narrow from now on. From the police I talked with, a lot of the perps are college-aged idealists who had no idea they were being played. Sad, really."

Johnny felt the fatigue of his lingering illness wash yet again over his cold, wet body.

"I'd better get back home," he said to the room. "I'm still sick."

"But not contagious?" Mona said hopefully.

"I hope not," Johnny murmured. "By the way, Tuck, did it strike you as odd that this is two cases in a row involving eggs?"

Tucker hummed to himself. "I wondered when you were going to notice that," he replied jovially.

"Noticed it long ago," Johnny said, his voice fading. "Wonder what it means."

"Probably nothing," Tucker replied.

Johnny began to move toward the door on his weak ankle, his arm around Mona's shoulders, his weight resting on her stronger frame.

"It never means nothing, my friend," he said with some resignation, hobbling out the door, weary and relieved. But a note of worry permeated his speech. "It always means something."

Across town, on a lonely, leafy lane in Cambridge, its heaving sidewalks split by trees hemmed with flared wrought iron fences, a flicker of light sparked inside a locked and empty academic office. The burning ember, no larger than a mote of dust, nestled in a pile of papers and smoldered.

Soon, a small plume of smoke puffed up. Then a small bright fire flickered to life and began to consume the papers.

Five minutes later, the office was engulfed in flames.

Acknowledgements

A number of generous people helped make this story and Johnny Denovo come together on the page. I owe them my deep gratitude. My wife, in particular, has helped immensely by finding weak spots in early drafts, arguing for a better Mona, and maintaining continuity throughout the novel. I'd also like to thank Chris for his input on Fenway and literary license; Carey, for his helpful suggestions and help finding plausibility gaps with both books so far; and Candy, for her very early support of this project and sage advice. I'd also like to thank Sharon for her notion years ago that metaphors and detectives might go together, an insight that helped spur this series. Finally, thanks to the readers, who have turned out at book signings and encouraged me to continue with Johnny's stories. I'm certainly happy to oblige.

Breinigsville, PA USA
04 September 2009
223588BV00001B/1/P